The Past is Never Dead

The Past is Never Dead

by
David Schulman

John F. Blair, Publisher
Winston-Salem, North Carolina

The paper in this book meets the guidelines
for permanence and durability of the Committee on
Production Guidelines for Book Longevity
of the Council on Library Resources

Design by Debra Long Hampton
Cover image courtesy of
North Carolina Collection, Pack Memorial Library, Asheville, North Carolina

Library of Congress Cataloging-in-Publication Data

Schulman, David, 1948-
The past is never dead : a Gritz Goldberg mystery / by David Schulman.
    p.   cm.
ISBN 0-89587-290-0 (alk. paper)
1. Asheville (N.C.)—Fiction. I. Title.
PS3619.C474P37 2004
813'.6—dc22
2004004334

Printed in Canada

This book is dedicated to Denissa Schulman, Louise Davis, Creighton Sossomon, Ron Morgan, William Paulk, Lynn Moser, Judith Bush, Abigail DeWitt, Tommy Hays, and Leo Potts, glorious teachers who, I suspect, are also really angels.

ACKNOWLEDGMENTS

I am grateful to

The late John Parris, for his actual notes, which he dug up for me from his reporting days
Evan Marshall, for being an agent *extraordinaire*
The staff of John F. Blair, Publisher, in particular Carolyn Sakowski and Steve Kirk
All the members of the "Hangers On" writers' classes and the other writers' groups to which I have belonged
The late Leo Finkelstein, for being Asheville's Jewish historian
Livingston Kelley, for listening to my whining for years
The late Sol Schulman, for being able to tell me he was proud of me after he read my stuff
Herbert Schulman, for being an overprotective brother
The late Lillian Schulman, for her unconditional love
Clyde and Barbara Andrews, for producing a wonderful daughter—my wife—and for loving me

Tom Slagle, for being the friend that he is

Charles Gershon, for monthly support lunches

The *Asheville Citizen-Times* editorial staff, for their excellence

The former employees and customers of the David's and Boo Boos stores, for giving me confidence

Betty Love, the late Mary Walton, and the late Gene Austin, for just being who they were

Jim Lister, for his research

And all those I have forgotten to list but who are in my heart

The Past is Never Dead

CHAPTER ONE

"Di tsung iz der feder fun hartz."
"The tongue is the pen of the heart."

"I hate Jews, always have."

My mom always said that there is some good in everybody, you just have to peel off more layers on some to find it. I knew that with the skinny thirty-three-year-old sitting opposite me in the worn burgundy leather chair, I was going to have to peel awfully deep.

"Why is that, Bobby?" I said, looking into his feline green eyes.

I was supposed to be the detached doctor, the analytical Jewish psychiatrist who showed no emotion. I glanced at the antique hourglass that sat on a corner of my desk. The sand had drained almost completely to the bottom half. I would momentarily be closing my memo pad of scribbled observations, indicating not so subtly to my patient—or rather my client, as we had recently been

3

instructed to call them by our new CEO at Highland Psychiatric Hospital—that our session was over. Through the years, I had become quite adept at casually turning over the hourglass just as my client crossed the threshold into my office. Sounds unprofessional, I suppose, but I saved a bunch of cheap glances toward my watch that way.

"I don't know why. They just crawl up my ass. Too rich, pushy . . . They control the whole damn world, you know. Granddaddy used to say, 'If you see a good Jew, you better get your eyes checked.' " He gave me a smile that asked for confirmation. I didn't oblige.

Bobby occupied a body that was starting to reflect his age. Though he was still trim, he had just the beginnings of a paunch. And above his Adam's apple, a double chin was developing. His conversational skills, however, reflected none of the aforementioned maturity. His outlook on life seemed to be stuck somewhere between high-school assuredness and frat-house humor. Bobby never let an opportunity pass to bring up the name of his grandfather Robert Rice Raby, the late United States senator from North Carolina. For those of us who grew up in Asheville or even just moved to town, the Raby name was part of the local vernacular. While in office in the 1930s, he'd been referred to as "Our Bob." From Raby Middle School to Raby Memorial Library, Bobby's family name was spoken daily by ordinary citizens.

"I loved Granddaddy. Everybody loved him," Bobby reflected.

It was obvious from his stare that he didn't like that I'd withheld the expected racist chuckle he was used to evoking with his grandfather's Jew wisecracks. It was also clear he didn't include Jews as worthy of being in the "everybody" classification. *Mamzer* was the term my family used to recall western North Carolina's former political wizard. Yiddish has such sweet ways to call an asshole an asshole. Dad said the *New York Times* dubbed the man "the Tar Heel Fuhrer." Besides his controversial seven marriages, Senator Raby had been one of the country's leading proponents of isolationism prior to World War II. He also made known his hatred of Franklin D. Roosevelt, in itself a criminal offense to Mom and Dad while I was growing up. Thankfully, Mom died peacefully before she witnessed my 1996 conversion to the Republican Party.

"Does it bother you that I'm Jewish?" I said, half for my benefit, half as part of confrontational therapy.

Robert R. Raby III looked down at his naked ankle. Dressed in the modern-day Confederate uniform of formerly well-to-do Southern aristocracy, Bobby wore no socks with his tan leather boat shoes, khaki pants, and rumpled red polo shirt. The collar rose on the back of his neck into a hairline that was very close to the same color as his shirt. There was a pause in our conversation, but I was used to that in my line of work. I just looked at his ankle, too. It had a clump of red-brown freckles on it in the exact shape of the freckles on his forehead. Sign of the beast, I figured.

Bobby finally came up with as bright an answer as he was capable of: "Hell, I don't know."

A sweet, familiar smell wafted through my ancient office. I always became aware of it when a client responded to one of my questions like Bobby just had—with anger, with defiance, with mistruths. I could never prove my wild premise, but I felt sure what I sniffed was Zelda Fitzgerald's private perfume, which she had shipped from Montgomery when she was a patient of ours at Highland in the 1930s and 1940s. Zelda died in a terrible fire at the hospital in 1948. Since it was part of Highland's history, I liked to read all the Zelda stories that were published. When I read of her favorite perfume and also found out that my office had been Zelda's own therapist's office, I came to the conclusion she'd never really left us. Not that I told many people about my theory.

I was really tired of Highland's propensity to admit patients like Bobby—repeat fuckups with deep pockets, as I unofficially called them outside of conferences; maladjusted borderline psychotic personalities with recidivist criminal tendencies, as I referred to them inside staff meetings. His still well-connected family had gotten him admitted, this time claiming bipolar tendencies, in an obvious attempt to stall some judicial proceeding on yet another marginally serious infraction of the law. Bobby had moved from "nothing little hate crimes they hung on me" in the early nineties to internet fraud of late. Best I could tell, he was not depressed or oppressed, but simply a run-of-the-mill pain in the societal ass. Once we'd become part of the Trinity University hospital system instead of a private mental facility, the voices of the staff barely made it out of our conference room, let alone to the other end of North Carolina, where Trinity made most of our decisions for us.

"Dr. Goldberg, I need to meet with a couple of my associates. Business matter. They can't get by the idiot at the gate. He told them you sent orders that I have no visitors."

There we sat, a warmed-over bigot and a burned-out shrink. Once, I'd been as passionate about my profession as Bobby was about hate, but now I mostly tolerated my career, hoping to reach early retirement before total disability. I'd been Highland's poster boy for what psychiatric hospitalization could achieve. I myself had been a patient at the hospital in my teens, battling obsessive-compulsive behavior. After going on to become a doctor, I had deep empathy for those who were troubled. Now, I still tried my best to help those assigned to me, but there were days when one neurotic merged into another, no matter how hard I tried. I changed my glasses frames to current fashion every few years, trimmed my full beard down to a graying goatee, and kept my tummy from dropping with weekly rounds of bad golf and mounds of tasteless salad. But deep down, I feared I was perilously close to doing what I had intensely fought against my whole life. Compromising.

"I think that a little break from your normal associations might do you good." Maturity had taught me to appreciate little things, like the final, tiny grains of sand that fall to the bottom of an hourglass. I closed my memo pad. "Give me a list of who you want to see and their relationship to you, and maybe we can work something out. Bring it in Thursday, okay?"

I finally gave Bobby that faint smile he'd demanded a few minutes earlier. This time, it was he who refused to return the expression.

He stood and turned to leave. Then he looked back at me.

"For some reason, Dr. Goldberg, you don't seem so much like the rest of 'em."

I glanced at the framed stitchery above the door behind Bobby. My ex-wife made it for me just before she hightailed it back to Long Island. "The past is never dead. It's not even past," it read. William Faulkner's famous quote about the South.

"See you Thursday, Bobby."

CHAPTER TWO

"Men ken nit kaien mit fremde tsein."
"You can't chew with someone else's teeth."

"Gritz, your aunt Fay called," Essie Coleman said, looking at Bobby Raby's skinny butt going down the stairway across from her desk. "She said it was important that you get right back to her." My secretary's voice had a distinct tension equaled only by the tightness of her gray-blue curls, which she had rolled the exact same way each Friday at the Quality Hair Salon.

Almost everyone called me by my nickname, even some of my clients. I was given it by Dad's sister, Fay, who would go to New York on buying trips for her business and return toting enormous plastic bags of bagels, once a Yankee delicacy not available in the South. Though my family loved the manna from the North, even as a toddler I would spit out the "holey" bread and demand my morning round of ground white hominy instead. "Some Jew!" Aunt Fay would grimace.

"Then I'd better give her a call," I said, smiling at Essie.

I'd tried out younger secretaries with tight skirts and loose cleavage, but I found most of them distracting and inefficient. Essie distracted no one. A 1950 graduate of Asheville's famed Candler Correspondence School of Wireless Telegraphy, she'd never married and was devoted to her job at Highland, her garden, and Macedonia Baptist Church. "I'll work as long as they let me" was Essie's only retirement plan.

I went back into my office and punched speed dial number three.

"You have reached the Miami Beach condominium of Solly Goldberg and Fay Cohen. We're brother and sister. Don't dare hang up before you tell us what you want."

"Hi, Aunt Fay, it's Gritz. I was returning your—"

"Gritz, don't hang up. I've got to talk to you!"

"Is Dad okay?" I said.

"And me, what about me? Don't I count?"

"Of course, you count, Aunt Fay, but I was—"

"Gritz, your dad is fine. You remember Big Fay, don't you? Big Fay, your dad's and my cousin from South Carolina?"

"Yes," I said.

Big Fay was five foot two. She was called Big Fay because she was older than her cousin Little Fay, who was almost six feet tall but six months younger.

"She's just moved down here from Charleston. I made the mistake of taking her to the temple sisterhood. Right away, she takes over the meeting. Suggests we all start writing about our personal histories—you know, Jews of the Old South, that type of thing. She wants to make a book of all our memories."

It sounded like a great idea to me, but I knew better than to say so. Big Fay and Little Fay competed at everything. A couple of months prior, I had volunteered to do a Sunday bagel-and-lox breakfast talk at our temple about Asheville Jewish *mishuganahs*. It was a combination of gossip and real history. It went well until I mentioned that ancestors of the Bloom family had been organizers of train heists across the United States in the early part of the twentieth century. I quickly found out genealogies are fun to talk about only if everyone in the family is long dead.

"Wouldn't you know, the *yentas* down here loved her idea right off the bat. By next meeting, they want us to bring information about where we used to live. Of course, Big Fay acts like Charleston is the Tel Aviv of South Carolina. Asheville Jewish history is better than her history. I got to thinking about W. D. Paully. You remember that story, don't you?"

Willard Dudley Paully was to Asheville Jews what Pharaoh was to Egypt. He showed up in town in the early 1930s. He was the self-anointed commander of the Silver Shirts, a pro-Hitler militia with reportedly as many as two million followers nationwide. From his Asheville home, he plotted to overthrow Roosevelt and cleanse the country of Jews, blacks, and lawyers. Every Asheville Jewish kid was taught this in Sunday school. Moses, Abraham, Isaac, and W. D. Paully.

"Sure, I remember Commander Paully," I said. The fewer words you spoke to Aunt Fay, the better, because within seconds she would interrupt you anyway.

"Moses Bloom should have a whole lot of stuff on Paully. That man saves fingernail clippings. Call the *alte kocker*. Is he still alive? Get me pictures, whatever he's got on Paully. Big Fay's going to *plotz* when she sees what I bring in."

Little Fay was eighty-eight, a year younger than my dad. He

moved in with her after Mom died and Wal-Mart came to town, ending his sixty-one years as proprietor of Goldberg's Department Store, "Where Low Prices Are Born, Not Raised." Dad and Little Fay mixed like oil and water, but for some reason they chose to live together. Aggravation bred security, maybe.

"I think I heard old man Bloom is at the Happy Valley Assisted Living Home. I'll do what I can," I said. "Is Dad around?"

"Your dad, he's in the ocean, always in the ocean. You'd think he was training to be a prune. I never get in the water. Too much seaweed down here. Gets in your crotch."

That was a visual I needed to block quickly.

"I'll get right on it, Aunt Fay. Tell Dad I said hi."

She hung up without a reply. That's how she always ended her phone calls. Aunt Fay taught me long ago that love means never having to say good-bye.

I had two more sessions before lunch. The first was with Cage Blevins, a dreadlocked teenager who always walked barefoot and toted a guitar on his back. He never played it, just carried it. He had been in juvenile detention centers four different times since his thirteenth birthday and stored so much anger I suspected that if I didn't handle him gently, he might end up a pile of ashes on my carpet from spontaneous combustion. He hated Highland, his father, his nose, and capitalism, though not necessarily in that order. The second session was with Sophie Watkins, a sixty-year-old housewife from Atlanta who drank too much, ate too little, and whistled at inopportune times. I could help with the first two, but whistling was not addressed by any textbook cure. The impreciseness of therapy used to represent a challenge to me. Now, it was just a hassle.

What wasn't imprecise was my lunch hour. Thankfully, I had

that part of my life all worked out. No matter what, at exactly 12:23, I had lunch at Possum's Café. I had hired Pearlie Gates to make sure of it. Pearlie drove a repainted surplus highway patrol car that Our Lord's Dependable Cab Company must have bought at auction. His boss was lenient when Pearlie added his own personal touches to the car. On the hood, he had painted— reversed, so the driver ahead could read it in the rearview mirror— the names of all the people he figured had plotted or were plotting to destroy America, including Madonna and the Jackson Five. All that mattered to me was that he loved to drive as much as I hated to. At exactly high noon, Pearlie's cab would be parked in the reserved space below my office window. If I wasn't outside waiting on him, Pearlie would sound the siren he had somehow managed to get reinstalled just for me. He even had a portable blue light, in case we got stalled in traffic. One way or another, Pearlie got me to Possum's at 12:23 five days a week.

Driving was the one vestige of OCD I never conquered. The disease affects people differently. Some wash their hands over and over again; some count steps to and from a destination. Me, I had the "Did I run over somebody and not know it?" mania. All of us blessed or condemned with OCD have a constant, irrational fear of harming somebody other than ourselves, and it seems we have to check out all the possibilities to make sure we haven't caused a calamity before we can rest easy, which is never. There is always this clinging, strangling doubt that just won't let go. All it takes is a pothole in the road to keep us driving in circles for hours, round and round, where we stop, nobody knows. I tell my patients that OCD is like a friend you sort of hate and sort of love but never totally get rid of. My solution is simple, if somewhat controversial —sometimes, you win by giving up.

I was literally driving myself crazy, checking my mirror for the hundredth time to see if I had flattened somebody, when I finally saw Pearlie at a traffic light one day. We were high-school classmates, though we'd never been buddies. Physically, Pearlie had changed little since I last saw him. He was still a muscular guy with a greased crew cut and thick eyeglasses in brown plastic frames. Now, whenever he pulled up beside me, he'd roll down the window and yell, "How's she runnin'?" That's what we'd always said to each other when we passed in the hallways of Asheville High. Neither of us knew what it meant, but it had sounded cool at the time.

At 12:20 that day, Pearlie and I pulled into Possum's gravel parking lot. A square plastic lighted sign provided by Dr. Pepper hung lopsided on a tall, rusty metal pole that seemed only half stuck in the ground. "Swine Dining—Best BBQ in Town," it read in bold black letters. Possum Jenkins lived upstairs in the cement-block building with Jennie Mae, his wife of sixty-four years. Behind the restaurant sat a squat three-room motel. Possum had once shown me an old postcard of the place. "Asheville's Only Colored Motel," it read. The motel sat on the edge of a ravine, and only the middle room seemed like it had a chance of not sliding off the property with the next hard rain. The café was unpainted, but the motel was a shade Pearlie called "titty pink."

"I'll be back in thirty," Pearlie always said as I exited his cab.

"Make it twenty-nine," I always replied.

I stuck my hand through the largest hole in the screen door, turned the handle, and let myself in.

Possum Jenkins always greeted me like he hadn't seen me the previous five hundred workdays: "Have a seat, Gritz! Good to see you again." The owner, waiter, and cook spoke like he really meant it, not like it was ordered by corporate directive. He wore a stained, not-so-white cotton apron over a green T-shirt and blue jeans. On his head was a maroon baseball cap. Possum had recently started wearing the cap backwards, like all fashion-conscious men these days. He was still as skinny as he always had been. Dad once told me that in Possum's youth, he'd been arrested for staging cockfights in the back lot of the restaurant, but they couldn't hold him at the jail. As the story went, Jennie Mae sneaked him a tub of lard, which he used to grease his naked body and squeeze through the cell bars to freedom.

I never changed my lunch order either. Barbecued pork with fried okra and sweet tea. When I told Possum last month that a gourmet food magazine quoted some anthropologist as saying the word *barbecue* came from an extinct tribe in Kenya that roasted captured enemies, all he said was, "I bet they don't spit in the stew like I do."

"Got your plate in the warming tray," Possum said, heading back into the kitchen.

Sometimes during the whole lunch hour, it was just Possum and I. Once in a while, a stray cop or a couple of dental hygienists would wander in. There had been a brief rush of customers last year when the *Asheville Citizen-Times* ran a feature on little-known local restaurants. Even the ladies from the Vanderbilt Country Club showed up to taste soul food.

Possum usually had the morning paper spread out for me. Sometimes, he circled items of interest, like the new French restaurant advertising quail and wild rice for $29.95. "Ain't enough meat on that bird to satisfy its mate, let alone the person eatin' it," Possum had said.

The place was very worn and slightly dirty—two components of really good eating. I'd even gotten over my compulsion to straighten Possum's Roy Campanella picture, which hung behind the bar half off its nail, as it probably had since the catcher gave it to the owner with the inscription, "Good Q is better than making love."

Possum brought my food out and sat down with me. "I'm kind of worried lately, Gritz. I just don't have the drive like I used to. I think I may close this place down and take a long vacation."

My security in jeopardy, I said what any good shrink would: "You can't do that. Where would I eat lunch?"

"It ain't that I'm overworked, but Jennie Mae says maybe we need a change of scenery." He looked at me with all seriousness. "I read in a magazine the other day that when a woman says that, she's really saying her man ain't satisfying her. You're a doctor of the mind and all. You think that's right?"

Since it was four months since I'd even come close to foreplay, I didn't feel comfortable advising an octogenarian about sexual frequency.

"Not necessarily," I said, stuffing my mouth with okra.

Fortunately, before I had to find a way to change the subject, my beeper went off.

"Emergency. Asheville Police," the text message read.

CHAPTER THREE

"Der ponim zogt ois dem sod."
"The face tells the secret."

Talmadge Livingston, chief of police of the Asheville metro area, our first with a genuine criminal degree, answered the phone.

"Gritz, we've got a subject on the roof of the old Battery Park Hotel. He wants to talk to you."

"To me!" I said. "Who is he?"

"I don't know, but he threw down a notepad off the roof. Has the name of Wilson's Funeral Home advertised on it, and written on it were the words, 'Call Gritz.' "

When you work for a mental facility, the local authorities get to know you personally. Anger, hysteria, and violence are all symptoms that scream for help. If the good cops distinguished that fact before the bad cops beat the hell out of the screamer, Talmadge usually got around to calling Highland for our expertise.

My first thought was that Cage Blevins had taken his rage to a rooftop and was about to fly.

"Young man?" I said.

"Can't really tell, that far up, but the handwriting seems awfully shaky. Don't think so."

"I'm on my way," I said.

I stood up, inhaled my last bite of okra, and put my sports coat back on. I don't know why. Suicides aren't usually dressy affairs.

The formidable fourteen-story Battery Park Hotel was only a few blocks from Possum's tiny motel. The hotel was in its second incarnation. The original Battery Park, built in 1886, sprawled high on a hillside, its wooden gables and shingles looking more like they belonged in an English countryside than downtown Asheville. In its day, the place was a favorite of genteel low-country Southerners trying to escape the summer heat, as well as a posh retreat for Northern industrialists. It is said that, from the veranda of the original Battery Park, George Vanderbilt first glimpsed the thousands of acres he would later accumulate to build his Biltmore Estate. Dr. Edwin Grove, a visionary who made his first fortune marketing the enormously popular, cocaine-laced Grove Tonic for malaria, tore down the hotel in 1921. Having come to Asheville to cure his chronic hiccups, he built the Grove Park Inn and the Grove Arcade. After a feud with his son-in-law, Frank Seals, Grove left the Grove Park Inn for Seals to operate and moved downtown, where he leveled the whole hill on which the Battery Park regally sat. In 1924, he completed a new Battery Park, beautiful in its own way with its dark red brick and top-floor ballroom, but more an erect, standard hotel of its day. Of late, the building was not a hotel at all, but a federally subsidized retirement building for low-income elderly.

Pearlie and I pulled up behind Talmadge, who was standing outside his patrol car, double-parked in front of the Battery Park. He was a massive man. Fifty-two regular, I'd say. Coming from a long line of clothing-store owners, I was taught at a young age how to size up people. Not their character, their suit size. His shoulders were jammed up into his neck, making his short blond hair appear to hang longer than it really did. He had a round, red face almost the size of a sliced, half-sweet August watermelon.

"Call me when you're done," Pearlie said as I climbed out of the backseat. He bulldozed his way through a small crowd of shoppers who had emerged from the Grove Arcade across the street.

Talmadge jammed the notepad into my hand. Something about the handwriting seemed vaguely familiar. The message was in pale pencil, and it read what Talmadge had said, nothing more. I looked up toward the man, who was now sitting on the edge of the roof, his legs dangling over the side.

"Lady inside said he just moved in a week ago," Talmadge said. "From Charlotte. African-American, old."

"Let's go up," I said. I might have sounded decisive, but that's as far as it went. I had no idea what to do. Sure, I had counseled hundreds of suicidal people, but their legs had never been dangling over the side of a hotel roof while I did it.

The lobby was about two flights of dirty concrete steps above the street. I reached the heavy glass-and-brass lobby door before Talmadge. As I opened it, I spotted a battered army-surplus metal desk and an even older lady sitting behind it, straddling the walkway to the elevators.

"How do we get to the roof?" I asked.

"Over there's the stairway. Elevator's been broke all morning," the tiny woman with teased white hair said. She had a black toy poodle clutched in her arms. "Never know about a person, do you, FuFu?" she said, kissing the dog on the nose. "He seemed fine at breakfast."

Climbing to the roof loomed as a considerable task, since both Talmadge and I were out of breath from just climbing to the lobby. Talmadge did all the cussing, as I didn't have even the energy for that. When we reached the top floor, we found the door opened to a hallway. At the far end of it was a door with the word *Roof* painted on it. It was time. Time for the good shrink to do his thing. If only a good shrink had been around.

I slowly opened the door. I realized we were on the back side of the roof, with the man opposite us facing the front of the hotel. He had a healthy wad of overgrown steel-wool hair bulging out from under a white golf cap. He wore a starched yellow shirt with wide, white vertical stripes, white suspenders, and beige pants. If he'd been a white man, I would have sworn it was an aged Jay Gatsby. He opened what appeared to be a tall, slim plastic bag of peanuts, dumped part of the contents into a glass bottle of cola, and then took a swig of the whole concoction. I felt a sympathetic burp coming up.

Talmadge looked at me like a dog that had just been slapped by a rolled-up newspaper but didn't know why. We watched the man pour more peanuts into the bottle and take another giant swig. If he intended to end his life, he was going on a full stomach.

"Excuse me, sir?" I blurted out.

The man turned his head slightly, like he'd heard something but wasn't sure where it came from. A fat older-model hearing aid stuck out of his left ear.

Talmadge whispered for me to go toward the man from his right side and mimed that he would go from the left. Just as we started toward him, the man swung his legs onto the roof, got on his knees, and lifted himself slowly. As he did, our eyes met.

"Holy shit!" I said. "T, is that you?"

This was not just an acquaintance. This was Theloneous Royal, a man who'd known me almost before the bleeding from my circumcision stopped. He had worked for us at Goldberg's, doing everything from sales to alterations, but he mainly "carried Gritz round town," as he used to say—to Little League practice, to orthodontist appointments, to spin-the-bottle parties at Gail Mason's house, to the fishing hole below Dillsboro Dam. T drove my brother and me all over Asheville in Dad's 1954 Buick Roadmaster, which we three dubbed "the Golden Chariot." Once, when he was accidentally shot by a fellow hunter during bear season, T told the doctor he had to survive because "who else is going to get Gritz to his bar mitzvah lessons?"

It was T, all right, sans tight skin and clear eyeballs and with loads more dots, spots, and crevices on his face than the last time I'd seen him.

"Are you all right?" I said, grabbing his hand to help him stand. His palm was cold and his handshake weak. Even so, gripping T's hand made me feel safer and calmer than I had in years.

T looked at Talmadge and then me.

"You fellers thought I was going to . . . Good Lord! I was just trying to escape a couple of women that can't seem to keep their traps shut downstairs. Their chatter is like hail on a tin roof." He looked at the notepad that for some dumb reason I'd carried with me all the way up the stairs. "That damn thing fell off while I was feeding my face. That's my to-do list for today. Believe it or not, I was meaning to call you." T chuckled. "Musta had a mind of its own, huh?"

CHAPTER FOUR

"As me est chasser, zol rinnen iber de bord!"
"If you're going to do something wrong, enjoy it!"

Talmadge and I followed T as he walked slowly down the hallway of the fourteenth floor.

"I guess I got the penthouse. There ain't no more apartments on this floor but mine. Just the old ballroom and me."

To my right and closed off by two large sets of French doors was the formerly popular Robert R. Raby Banquet and Dance Hall. It was Arthur Murray—who started his dance-business career in Asheville at the original Battery Park Hotel, teaching rich widows to waltz—and not Asheville's infamous politician who the room should have been named for. The ballroom was important to my personal history because it was here that I had, with intense trepidation, walked up to Marci Dubinsky, seventh-grade cheerleader *extraordinaire*, and asked her to do the watusi with me at my bar mitzvah.

From what I could see through the gathered curtains on the ballroom's doors, the décor was shabby chic, heavy on the shabby. Obviously not as remodeled as the rest of the building, the room retained some of its past charm—namely, the hardwood floors and the faded velvet draperies hung over large, arched windows.

"I think they're going to have bingo in there tonight. I've got to check my schedule," T said, reaching in his pocket for his key.

He stopped in front of a door with a fresh coat of chocolate-colored paint slapped on it, the old layers bubbling up beneath it like they were hiding giant hazelnuts.

"I'm in the mood for nomnom, how about y'all?" T asked, inserting the key. The door stuck for a moment and then popped open.

Nomnom was the secret name T and I had made up for pork rinds, their consumption being strictly forbidden in my kosher household. Only God and T ever knew of my weakness for T's private stock. He made his own, stirring a big pot on his stove, heating the oil to just the right temperature with the care of a trained chef. We always kept a bottle of mouthwash hidden in the spare tire of the Golden Chariot to cover my waywardness. In the days when we regularly downed those greasy suckers, I debated renouncing Judaism, thinking of all the allowance money I could save by not having to buy so much Listerine. I even sold my 1955 Sandy Koufax rookie baseball card just to keep up my habit. Every now and then, Possum would make his own version and have a bowl of them waiting with my newspaper at lunch, but no one could come close to T's nomnom.

"I think I better get back to headquarters," Talmadge said suspiciously, like he'd just got an inkling of a bong party.

"You ever had rinds?" T said seriously, looking at Talmadge. "Pork rinds?"

"You bet. Just sit a minute with Gritz. Let me fire up some butter to drizzle over them. You can take 'em with you. That Indian fellow downstairs stocks the packaged kind. Those give bad indigestion. I have to make my own."

Talmadge and I filled T's tiny rust-colored corduroy couch, sitting next to each other like puppies waiting for our biscuits. Rinds take a man back home. Even Jews, but only Southern members of the tribe.

I watched T hobble around his tiny kitchen. He had an eight-by-ten picture of Jesus hung over the stove, and a small oak table with one yellow place mat. A plastic bowl sat in the middle of the table with one banana and one apple inside. I would have gotten up to help, but two people in the kitchen would have made a crowd.

Sitting close to Talmadge on the sofa was a little too intimate. The coffee table rubbed our knees. A large, old, and very used Bible with gilt lettering sat prominently on it. The *B* was rubbed off, so it read *IBLE*.

T dropped a metal ladle. "Doggone it," he said loudly. "My body ain't keeping up with my mind anymore."

Reuniting with T was great, but it also made me recognize how empty my life had become. And seeing T that day, I knew our reunion would not last as long as our early years together.

I tried to tell Talmadge how T and I grew up together, T with a thirty-five-year head start. Talmadge fiddled with his socks and didn't seem interested. Maybe cops aren't nostalgic—too many nasty things in the present to deal with.

Talmadge picked up the Bible. "I like to see people who give this book a heavy workout," he smiled, flipping through it like it was a *Field & Stream* in a doctor's office.

"I'll be right there!" T yelled from the kitchen, much louder than he needed to.

I noticed a folded section of newspaper lying on the coffee table. The Bible had been sitting on it. I carefully picked it up. The paper was dated September 16, 1993. It was a section containing the *Asheville Citizen-Times* Sunday feature called "Remember When." The year featured was 1939, and the column listed some of its momentous happenings, such as President Franklin Roosevelt's declaration of United States neutrality in the European war, the opening of the New York World's Fair, the rally held in New York by twenty-two thousand American Nazis, and the movie release of *The Wizard of Oz* and *Gone With the Wind*.

Also featured was a picture of a tall, slender, young black man in a hotel bellboy's uniform scaling the front of the Battery Park Hotel. He clung to the ornate, white front-porch balustrades that were still part of the facade while two short, bloated white men in Panama hats stood below smoking fat cigars.

The article described the scene as "a reenactment of the famous September 1939 Battery Park murder escape." The skinny black man was identified as Mordecai Moore, an elevator operator who, the article said, had confessed to the murder of Evangeline Sardano, a New York University coed from Fishkill, New York, who was traveling through the North Carolina mountains during summer break with her uncle, Hieronymous Sardano, professor of animal husbandry at North Carolina State College of Agriculture and Engineering. The two lawmen in the picture were identified as Sheriff Harris "Hurt" Bailey and his deputy, Love Andrews.

The article noted that Moore had retracted his confession during a three-day trial, claiming he was beaten into submission by a New York City private detective the Sardano family had brought to Asheville when there was no immediate arrest in the case. The bellboy was convicted and executed, all within four months of the crime. The last sentence of the article read, "Many people in the community, even today, believe the wrong man was executed for this hideous crime."

"I keep that article right under my Bible. Pray about it every night of my life," T said, bringing in a plastic bowl of nomnom, as well as a bag to go.

"Why's that?" Talmadge asked, taking the bag, which already had a large oil stain on the side.

"Mordecai didn't kill that girl."

"Sounds like a lot of people still believe that," I said, looking at the article.

"I don't just believe it. I know it."

CHAPTER FIVE

"A shver hartz redt a sacht."
"A heavy heart talks a lot."

.

Have you ever felt like time is a conveyor belt of everything that has ever happened, stopping for no mortal, for the most part carrying things, all kinds of things, moving along in a monotonous hum that you can't dance or even sing to? Things packed in unmarked dull brown boxes, some neatly sealed, some bursting at the seams. Herman's life's things or Mary's life's things, intensely important to them, but just boxes of stuff to you. You can't quite see this ever-moving line of life, but still you know it's there, always there, never stopping, not for pauper or for king. And then out of the blue on a September afternoon, one of those other people's boxes falls off that conveyor, contents spilling at your toes, waiting for you, only you, to pick them up and send them on their way again. Dirty stuff, sticky stuff, sweet stuff. Stuff you have no choice but to pick up and do something about.

Talmadge and I had a very fat box of Mordecai Moore's stuff fall at our feet that day.

Thankfully, the chief went first.

"How's that?" he said with the right amount of uncertainty.

"I know the boy didn't do it 'cause I was with him all that night."

"Why didn't the police believe you?" I said.

" 'Cause I never told them," T said, putting his hands in his back pockets and walking to the apartment's front windows. "I couldn't tell nobody. You got to remember, this was nineteen thirty-nine in the South. Colored people couldn't just open up to anybody and everybody. It wasn't just your own self you had to worry about. I mean, there was your family, your church. There was always those"—T paused—"those complications you had to think about."

A psychiatrist knows there are times when he has to keep his mouth shut and let all the words that need to be said fight their way out in the open. Talmadge followed my lead. We simultaneously reached for nomnom and waited for T to tell the rest of the story. When he was ready. If he could.

Still facing the windows, T began: "Mordecai and I worked together here at the Battery. We were both teenagers. He wasn't from here. Somewhere down in South Carolina. Shy kid. Liked to read all the time, Western dime novels, Kit Carson and the likes. Always kept a stack in his locker like some boys kept liquor. Anyways, Mordecai and I went over to McCormick Field that night. Just the two of us. They was having one of those barnstormer baseball games, colored teams playing each other all over the South, long time before anybody heard of Jackie Robinson. Cool Papa

Bell was playing center field. He was a damn good pitcher earlier in his career. Philadelphia Monarchs versus the Pittsburgh Crawfords. Can't remember where I laid my boxer shorts yesterday, but I remember every inning of that game, all right."

T took a deep breath and turned to look at Talmadge and me. "After the game, Mordecai and I went on over to Fannie Jackson's house in Stumptown. She was having a surprise birthday party for her mama. Some fool brought a jug of corn liquor, and Mordecai and I both got skunk-drunk. Next thing I remember, I wake up the next morning lying on Fannie's back porch with Mordecai curled up on the swing above me. Fannie comes out with her big feet at my nose and says we got to get on up, wasn't we missing work? Then she brought us a couple mugs of black chicory coffee to spark us back to the living."

"This was the morning after the murder?" Talmadge asked.

"That's right. We got to work by noon or so and tried to sneak into the basement of the Battery Park to our lockers, but the cops were swarming like flies over hot Brussels sprouts. They told us a girl had been murdered during the night and nobody was to enter or leave the place just then."

"And so how did they decide so quickly that your friend killed the girl?" I asked.

"They didn't charge nobody right then. It was a couple weeks before they come down on him. The town was in one major snit. Crowds were hanging off the police-station steps waiting to hear who done it. Rumors circulated about every man or boy old enough to spank his monkey. I mean, it was real panic around this town."

"Girl was raped," Talmadge said.

"No, she weren't. I mean, they found her on the floor in bloodstained silk pajamas, but the coroner said she was not messed with in that way."

"How did she die?" I said.

"Shot, once in the face, once in the stomach. Slapped across the face with a pistol, too. Bled to death."

"I guess we've got a full file on this one somewhere," Talmadge said, jotting something on a tiny piece of paper he pulled from his shirt pocket.

"Maybe, but the sheriff took over the investigation. Not the police."

Talmadge didn't seem surprised that the county sheriff would be in charge of a crime in the city's jurisdiction. "The sheriff and the police chief hated each other's guts, huh?" he asked.

"How did you know?" T said, smiling.

"Happens more times than not."

"Pete Reid could tell you all about it. Is he still kicking?" T said, looking at me.

Pete Reid wrote a column called "Roaming the Hills" in the *Asheville Citizen-Times*. He was about the same age as Dad and T, I guessed, but he was still writing for the paper, although his three-times-a-week column was down to one lately.

"He still writes. Haven't seen him since Dad moved to Florida," I said.

"Pete covered the whole thing for the paper," T said. "As I remember it, he questioned why Chief Mills wasn't in charge. Day after the murder, he wrote up in the *Citizen* that the police chief was fishing on the French Broad that morning, when he was supposed to be on the job. I heard the chief threatened to get Pete fired, but nobody was really that concerned about the police chief playing hooky anyway. This was Sheriff Hurt Bailey's town."

"From the stories I've heard about Bailey, nothing would surprise me," Talmadge said. "His oil portrait greets me every day at headquarters. There's something about the man's eyes that bothers me."

"Dad always said Hurt Bailey couldn't help being ugly, but he could have stayed home more," I said.

"Amen," T said, smiling. Then he realized he needed to finish his story, and the grin fell off his face faster than a boy's first sexual encounter. There were a few seconds of silence before he continued. "At first, some people thought maybe the girl's uncle could have done it. You know, maybe he wanted more than a good-night peck. The hotel was nearly full that night, but it wasn't long before they started on the help. One by one, we was all called in to tell what we knew. When they pinned it on Mordecai, I told him I would testify about him being at the ball game and Fannie's party with me, but he said for me not to dare say a word. He said he was going to be six feet under soon enough, and there was no reason I needed to join him. He made me promise not to speak to anyone about that God-awful night. He said Sheriff Hurt told him he didn't need but one nigger to fry at a time, and if anyone tried to save Mordecai's ass, he'd take him down, too. Lord, sometimes I think it would have been better if I talked, even if they killed me, too."

T took a deep breath. He was done. I knew it. Talmadge knew it.

"I like the way you add butter to the rinds," the chief said. "I'd better get back to the station. Don't want anybody thinking I've gone fishing." As if on cue, his cell phone rang. "I'll be there in five minutes," he said, using his free hand to pick up the bag of pork rinds. T opened the door. Talmadge waved good-bye and left, still talking to the dispatcher.

T looked at me.

All I could think to say was, "I'm sorry, T."

"You know, he's still here," T replied. "I've seen him."

"Seen who?"

"Mordecai. He might be dead, but he sure ain't in heaven. Twice. I've seen him twice since I've been back. Sounds crazy, I know it does. That's why I wanted to talk to you."

Actually, I was thrilled to hear that someone I knew believed in ghosts, or at least the possibility of them. *Haints* was what they were called in New Orleans. At Tulane Medical School, my adviser, Professor Geoffrey Baines, had talked about haints like they were as common as crawfish. The whole town seemed like a commune for the reluctantly departed.

"Actually, T, I think I may have something like that dogging me. I don't see her, a former patient at Highland, but I know when she's around. Zelda Fitzgerald?"

"Burned up in that fire, didn't she? Writer's wife."

"I haven't told many people, T."

A broad smile crept across T's face, exposing teeth too perfect to be natural. I smiled back. It didn't have anything to do with Zelda or Mordecai. It had everything to do with T and me.

"What does Mordecai do when he sees you?"

"Looks at me."

"That's all?"

"He looks at me and then disappears. Makes me wonder if I'm touched."

Trinity didn't like us to use the word *touched*. I found this out at a staff retreat. I personally liked the word, but it was far too nonclinical, too Old South, for Trinity. I'd decided that at least a percentage of mental-health flareups occur when God gets so close to people—close enough to touch—that they can't stand it, the pressure and the beauty, and then all the craziness just bursts out, flooding, overloading a fragile system of nerves and thoughts. That was a theory I never told anyone about, but it made perfect sense to me.

"There's not a thing wrong with your mind, T. I'm sure of that."

"I hope so."

"I know so," I said firmly. I stood up to go. "I'd better get back to the hospital. How about coming over for supper sometime this week? I'd like you to meet Arlene and the kids."

"I thought it was Nona," T said hesitantly.

"Nona and I split up four years ago."

"You remarried or just warmin' it?"

"Arlene's not my lover, she's my housekeeper and my ex-mother-in-law."

"Come again?" T said.

It was hard for most people to understand my domestic life. Not every divorced man allows his former wife's mother to move in. But one week after Nona took off with Sunshine Smith, the non-circumcised lifeguard at the Jewish Community Center, I got a call from Arlene. "I'm at the Asheville bus station," she said. "My daughter might be a little tramp, but I've got grandchildren to take care of. Come get me."

"I normally stayed at least six miles from my mother-in-law," T said, picking up the nearly empty bowl of nomnom and carrying it to the kitchen.

She'd been bored living in Boca Raton—Boca, as she called it—collecting age spots and dividends from her late husband's stocks. But Arlene fit right into my household. My kids—Nate, now sixteen, and Stef, seventeen—loved their seventy-five-going-on-forty-five-year-old grandmother. Whether thanks to my kids' free spirits or Asheville's New Age atmosphere, Boca's mah-jongg queen fast became a leader of rebellion in our town. Though she still made the meanest chopped liver known to Jewish mankind, Arlene donned a new wardrobe of tie-dyed T-shirts and purple Birkenstocks and started organizing citizens' groups to fight everything from pollution on the Blue Ridge Parkway to highway patrol profiling stops. She even made the front page of the *Citizen-Times* by standing in front of a bulldozer at the Wal-Mart Super Center site. "Somebody has got to stop those *goyim* from Arkansas from taking everybody's business," she proclaimed. Dad saw her picture on the internet and sent a lovely bouquet of flowers.

My only conflict with Arlene came one time when she tried to fix me up with the Jewish hippie from New Jersey who led her yoga class. "So what she doesn't shave her legs?" Arlene said. "Buy her tights for Valentine's Day."

T agreed to call me if Mordecai showed up again. I told him I would requisition some anxiety medication from the hospital pharmacy and courier it over to him, though he seemed a little hesitant about that. We shook hands and said good-bye. I really wanted to hug him again like I had as a kid, but even shrinks hold back emotions. The door closed behind me, and I heard T lock it, and chain it, too.

CHAPTER SIX

"Az me ken nit vi me vil, tut men vi me ken."
   "If you can't do as you wish, do as you can."

There was plenty of time to call Pearlie as I trudged down the fourteen floors of mercilessly hot stairs back to the lobby. I still owned the Jeep Commando that had been my first car in high school. Stef actually thought it was cool, and took up driving it for her first car. She didn't like having to kick the driver's door to get it open but otherwise claimed to her friends that it was an authentic Beach Boys car. Most of my colleagues had Mercedes coupes or Jags. They made no comment about my taxi, but I could tell they were never going to make me chief of staff. That train of thought reminded me I needed to call the office.

"Essie, I had an emergency, but it was a false alarm. Anything urgent?"

"It's been real quiet," she answered.

That was always an ominous sign for a mental facility.

She read me my afternoon itinerary—one unimportant staff meeting and a few stacks of inane insurance filings to wade through. "Oh, Perrier Skyhawk called. She said you told her to call if she had any cancellations, and she has one at three," Essie said.

"Great. I'll take it. Call Dink and tell him I am unavoidably detained." He wouldn't be surprised. I came up with some excuse to miss almost all of his meetings.

Dink was Dr. Denver Montague, Highland's nationally acclaimed psychiatrist and chief of staff. He spoke to groups all over the country on his specialty, kleptomania, but after I observed him pocket a CD in Wal-Mart one Sunday, I didn't have much use for the man. The feeling was mutual.

My friend Perrier Skyhawk was one of Asheville's many certified massage therapists. One news report said we have more CMTs per capita than any city west of Hong Kong. When she arrived in Asheville, Perrier had the name Esther Goodkind. A contemporary of Arlene's from Boca, Esther moved shortly after her husband, Benjamin, died. According to his wife, Benjamin had been a "major player" in the multiple-sized men's sock market, but he dropped dead just days after one-size-fits-all socks hit the market. Within a year after showing up in Asheville, Esther became acquainted with Arnie Bigmeat, a Cherokee Indian from the neighboring reservation. Arnie, though twenty years younger, fell hard for Esther, and she for him.

"Tradition is so important to them, like it is to us," Esther explained to Arlene. "It's like *Fiddler on the Roof* with face paint."

Esther began studying ancient Indian ways of curing ailments but took an Oriental turn when she enrolled in The Land of the Sky School of Massage on Lexington Avenue. Upon graduation, she legally changed her name to Perrier Skyhawk, and Arnie moved in.

Perrier's place of business was handy for me—close to my office and also my home, all three sitting on various corners of Montford Avenue. One of Asheville's oldest streets, Montford was lined with authentic Victorian homes and lovely old oaks with enormous roots that erupted under the sidewalks and into the road. These old painted ladies, once small tuberculosis sanitariums at the turn of the twentieth century, were now brightly restored bed-and-breakfasts catering to rich Atlantans on weekend escapes. A few were decaying boarding homes for petty thieves and lost-forever sots.

Highland was located at the dead-end of Montford. When Dr. Robert Carroll established his private hospital with its campus of walking trails surrounded by dense forests and volleyball courts scooped out of steep hillsides, his unique approach to mental health gave Highland national notoriety. He demanded fresh air and daily exercise as part of his strict mental rehabilitation. He also thought pumping pig's blood into the spinal area of his patients gave them a better outlook on life. Once, while Zelda Fitzgerald was a patient, Carroll took the whole hospital to Cuba for a weekend. He also purchased several homes surrounding the hospital and made them free housing for his staff. Eighty years later, one of those houses— mine—was still used for the same purpose. Though the water pipes sounded like howling coyotes and the floors creaked and swayed, my current family unit—the kids, my ex-mother-in-law, and I— liked living in what we called *Kleina Shmahta*, "the Pretty Rag."

Pearlie seemed in a good mood when he pulled up in front of the Battery Park. He even reached behind him and popped open my door.

"Where to, general?" he asked.

"Perrier's going to squeeze me in at three," I said.

I knew this would not make him happy. He had made it quite

clear several times before when he drove me to her office that the Bible did not include women when it told of the laying on of hands.

"Oh," he said. "Are you sure?"

"Yes, I'm sure."

I hated to disappoint Pearlie, but I really needed the rubdown. He mumbled a little but made no conversation the rest of the short trip. Nor did he make an attempt to pop my door open when we got there.

"See you in an hour," I said, stepping out.

Pearlie didn't reply, but I knew he would be there.

"Glad you could make it," Perrier said as I entered her living room from her front porch, which had more rotten planks in it than not. She wore one of those bright Southwestern smock house dresses wide enough to hide three Mexicans immigrants. Barefoot and without makeup, she made casual Fridays at the office an understatement. "The sunroom awaits," she said, smiling.

The room was small but adequate. It had curtains that went only halfway up the windows. I took off my shirt and pants and laid them on the couch. The curtains covered all they needed to, but my head and part of my bare chest could be seen above them. I noticed an old lady battering a rug on her porch next door and wondered what she thought a certified massage therapist did all day.

I climbed onto the table, lay face down, and covered my butt with a sheet that had palomino horses romping all over it.

"Ready, dear?" Perrier said in motherly fashion, poking her head into the room.

From my vantage, I noticed that she had pretty good feet for a retiree. My favorite third-year seminar at Tulane was the one covering foot fetishes. Each of her toenails was painted with a colorful tiny scene, the big toe with a bigger sunset than the pinkie.

I guessed the bunion on her left foot was supposed to be a rugged mountainside.

Some people visit bartenders to relieve stress. Others come to doctors like me. I like venting my frustrations with small talk while my tush is kneaded.

"You must be having a rough week. Your body is really tight," she said.

"I sort of ran into an acquaintance at the Battery Park today who swears he sees a man who died in nineteen thirty-nine."

"Doesn't surprise me. The ghost has a connection to the place, right?"

"Definitely."

"Poor soul's probably trapped down here until the right person frees him," Perrier said, digging into my cross-trapezoidal.

I proceeded to tell her the story of Mordecai Moore. She was particularly interested in Moore's liking for cowboy novels.

"Can you find an old copy of one of those books?" she asked.

"I think you can locate Methuselah on the internet if you look hard enough. Why?"

"We could use it as a bridge. To Mr. Moore. I mean, if you want me to help in this. Arnie and I just came back from Oklahoma. Visited his grandmother. She's a medium—you know, channels souls. She taught us how to communicate with the dead. Fascinating. We're just novices right now, but I'm sure Arnie and I could try and reach the man for you and your friend. Especially if we could find one of those Westerns. Departed souls like common ground to be presented before they intermingle with the living. We could just leave the book on a table nearby and see what happens. No guarantee, of course."

I knew she meant business. Her thumb dug into the muscles near my kidney a bit too hard.

"I'll certainly ask T," I said. "What about Zelda?" I had mentioned my own possible encounters with the supernatural during a previous tush push.

"You can't do two at a time. Privacy issue among the dead."

I turned over like a turkey ready to be basted, in this case with oil instead of butter.

"Gritz, how do you feel about local politics?" Perrier said, filling her hand with a new puddle of coconut oil.

"I like it about as much as singing 'Jesus Loves Me.' "

"I've been asked to serve on a citizens' committee for the election of Mayor Bloom for the United States Senate," she said while doing a long, slick run down the underside of my arm all the way to my fingertips. "He's going to officially announce during the dedication of the new Raby Justice Center on the twenty-eighth."

"We need another Raby building about as much as we need another McDonald's," was all I could honestly say about the topic. I thought about singing, "If you knew Smelley like I knew Smelle . . ."

I should have been thrilled that a member of my minority was doing so well in politics. Shelburne Bloom, son of the same Moses Bloom who Aunt Fay called about, was affectionately known to his constituents as "Shel," but those of us who had attended Asheville Elementary and High with him knew him as "Smelley." He had an odor about him. I'm not sure what the smell thing was with me, but unlike my shadowy friend Zelda, Smelley stunk like unflushed waste sautéed with garlic.

Politics was a good life slot for the guy. He cheated at everything, even his bar mitzvah, after which Shel had bragged about how he lip-synced the Hebrew from a hidden tape player. He was also one of those people in a small town you get thrown together with just because you're the same age or same religion—

or in my case both. It was like a life sentence. For example, the one time in my life I hadn't seen Shel for an extended period, out of the blue, his wife, Marsha, showed up at the hospital wanting outpatient treatment, and who got assigned to her? She was obviously depressed—and who wouldn't have been, married to him? It seems "the mayor," as she called him in therapy, was playing Pokémon with one of his father's nurses at Happy Valley Assisted Living. Marsha wasn't sure the girl—one Candace "Candy" Kane— was assisting her father-in-law but was confident she was doing a great deal for her husband. I was leaning toward believing my patient. I've never met a Candy who didn't have an extremely strong libido.

"I'm sorry, Perrier, but I just can't stand the man."

"I did have my doubts about him after I saw his toes," Perrier said thoughtfully.

Perrier had previously coached me on toe analysis. She claimed that the shape, size, and bend of one's little piggies were better ways of judging people or predicting what they might do than were palms. I wondered whether they might also give more insight than psychotherapy.

"He came in for a massage awhile back, and when I saw that his middle toe—you remember, the anger one—curved sharply into his fourth toe . . ." She waited for me.

"The gauge-of-sincerity toe?" I asked like a good student.

"Exactly. When I saw the arc of those two toes, it did make me uncomfortable."

"I never noticed his toes, but he used to make the overweight girls in school cry. He was a wizard at coming up with horribly hurtful names." I figured that would cost Smelley a vote, since Perrier had been hitting our corn fritters a little too heavy since leaving Boca.

"I heard that his dad used to be the local kingpin of the Democratic Party without ever being elected to office. I thought that was kind of odd," she said, pressing a little too close to my liver.

"Perrier, in Southern politics, odd is perfectly normal."

When she got to the tips of my toes, I knew the good times were about to end. She once told me that my toes were sensitive and kind, and that the only warning sign was that my pinkie indicated my career was not going in the right direction. My pinkie was a perceptive little digit.

"I'll talk to Arnie when he gets home about the Battery Park thing," Perrier said, gathering her towels so she could leave the room and let me get out of my Julius Caesar attire.

Hopping off the table, I thought I saw the old lady across the way peeking at me. I waved, but she darted inside.

I dressed knowing that the stack of insurance forms I had been restacking for weeks awaited me at the office. Still, I felt a tad energized, and not just from the massage. I had this funny feeling deep in my gut. Though I had no idea what to do to help T, I had stirrings of what vaguely felt like a purpose, a feeling I hadn't had in a very long time.

CHAPTER SEVEN

"Yeder aizel hot lib tsu hern vi er alein hirzhet."
"Every ass likes to hear himself bray."

I slept hard that night but had disturbing dreams. People who had died years earlier were back in my life, but in skewed ways. Uncle Jack, who in real life had converted to Catholicism, was a rabbi, and Emily Tompkins, my sweet first-grade teacher, was a stripper at Possum's during spicy lunchtime buffets. I awoke to a typical early-September day in Asheville, hazy and hot. The chamber of commerce promoted "Cool, Green Asheville," but if you didn't have air conditioning, which my house didn't, you were sweating by the time you got to the breakfast table. I didn't take the time to analyze my dreams as I might have suggested a patient do. I blamed it on the late-night leftover pizza I'd grabbed before bed and left it at that.

Everything was quiet downstairs. Stef and Nate slept until the very last minute before going to school, and Arlene was usually out early. I showered, grabbed a cold Pop-Tart, and headed for work. Since I lived almost on Highland's grounds, I walked. Pearlie could be grumpy in the mornings, and I used the few minutes it took to reach my office to organize myself.

There were several things I wanted to accomplish that day, most of which had nothing to do with work at Highland. I wanted to visit Moses Bloom at Happy Valley and get Aunt Fay her information on Willard Paully. I didn't need her calling me every half-hour in a panic to outdo Big Fay. But my first hour was already committed to another Bloom, Moses' daughter-in-law. I liked Marsha and wanted our therapy sessions to succeed. Maybe she and the mayor had actually had sex, usually a solid short-term solution to making couples think they were salvaging their relationship. Of course, for that to happen, Nurse Candy would probably need to be out of town or having her period.

I greeted Wayne, our newly hired blond entrance guard. He was young and muscular and had hair longer than Lady Godiva's, worn in a ponytail. I rubbed my bald spot and tried to hide my resentment.

"Another hot one," I said as I walked by his booth.

He nodded. I could tell his focus was the teenage girls on the volleyball court within his sight. Highland had mandatory competition first thing in the morning, five days a week, rain or shine. Though it had been years since I was a patient myself, just the faint sounds of screaming, overly enthusiastic orderlies prodding lethargic souls with no desire to play volleyball at eight in the morning sent my stomach into a sympathetic knot. I'd forgotten the faces of most of those I shared a sandy court with, but Carter Holliman's countenance had never left me. A gray-haired, distinguished-looking middle-aged man, a severely depressed insurance executive from Tampa, he never uttered a word to anyone, walking everywhere with shoulders slumped and eyes firmly on the ground. Still, the guy showed up promptly for every volleyball game. He would stand at his position, oblivious to who was winning, responding only when the ball was slammed directly onto his head or into his chest, and then only to pick the ball up and throw it blindly to the nearest person. I never knew if he didn't care or couldn't care. Of late, I was getting scared Carter Holliman's view of life and mine were similar.

Von Ruck Hall, which housed my office, sat in the middle of the Highland campus. It was one of the original buildings, a handsome Greek Revival structure of dark burgundy brick with large white columns holding up a small, rounded balcony over the front entrance. The main floor housed a few older female patients. Doctors' offices were on the second and third floors. Von Ruck was named for one of Asheville's early tuberculosis physicians. "Lungers" had flocked to town in the late 1800s and early 1900s for his miracle cure, which wasn't much more than milk and mountain air. The fallacy of that legacy was that we now know milk causes more lung congestion that it cures, and that our mountain air has so many allergens that medical schools all over the nation advise their brightest and greediest pulmonary graduates to head to our hills. I had a nagging belly pain that my profession didn't deserve its reputation much more than Von Ruck and his cohorts. Like politics, psychiatry is as much spin as science.

Ophelia Walton turned her giant vacuum off as I passed, heading for the stairway. She had been an employee at Highland for decades. As a matter of fact, she had just started work about the time I was bitching about having to play volleyball. We didn't cure as many patients as I would have liked at Highland, but we

44

definitely had fewer dust mites than any hospital in the country. Ophelia loved to vacuum. Highland's star exterminator of minute creatures and collector of carpet fuzz still seemed confused at how I was once a patient and now a doctor.

"Doing okay today?" she asked, as if it was just a matter of time before I'd crash again.

"Feeling great, Ophelia. How about you?"

"Just doing my best till the Lord calls," she said. "Don't you work too hard today, Dr. G." She turned on the vacuum again.

That's what I love about the South. Southerners never forget who you are, even if you do.

I was a few minutes late, so I hurried up the steps to my second-floor office. As I reached the top stair, I saw Marsha Bloom sitting on our torn, puke-green fake leather couch in the waiting area facing Essie's tiny desk. She was reading a paperback with her legs crossed, her top leg kicking back and forth nervously. Marsha was a pretty woman, probably about my age, a touch on the *zaftig* side, but still actively working at looking put-together.

"I'll be right with you," I said, smiling at her.

The look she gave me with raised eyebrows indicated my wish for good sex for her and Shel probably hadn't happened.

"Good morning, Essie," I said.

She smiled and handed me two or three post-it notes of phone messages. She used her own supply, ones with "Jesus Saves" on each note. I didn't mind her trying to convert me, but I didn't have the heart to tell her about Stef's new bumper sticker on the Commando: "Jesus loves you, but everyone else thinks you're an asshole."

I pulled my office keys from my pants pocket. I unlocked door one, which opened to door two, which I also unlocked. That was one thing I liked about old Von Ruck. It still had the two doors back to back that shrinks' offices used to be known for. They were great for ensuring privacy. Patients didn't have to worry about being heard outside the office, and I didn't have to worry about sounds escaping on days after I'd ingested bean burritos the night before.

My messages were not urgent. I quickly came back out to formally invite Marsha in. You don't keep a Jewish princess waiting a second longer than you have to. We learned that in Sunday school, right after they taught us about Paully.

She wasted no time. Plopping down hard in her chosen chair, she kicked off her Cleopatra-style gold lamé sandals, tucked one bare foot under her pear-shaped bottom, and began to reel off Shel's indiscretions. I noticed her second toe was longer than her big toe. Perrier said that meant a severe lack of sexual fulfillment.

"He did it again," she said, running her fingers through her long black-dyed hair and pushing it with supreme agitation off the nape of her neck.

I'd been a therapist long enough to know the meaning of commonly repeated phrases among my patients. In this case, "He did it again" meant an attempt at sex had led to premature ejaculation and further damage to the antique Battenburg lace duvet she'd bought in New York. Though I enjoyed hearing about Mayor Smelley's failures, I tried to show patience and understanding for Marsha.

"Didn't we discuss putting the antique duvet up for a while and just doing with a Kmart variety?" I said. "Martha Stewart's not bad. Just for practicality."

"Why the hell should I? He's using up his good stuff on that damn nurse, and I have to put up with what he's got left over."

Marsha was obviously unaware that semen production wasn't

exactly akin to the giant water reservoir on Town Mountain, but I didn't want to get into a discussion of prostate dynamics.

"He still won't join you in therapy, will he? I'd like to treat you as a couple."

"Never. That's exactly what he says. Never."

Marsha swapped the foot she had under her butt and fiddled with her uppermost blouse button. Her plump cleavage showed more than a few age spots. The more I heard about Shel, the more I knew his symptoms of toxic jerkitis had only gotten worse since school.

It wouldn't have been professional for me to tell her to flat out leave the bastard, but I wished I could have. After all, I'd known her man was hopeless ever since the two of us were Asheville Bears teammates in Little League. Once, after he released his bat into the stands on a wild swing, a young girl was bashed in the head. As she went down, everyone gathered around trying to do something to ease her pain. Everyone but Shel, of course. He'd connected with the ball, you see. He rounded the bases laughing like a hyena and jumped on home plate like the winner he would never be.

"How long have you been married, Marsha?"

"Thirty-some years. It used to be good. I mean, pretty good. I guess."

"I just heard a rumor he's heading for the Senate."

Marsha sighed. "And now I'll have to be the smiling wife by his side. It hasn't mattered much since he's been mayor, but this is a statewide election."

She took a tissue out of her pocketbook and dabbed her eyes, being careful not to mess her mascara. I tried to casually observe her feet, wanting to make sure I hadn't mistaken her second toe for her third, thus causing a major misdiagnosis.

We spent the rest of the appointment discussing self-esteem and ways she could live her life in spite of her husband, though I didn't couch it in that manner. Having no immediate solution, I turned to the only sure help I could give her.

"I recommend you give this lady a call. I'm sure she can give you some relief."

I handed her one of Perrier's business cards.

I didn't mention to Marsha that I hoped to visit her father-in-law later that day. She didn't like the old man but put up with his constant controlling attempts because, as she put it, "the money's good." I hadn't pursued the comment. That was another downside to being a therapist in a small place. You had to keep straight in your head what people told you about others in the community, in addition to sorting out their illnesses. In the case of Moses and Shel, I assumed the maxim about the apple not falling far from the tree was valid.

Though I still had to see an alcoholic patient and a pyromaniac after Asheville's first lady, I asked Essie to get Moses on the phone for me.

"Gritz? Gritz Goldberg? Hell, I haven't seen you since you and Shel used to fuck around together."

Loose talk like that could kill a career.

"Mr. Bloom, I—"

"Call me Moses. I ain't never been much of a mister-type guy."

"Moses," I said, "do you remember my aunt Fay?"

"Your aunt Fay? Sure, who doesn't know Fay Cohen? *Ballebosteh*, that woman. You know what that means?"

"A woman in control."

"More like a controlling woman, but yeah, something like that. So, Fay is still alive?"

I didn't want to tell him she'd asked the same about him.

"She lives in Miami Beach with Dad. She said that you might have some pictures or articles on Willard Dudley Paully. She's doing a synagogue sisterhood project. She asked me to call you."

There was a pause, then a sharp cough. "Son, I know every bit of Jewish history in this town. I made most of it." He laughed. "You ever see my albums?"

"No."

"If it was ever in the paper, anything about a Jew in any corner of these mountains, I got it pasted up in those albums. I was the unofficial historian for B'nai Brith. Those albums are stuck somewhere in this damn closet out here. You can come out and look, if you want. Nobody else gives a shit about them anymore."

"I could come out in a couple hours, if that's not too soon."

"Hell, at my age, soon is too late. Come on out. Hey, do me a favor."

"Sure."

"On your way, stop at Heavenly Ham. This place is Seventh-Day Adventist, no meat. Bring me a ham sandwich. They know how I like it fixed."

I laughed as if he were joking.

"Ain't funny, son. Bring me a damn ham sandwich." He hung up abruptly. Aunt Fay must have taught him phone etiquette.

I tried not to seem impatient with my next patients, but I was itching to get out to Happy Valley. You didn't want to disappoint Little Fay, and being that I was sort of an amateur historian myself, the idea of finding some new tidbit of Asheville history interested me. And in the current malaise I seemed stuck in, that was notable.

On my way out, Essie reminded me that Dink had rescheduled the staff meeting I thought I'd gotten out of the day before.

"Tell him I—"

"He said for you to be there, no excuses."

"I'll do my best, Essie."

I knew I'd regret not turning Dink in on that shoplifting incident.

Pearlie and I picked up Moses' sandwich on the way. Moses was right. The employee at the drive-through window knew exactly what he wanted.

"Those people at Happy Valley are damn good customers," she said, stretching to look at the writing on Pearlie's hood. I watched her hunt for my order among ten or so all in the same size brown paper bags. "What kind of crazy shit is that?" she said, looking at the cab and handing the change to Pearlie. I wished I could be so honest with my customers. Pearlie acted like he hadn't even heard her.

Happy Valley attracted a lot of local Jewish elderly. As my uncle Dave said before he died there, "They're *goyim*, but they eat like Hasidics."

On the drive out, I recalled the stories I'd been told about W. D. Paully. Mrs. Rubin, my aged Sunday-school teacher, said that if it hadn't been for her and her friends in the Jewish community, Paully might have succeeded in taking over the United States from within. Observing Mrs. Rubin, a tiny, rotund lady about the size of Dr. Ruth, I had serious doubts about how she and her friends could have stopped such a notorious man. She never gave details, and none of us asked. All we wanted was for the hour to pass as quickly as possible. Seeing Mrs. Rubin's thick hosiery rolled over her knobby knees made us all quite sick each Sunday.

Pearlie dropped me at the front door of Happy Valley. A young nurse was leaning over the white wooden porch railing smoking a cigarette. It had to be Marsha Bloom's nemesis, Candy Kane. With the sun just past high noon, it was easy to see through her sheer white uniform to the black thong panties riding her slightly bulbous ass and the microthin black bra holding up her small but perky breasts. She turned toward me and licked her generous lips as if she were auditioning for a naughty movie and the director had just pulled up. I saw why the mayor was attracted to her. Slutty blond *shiksas* attract Jewish men like salt licks do deer.

"You must be that Dr. Goldstein who Moses said was coming."

"Goldberg," I said.

"Same thing," she smiled. Her gold badge confirmed it was Candy; she even had a red-and-white candy-cane design on it. She looked at the grease-stained bag I was carrying. "Oh, Lord, more contraband, huh? Moses is one cutie. I like old Jew men. Young Jews aren't too bad either," she said with a wink. "Follow me."

As I watched her bottom swish down the hallway, I had to remind myself that I was supposed to dislike this woman. After all, she was probably destroying one of my patient's marriages. On the other hand, if I followed my carnal desires, I might save my client by stealing the slut from the mayor. *Wait a minute!* I yelled quietly to my bad self. *You are a doctor.* The reply came to my mind in the voice of Aunt Fay: *Some doctor.*

Candy and I walked through a spacious, well-decorated lobby, then down a long hallway. Whoever owned the place had spent a ton of money on coordinated pink and green chairs, wallpaper, and prints. But the absence of urine smell was what impressed me the most.

"How come I haven't seen you before?" Candy said, slowing and turning her head back toward me.

"First time I've been here," I said.

"That's a good reason," she said with a giggle. "Moses has another visitor at the moment. He came in just before you pulled

51

up. Your Jewish preacher man." Candy waited a step, took me by my arm, and whispered into my ear, "That man acts like he's got a corncob stuck up his ass, if you know what I mean." I thought I felt the slightest flick of tongue on my ear.

Just before we got to the end of the corridor, we saw an old woman slumped over in a wheelchair in the middle of the hall. She looked like a defensive end guarding the goal line, except this player wore a sleeveless yellow cotton nightgown and matching, very worn terry-cloth slippers.

"What is Mrs. Levitz doing out here all alone?" Candy said sweetly.

The old lady looked at her and then at me. Her jaws were drawn tightly, and she said nothing, but her sad, dark eyes seemed to grow larger as she stared at me. She hugged herself as if she might be embarrassed to be seen in her nightgown.

"This is Dr. Goldborrow. He's a friend of Moses."

The woman suddenly backed her chair out of our way, bumping the wall.

"Estelle and Moses, they don't much like each other," Candy said.

The old lady disappeared into what I presumed was her room. I glanced inside as I passed and was surprised to see a computer sitting on a desk next to a bare hospital bed.

"Mrs. Levitz knows how to use a computer? In her condition?"

"She can't do a lot of things, but she can work her hands pretty well," Candy said. "She can't speak, but her mind is all there. She and I communicate better than I do with my own mother. That little lady is on that computer day and night. She sends e-mails down to the computer at the main desk."

We finally got to the last room on the hall. The door was cracked.

"Moses, honey, are you decent?" Candy called.

"I ain't been decent since the third grade," the voice of an old man called back.

"You are one busy fellow today," she said, pushing the door all the way open and holding it for me. "You boys be good now," she cooed before she left.

In contrast to the rest of Happy Valley, Moses Bloom's room smelled like an unattended bathroom. Moses sat upright on the bed in a white sleeveless undershirt and white boxers. On the nightstand was a white felt Stetson hat. I felt awkward, but he seemed completely comfortable greeting me in his skivvies. In a chair at the foot of the bed sat Asheville's lone rabbi, Shlomo Weiskopf. A single man in his early thirties with a wild red beard and curly red hair, he looked like a backpacker in his plaid cotton shirt, khaki shorts, and expensive hiking boots. Shlomo had been in Asheville for about three years. We hired him his first year out of the New York *yeshiva*, bringing him straight from his whitefish and smoked kippers to our cornbread and beans. Our congregation couldn't afford a seasoned leader, so we had to settle for newly ordained rabbis and for being a steppingstone as they worked their way up to bigger and better-paying positions. Shlomo was fond of describing himself as being "in a constant state of culture shock." He fit in Asheville about as well as Candy would fit in a convent.

"Hi," I said, reaching to shake Moses' hand. Shlomo didn't offer his.

It confused me that our latest batch of men of the cloth were no longer satisfied with using regular biblical name such as Samuel or Isaac but were now demanding to be called by Hebrew names. Shlomo grinned like the room didn't really smell of spilled bedpan. That was the other thing I disliked about young Jewish spiritual leaders: most smiled entirely too frequently. I missed old Rabbi Youngman, our last leader over age fifty. He had never smiled at anything but had at least seemed genuine in his negativity.

"Got my sandwich?" Moses bellowed.

"Sure do," I said, glancing at Shlomo.

The rabbi stood and turned toward the window. I guessed he was trying not to see what Moses was about to eat. Not many Jewish people follow the *kashruth* dietary laws anymore, but rabbis seem to fantasize we do. Sort of our own don't ask, don't tell policy.

I set the bag on the foot of the bed and took off my jacket. Moses sprang for the bag like a cat at a mouse. He took the sandwich out, threw the bag on the floor, and bit into his food almost savagely.

"*Gashmack!*" he said. The Yiddish word for culinary orgasm. It always surprised me how much Yiddish I recalled from hearing my parents, though I never used the language myself.

"Those albums you talked about, they sound like what Aunt Fay needs," I said. I wanted to get to the point and go anywhere it didn't stink.

Moses' mouth was fully stuffed, but he pointed to the closet and grunted, "Over there."

"Behind the urinary pads," I heard Shlomo say softly, still looking out the window with his back to Moses and me.

"Get me a drink! Don't want to die with *treif* in my mouth, now, do I?" Moses said with a chuckle.

Shlomo didn't laugh but turned, reached for a cup on the sink, and started filling it with water.

"Not that, Shlomo. The good stuff's under the sink. Pour me a shot of Jack Daniel's!"

I guessed Moses' age and the fact that he was a big contributor to Beth Augudus Synagogue gave him the luxury of bossing the rabbi around.

Once I got beyond the year's supply of leakage pads, I found three albums sitting on top of each other. They had wooden covers with crudely formed letters burned into them. Each read *MY ALBUM*. The pages were dusty black construction paper with mostly newspaper articles taped to them.

"They're not in order. Pull out all three," Moses said, clearing his throat.

I fetched them out of the closet and set them at the edge of his bed.

"Look in the one with the wormy chestnut cover. I think Paully's in that one. Real *shmegegi*, always wore a gray military uniform and black riding boots, like he thought he was Robert E. Lee or something."

Shlomo came over to my side of Moses' bed. "What are you looking for?" he said.

"His aunt is doing some kind of show on Willard Dudley Paully for the sisterhood. Down in Florida. Gritz, women like your aunt Fay are why I'm not in Florida. Goddamn nightmare. The whole state is full of them."

"Why's that?" I asked, more interested in flipping the pages than talking to him.

"That's why I stay in Asheville. All those *yentas* are ganged up down in Florida. When I was little, I always thought that before I grew up, all the *yentas* would be dead. But you know, there are just as many as there ever were."

"Now, Moses, let's be kind," Shlomo said, looking at one of the albums himself.

Moses acted like he didn't hear him. "Gritz, you know what a *yenta* is, don't you?"

I just smiled. Opinionated gossips who need to know everything about everybody. From my visits to south Florida, I had to admit Moses had a point.

Not surprisingly, most of the articles and pictures in the first few pages of my album were of Moses himself.

"You see, rabbi, I always gave away lots of my money—this charity, that charity. So tell me, why does God let me sit here in vegetarian hell?"

This time, it was Shlomo who focused on the album.

Finally, I came to a page with a copy of *The Libertarian* stuck to it. It was a small tabloid newspaper with the headline, "Roosevelt's Secret Jew Cabinet."

"Starts there. That was Paully's paper," Moses said. "Dumbass tried to make money selling shit like that. There's no money in newspapers, I don't care how many he shipped all over the country. I told him so. He could have made a fortune selling liquor during Prohibition, but no, he had to publish his damn paper. *Goyish kup*, no brains."

"You knew him personally?" Shlomo said.

"Played poker with him every week. He didn't have a problem taking money from a Jew, I can assure you that. He came almost every Wednesday. Always marched in wearing his fucking Silver Shirt uniform. Acted like he was some kind of general or something. Had a bodyguard stand outside the room, like he was important enough for somebody to kill."

"Where was this poker game?" I asked.

"Did your daddy never talk about the Battery Park poker club? He came pretty regular."

"My dad played poker with Willard Paully?"

"Sure he did. Leo Finkel from the pawnshop, he always came. Senator Bob Raby, he played when he wasn't in Washington.

56

Traveling salesmen dropped in on the game. Eddie Levitz, my brother-in-law, he came. Man was like my shadow, couldn't get away from him." Moses glanced at the hat on the nightstand. "And that writer, he came a time or two. That was before your dad was even married, I guess."

"Thomas Wolfe came to your poker club?" Shlomo said in awe.

"No, he was a *shmendrick*. Maybe he could write books, but he didn't have sense to get out of the rain. No, I mean Pete Reid, who wrote for the *Citizen*."

"Weren't you scared of a man like Paully? Seems like it would be like playing poker with Hitler," I said.

"You've never played poker, have you, Gritz?" Moses looked at me with his eyebrows scrunched, like I'd just missed a urinal and didn't know I was peeing on my shoes.

"Once or twice," I said.

"Saints don't play good poker. The best games are with people you wouldn't normally be seen with. Ex-cons, they're the best. They've had time to practice. You don't have to be bosom buddies to play poker."

I turned a page of the album.

"Is that a real wanted poster?" Shlomo said.

"Took it off a telephone pole myself," Moses responded. "Only thing is, that picture made him look too good."

WANTED was printed at the top of the sheet in bold black letters. There was a black-and-white head shot of a man with a white Vandyke beard. Under the picture, it read,

> Willard Dudley Paully. Description: Age 55, five feet, seven inches, 130 pounds. Has heavy eyebrows, straight Roman nose, dark eyes, very penetrating, good talker, highly educated,

interested in psychic research. Capias has been issued by the Judge of the Superior Court of Buncombe County for the arrest of the above-named party for felony, making fraudulent representation, and engaging in, among other things, UN-AMERICAN activities.

Notify Harris "Hurt" Bailey, Sheriff

"That is one fantastic relic of history," Shlomo said.

"Is it? I thought it was funny at the time. He deserved what he got, cheating like he did every Wednesday night. We finally ran the S.O.B. out of town."

"How did you do that?" I asked. "Mrs. Rubin used to say she and a bunch of her friends made that happen."

"Well, if you count bumping uglies with Eddie Levitz when her husband was on the road, Hilda Rubin participated," Moses said in a spiteful tone.

"What did y'all do to Paully?"

"I guess you might say we maneuvered him into a corner and let the Feds stick it to him. I didn't really see what the big fuss was. The women, they all said we shouldn't be associating with a Nazi, but I told them that poker was one game that made all men equal. I told them that even Nazis had a right to play poker in a free country. Anyway, the women kept bitching until they made the B'nai Brith hire a couple of attorneys— Jewish boy and a *goy*. Those two dug up whatever shit they could find on Paully."

"Sedition," Shlomo said, nodding.

"Yeah, that, too, but what tripped him up in Asheville was more like a technicality of the state laws. I think Paully had sold shares of stock in his newspaper without getting approval from

58

the state first, or something like that. Paully took money from a lot of widows and diverted it through his paper to his militia. He could charm the panties off a nun."

"Can I borrow these albums for a few days? Make some copies of the Paully articles? Aunt Fay will love you forever."

"How many days do I have left anyway, Shlomo?"

"Only God knows, Moses," Shlomo said, putting his hand on Moses' shoulder.

Moses wiped it off immediately.

"It's a shame you can't ask Estelle Levitz about how they nailed the bastard. She was one of those women who broke into Paully's headquarters for the lawyers, stole the bastard's files. Our own little Watergate." Moses smiled.

"She passed away before I came to Asheville, I suppose," Shlomo said, shaking his head.

"I should be so lucky. You must have passed her ass in the hall. Damn woman is always in somebody's way. She's still alive, she just can't talk. Stroke. God got tired of listening to her, I guess. She was married to Eddie, my wife's brother. In-laws, outlaws, one and the same." Moses started coughing and reached for a dirty coffee cup on the nightstand to spit into.

"When exactly did all this Paully stuff happen?" I asked.

"I don't remember. He hung around four or five years. I think they nailed him in thirty-nine."

"Nineteen thirty-nine?" I said. "So that poker game was going on when they had that murder there, at the hotel."

Moses stared at me for a few seconds. "How do you know about that?"

"Do you remember T Royal? Worked for Dad when Shel and I were kids?"

Moses nodded but kept staring.

"He's moved back to the Battery Park retirement apartments, and we were talking about hotel history the other day."

Moses finally quit staring and moved to roll off the bed. "Make way, boys, I gotta pee."

"I'll get these albums back to you as soon as I can, Moses."

"Leave a check on your way out," he said from behind the tiny bathroom door.

"Sure," I said.

"I ain't joking. A check. For Shelburne's campaign. Leave a check."

Intimidation is a powerful force. It's a shame I couldn't use it with my patients.

"Gritz, I haven't seen you or the kids at Friday-night services lately," Shlomo said as I painfully wrote a check for twenty-five dollars. Fund-raising always makes a clergyman perk right up.

I didn't look at him. Nate was toying with Zen Buddhism, Stef had her eyes on at least two different Presbyterians at Carolina Day School, and I still couldn't get my mind off Candy's ass, so it was not a good time to talk to me about being a good Jew.

"We've grown by fifty members since I came," Shlomo stated proudly. "Pretty soon, we're going to need an addition to the synagogue."

Suddenly, it was as if I saw the words *Capital Campaign* flashing in red letters across Shlomo's forehead. It was definitely time for me to get back to the hospital. Fortunately, Candy popped her head through the door just at the right time.

"Rabbi, the church called and said you have an emergency. To please call your secretary."

Shlomo sneered at Candy as he put on his jacket. "*Shalom*," he said, shaking the hand of Moses, who'd emerged from the bathroom, but bypassing his nurse and visitor.

"Speak English, dammit," Moses shot back. "This is Asheville, not Jerusalem."

"You and I have a little date at the hot tub, young man," Candy said to Moses. "Got to soak those muscles every day. I'll be back in a little while," she said, backing out the door.

"I'll be naked in a flash," Moses said in a tone of voice he'd never used once with Shlomo or me.

Being alone with Moses felt uncomfortable.

"Gritz, you know that rabbi is a *schmuck*. Odd people, those rabbis. Bad state of affairs when the only company you get is company you don't want."

I didn't want to get touchy-feely. "I enjoy hearing about Asheville Jewish history," I said. "I'll enjoy looking at these albums."

"Don't," he said.

"Don't what?"

"Don't get too interested. History is like wet shit. You step into it before you know what you're doing, and then you can't get it off your soles. Trust me, I'm an old man. I know what I'm talking about."

He turned over on his side and pulled the covers almost over his head.

"You take care now," I said, going out the door with his albums.

Moses didn't reply.

Not three full steps out his door sat Estelle Levitz, causing me to almost fall across her wheelchair.

"Excuse me, Mrs. Levitz. I didn't see you there."

If she could have talked through her eyes, she would have been one chatty lady. She was shaking her head as if to say *No, no, no.* Her fists were clenched.

"You take care now," I said, putting my hands under hers.

One of her palms loosened, and I felt a small piece of paper being transferred from her hand into mine. I took hold of it, but it felt awkward to stop and read it right then. I gently lowered her hands back to her chair, smiled, and hurried down the hallway. I pulled out my cell phone and messaged Pearlie to come get me. The fresh air felt good, even if it was filled with mountain pollen. I had an urge to walk until Pearlie arrived. Mom used to call it "having *shpilkes*"—Yiddish for having ants in your pants.

As I headed down a gravel path to what looked like a garden full of tomatoes and cucumbers, I unfolded the slip of paper Estelle had jammed in my hand. It was neatly printed from a computer.

"Don't believe the *ligner*," it read.

Mom and Dad had used that word when salesmen came by to sell us merchandise for the store. Yiddish for liar.

CHAPTER EIGHT

"Oif a fremder bord iz gut zich tsu lerner sheren."
  "It's good to learn to barber on someone else's beard."

I called Essie on the way back to the hospital.

"Bobby Raby's been a real pest this afternoon. Says he needs to talk with you before his scheduled Thursday appointment," she said.

"What's tomorrow look like?"

I should have known that any thirty-three-year-old still called Bobby would have unresolved issues. I let Essie have as tight a control over my appointments as the Quality Hair Salon did over her perms.

"I think you could squeeze him in first thing. Dr. Montague called to tell you he didn't appreciate you missing his meeting, and to remind you that Trinity is sending their legal team up tomorrow for briefings in the afternoon—some new proposals in the legislature on mental-health treatment they're worried about. He said absence is not an option."

"Set up Bobby for nine, then. Tell Dink I'll try real hard. Anything else?"

"Everything is copacetic. The Lord's been hovering close today."

Since the Lord was doing such a good job, I decided it would be presumptuous of me to interfere. "Why don't we take the rest of the day off? I've got a few personal items to take care of while I'm out."

"Bless you, Gritz. We've got our revival starting this weekend. I'm in charge of fans again. It gets pretty hot inside that place. It's Friday and Saturday at seven. Maybe you could come. Yellow-top tent by the river."

"I'll keep that in mind, Essie."

The idea of revivals scared me. I was much more comfortable being unrevived.

I decided to swing by T's place to see how he was doing. He hadn't called, so I figured Mordecai Moore hadn't been in a visiting mood. But Moses had piqued my curiosity about the Battery Park poker club. If he was accurate about the dates, the game would have been going strong around 1939, and T would have been working at the hotel at the time.

It was about three when I found a parking space in the back lot of the Battery Park. A couple of teenage boys with raspberry-colored spiked hair and spaghetti-stained cooking aprons stood just outside the basement entrance smoking tiny rolled cigarettes. I tried to hold my breath as I walked through the stilted air into the bottom level of the hotel. The kids acted like I didn't exist.

I recalled how the Battery Park's kitchen had always been in the basement. When I was a kid, the hotel's dumbwaiter had fascinated me, delivering trays of crisp duckling covered with orange sauce up to the opulent Carolina Dining Room on the mezzanine. On Sundays, Dad brought the family to the Battery Park for brunch. He always asked for Pauline Kelley to wait on us. A tall, stately lady, she would greet us in her starched black-and-white uniform and chat with us, seeming to actually care about our colds and school marks. All I could smell from the kitchen this day was overcooked greens and burnt bacon, but even that seemed pretty good. My chat with Moses had caused me to miss my rigidly scheduled lunch, but I surprised myself by not being ruffled by it. Maybe a few interruptions in my overly planned life were therapeutic.

When I got up to T's apartment, his door was wide open.

"T? It's Gritz," I called. There was no answer. "T, are you home?"

No one responded, but I did hear music. Not from his apartment, but down the hall. The music seemed to be coming from the Raby ballroom. As I got to the entrance, the old French doors were wide open, and I could see that the music came from an old LP player sitting on a straw stepstool in the middle of the floor. Above the Glenn Miller Orchestra, laughter echoed loudly. T and a heavy black lady about the same age were dancing around the room, not in stuffy box steps but some kind of swing. Dressed in his Sunday best, T twirled his partner with no signs of the arthritic limp he had displayed the day before. Dad's brother Earl was like that, too. On the street, he resembled a midget Saint Nick, but on the dance floor, my uncle transformed into Nureyev Goldberg.

The woman saw me and tapped T on the shoulder. He raised his hand and waved but didn't miss a step.

"We're just seeing if we can still cut the rug!" he yelled over the music.

"Beats bingo by a mile," the woman said.

"Don't stop for me!" I yelled back.

"Look on the stove," T said, short of breath.

I knew what he meant.

I found fresh nomnom and happily plopped down on T's tiny couch with a big bowl. I lifted his Bible once again and reread the newspaper piece on Mordecai Moore. "A reenactment of the famous September 1939 Battery Park murder escape," the paper called it. I could imagine what would happen now if the cops made an alleged perpetrator reenact a crime for a picture in the local paper.

Soon, T walked in, minus his dancing partner.

"I'm sweatin' like a pig," he said, wiping his forehead with a plaid handkerchief.

"And I'm eating one," I said, reaching for another rind.

"Give me a minute and let me change clothes. Mary Mag has been bothering me to show her some steps. Mary Magdalene Perkins. The old ladies here give you all kinds of attention as long as you have decent teeth and most of your hair. She's pretty nice— I mean, for an old woman." T undid his tie. "All her family's up in New York somewhere. She's missing them pretty bad."

T had his limp back as he went to change. He soon emerged wearing a black golf shirt, white Bermuda shorts, long black socks, and gold corduroy bedroom shoes.

"Glad you came by," he said, still a touch out of breath.

"I've been out to visit Moses Bloom today. He was telling me about a poker group that used to meet here."

"Sure enough, the card club. I used to tote those boys a big ol' bucket of ice or two every Wednesday night. They furnished their own beverages, if you know what I mean." He smiled. "And I don't mean ginger ale either. Sheriff Hurt's brother brought some of his moonshine, made with just the right amount of bleach."

"Remember anything about one of the players, Willard Paully?"

T lost his grin. "That man never would look me directly in the eye. That was okay, though, 'cause his eyes were full of nothing but meanness. Paully came much too regular for me, but I just did what I had to do and left the room."

"Moses said Dad played."

"That was before he married your mom. Mr. Leo from the pawnshop, Pete Reid, Senator Bob, they all played. Some travelin' salesmen and such who stayed regularly at the Battery, they would join in."

"I'm trying to get some information about Paully for Aunt Fay. Remember her?"

"Miss Fay, now that's one scary woman. It seemed like she got up in the morning and wound herself up as tight as she could and then let it rip. Drove everybody crazy until she ran down about nightfall."

"She's still like that. Lives with Dad in Miami Beach."

"Jesus!" T said, then looked at me from the corner of his eye to see if he had overstepped his bounds. "How's your dad takin' it?"

"Better than I expected. Aunt Fay wants all she can find about Paully—all I can find for her—for an Old South history program she's involved in down in Florida. I went out to see what Moses had at his place at Happy Valley. Did Paully play in the poker games for a long time?"

"Well, let me see. I was there from thirty-four to late thirty-nine. I think he played most of that time. He would leave

Asheville for a while and then come back. I left the hotel a few months after Mordecai got done in. It all blew up in the middle of September, and they charged, convicted, and executed the poor boy before Christmas. Didn't hang onto death-row folks like they do now."

"I wouldn't think Dad and Leo Finkel would want to be around Paully. I can see Moses not caring that much, but Dad?"

"True, Paully didn't much cotton to Jews or blacks, but you know, the man put most of his hatred on President Roosevelt. He was always making nasty comments about FDR. I remember one time I was bringing in the ice bucket, and Mr. Leo, he mentioned that he was looking forward to President Roosevelt traveling to Asheville on an early campaign swing for the nineteen-forty election. Paully throws down his cards, says the country don't need the president's 'Jew Deal'—right in Mr. Leo's face, mind you. Mr. Leo and your daddy, they cashed in their chips and never came back. But Mr. Moses and his brother-in-law, they never got real riled, just kept playing their hand like they never heard a thing."

"That was strange of them, don't you think?"

"Gritz, at eighty-eight, there ain't much that surprises me." He reached for my almost empty bowl. "Besides, nobody ever accused Mr. Moses of not being one strange bird. You hungry today, huh?" T smiled, pleased at the success of his latest batch of cooking.

"What about Eddie Levitz? What was he like?"

"I remember he was a big shot at some corporation off somewhere, like for General Electric maybe. After he married Miss Estelle, they came back to Asheville and started that salvage company. Mr. Eddie, he seemed like he wanted to be just like Mr. Moses. I mean, he even wore the same style cowboy hat, except his was black and Mr. Moses' was white."

"Cowboy hat?" I said.

"Yeah, and when they talked to each other, they would talk in that language—you know, like your mom and dad did so their customers wouldn't understand what they were saying."

"Yiddish," I smiled.

"Yeah, it was queer as hell, Mr. Moses and Mr. Eddie chatting up a storm in Yiddish, both wearing their cowboy hats. Still, folks said it was Miss Estelle that was the brains behind that salvage business."

"You know, T, in my business, strange is kind of normal."

"The more I live, the more that's the gospel truth," T said.

"I'd better be getting home, but how about I call Arlene and see if she has a little extra for supper tonight? I'd like for you to meet the kids, and her, too. They've heard me talk about you all their lives."

"Sounds great, if it ain't too much trouble," he said hesitantly. "I don't mind the bologna they serve here, but when they try to cover it with gravy and call it London broil, I start losing my appetite. You sure it's okay I eat over at your house?"

"Of course," I said.

I liked the sound of *my* house. T had never eaten at Dad's. It's strange how the strongest barriers can be the ones that are never acknowledged.

I called Arlene from T's phone.

"Sure, bring him on," Arlene said. "I'm doing Italian tonight. Pasta always goes a long way."

I held the phone from my ear. I hadn't noticed T's amplifier on the receiver.

"We'll be there in a half-hour or so. I finished early today," I said.

"I ran into Elliot Fineman at Good Earth. I promised him you and I would send him a hundred for the mayor's campaign. That's okay, isn't it?"

Shel was playing the Jewish angle for all it was worth. Unless the KKK ran a candidate, I'd support anyone who ran against him, but I figured I'd fill in Arlene later.

"We'll talk about it," I said.

Just as I hung up the phone, T and I heard a high-pitched shriek from down the hall.

"Help, Lord God, someone help me!"

The scream emanated from where I'd last heard Glenn Miller, but this was no Big Band sound. I led the way down the hall with T just behind.

"Got to be Mary Mag," T said. "Lord, what is it now?"

T's dancing partner was screaming at the top of her lungs. She stood on the small stage hugging herself and shaking like a Canadian cold front had just whipped through the room.

"Where did he go?" she said. "Where is he?"

"I'm right here, Mary Mag! I'm coming," T yelled back, a few steps behind me.

"Not you, the boy."

"What boy?" T said, stepping up on the stage and putting his long, protecting arms gingerly around her shoulders.

"He was standing right over there, I tell you."

T and I scanned the room, but we didn't see anybody.

T helped Mary Mag off the platform. "Sit yourself down right here, Mary Mag. Catch your breath, now. You don't want to have a heart attack."

She sat and looked up at us. "I was giving my feet a rest after you left, T. Just kicked my shoes off and sat down right here. Then I noticed what I thought was a paperback book over there on the floor, near the window, just in front of those drapes. You know how I like to read, so I figured somebody left a book, and I'd read it and find its rightful owner. I walked over to pick it up, and just as I got to that window over there, I saw him. Just staring at me, not twenty feet away. His eyes weren't mean, more sad-like. Skinny colored boy." Mary Mag looked at T. "If I didn't know better, I'd say he looked like that poor soul you showed me in that newspaper article." She took a deep breath, shaking her head. "I didn't mean to, but all I could do was squish my eyes tight as a Presbyterian and start yelling my lungs out."

"We better call the office. Kid musta been lookin' to steal what he could find," T said. "Druggies. You'd think they would let old people just be." T acted like he hadn't heard Mary Mag.

"The book," Mary Mag said, distracted. "Where is it?"

All I saw on the floor were her big red pumps. The sides of both shoes had large razor cuts through the leather near the big toe.

"Don't see it," T said.

I pulled the drapes back in case Mary Mag had thrown it when she got startled, but I didn't see anything but dust bunnies.

"Now, you think I'm making this all up, but I tell you, the book was lying on the floor right here. It looked really old. Had a cowboy on the front."

T's eyes met mine, and this time I knew he'd heard.

CHAPTER NINE

"Az der soineh falt, tor men zich nit fraien, ober men haibt im nit oif."
"When your enemy falls, don't rejoice, but don't pick him up either."

T accompanied Mary Mag back to her room. I went downstairs and stood on the wide brick front porch and leaned against a very old wooden column that helped hold up an equally old white arbor as I waited for Pearlie to pick up T and me and take us to my house. I watched the sun setting behind the blue, mountainous Asheville skyline. You couldn't see Biltmore House, but you knew it had to be there, glimmering in its European elegance, while the same sunset enveloped the old Stumptown area of Asheville where Mordecai had lived. It was the very same sun that had shone over the Battery Park in 1939, the exact sun that came over the mountains the day they made Mordecai reenact his "escape" from the crime scene. Now, that sun shone over me and over the building that still housed the same innocent man, absent his physical body.

There was no explanation for what had just happened upstairs. It had taken me almost a half-century to get comfortable with the idea that it's not necessary to have an answer for everything that happens in your life, but even a seasoned shrink gets unsettled when an executed man hangs out near a murder scene over six decades later. If Mary Mag really saw Mordecai Moore, if what T saw was truly his dead friend, could a scientific mind accept that as fact? And if so, was the haint demanding attention to finish unsettled business or just to scare the crap out of us? If Mordecai had been a normal, breathing human, we at Highland would have said he was acting out. But when the one acting out died sixty-five years prior, well, that called for a different diagnosis.

When T finally emerged from the lobby door, he definitely had lost his agile dancing form. He descended each step ever so slowly, holding onto the railing like his life depended on it. Pearlie pulled up in front of the building as if on queue.

"Car in the shop?" T asked.

"Not exactly," I replied.

T looked at me like he knew something was wrong with my transportation arrangement, but he also knew not to question it. We had always been that way together—sensing each other, hardly needing words to understand.

"Gritz, this haint thing is getting out of hand, ain't it?"

"To be honest, I don't know what to think about it," I said. "Maybe Mordecai is just tired of this place and wants to leave."

It was a stupid answer, but it was all I could come up with.

"Yeah, well, I'm getting pretty tired of it, too, and I ain't been back a month yet."

I opened the door for T and waited until he gingerly sat. I got in the other side.

"Pearlie, this is T Royal. You remember T, don't you?"

"Related to Sergeant Girsten Royal, U.S. Army Signal Center?" Pearlie said, jerking the cab into drive.

Pearlie's family didn't trade at Goldberg's much, so he didn't remember T.

"Don't think so," T answered.

Neither one of us was interested in chitchat, but that didn't stop Pearlie.

"He was of Italian descent, I believe. Yeah, Italian and Hawaiian, I believe it was." Pearlie stretched the *I* in Italian. "It's good you're not related, 'cause he was the meanest bastard at Fort Gordon. Made us crawl through mud so thick you could hardly keep your eyes open. I kept telling him about the renegades, but he never believed me, not until I got this bullet stuck in my neck—my brain, actually."

T looked at me as if to ask, *What the hell did he just say?* and I answered with a slight smile that begged, *Just let him go on.* Shortly after high school, Pearlie had been drafted. Vietnam changed him. Not that he ever got close to Southeast Asia. He was sent back to Asheville on a medical discharge shortly after boot camp when he made a stink about gooks coming over the base walls near Augusta, Georgia, and shooting soldiers. When Pearlie had his head x-rayed and a bullet showed up at the nape of his neck—a bullet that was inoperable because of its location—the army sent him home with an honorable discharge and permanent disability payments. That was when he started driving for Our Lord's Dependable Cab Company.

T and I listened quietly as Pearlie gave us his solutions for AIDS, bad air, and Siamese twins. It was a relief to pull up to my driveway and hear Stef trying unsuccessfully to start my old Jeep. It kept backfiring like it had swallowed some indigestible gasoline.

T looked out the window and chuckled. "I remember the Commando. Can't believe you still got that thing."

"Stef actually likes it."

"I taught you how to drive in that thing. Remember when you and I almost tilted into the wood flume at Mead, going around that sharp corner on Tannery Flats? I thought we were going to be brown boxes before I got you to stay to the middle of the road."

Pearlie seemed a bit jealous. "Gritz and I go back a long ways, too."

"Sure do, Pearlie. I'll get Stef to run T back to the hotel later. I'll see you bright and early tomorrow," I said, exiting the car while T pulled himself out the other side.

"Ten-four, *el capitan*," Pearlie answered, jotting down my fare on his clipboard.

I paid him once a month. I'd offered to swap my services as a shrink for his driving, but he seemed confused about what I had to offer, so I just paid him in cash.

My neighbor's German shepherd ran over barking. I don't know how it knew I was Jewish. It never seemed to bark at Christians or even Muslims, but it went berserk when anyone in the Goldberg household came within sniffing distance.

"Adolf, get away," I snapped as the dog burrowed under the hedge fence and tried to eat my socks.

To the side of the carport, where Stef was in her eighth try at coaxing the Commando to life, sat the Goldberg family garden. It was a joint effort. Arlene did all the work. I ate from it. At that moment, Arlene's rather full bottom faced T and me as she bent over pulling the few weeds she had let get by her the day before.

"She grows her own herbs," I said to T, who seemed focused on her *zaftik* cheeks.

Arlene had on khaki shorts, a white tank top, a large straw hat, and red rubber clogs. Her legs were not girlishly skinny but showed not the faintest purple veins either. She looked as cute as a Medicare recipient can on a hot Asheville day. She could easily have been a cover girl for one of those seed catalogs that always show a proud mature gardener holding an example of her record-breaking tomatoes. She stood up, turned around, and smiled at T, who tipped his white golf cap, as any good Southern gent left from another time period might.

"This must be the famous Theloneous Royal I've heard so much about," Arlene said, wiping her free hand on her shorts and then sticking it out to shake.

"The one and only," I said. "T, meet Arlene Davidow."

T seemed unusually shy as he took her hand.

"Supper will be ready in fifteen minutes. Gritz, take Mr. Royal inside and show him where he can wash up. Stef is going cruising down Patton, and Nate called to say he'd be late. You don't want to know, trust me."

Just as I opened the door to the kitchen and pointed T toward the bathroom, the phone rang.

"I'll get it," Arlene said behind me. "It's probably for me."

It usually was. Unlike me, Arlene was a joiner. Immediately after coming to save her grandkids, she'd joined Asheville's Save Tibet Council and the League for Creative Retirement. Arlene had been asked to leave the latter group. She said she couldn't stomach half the members, who loved telling people all they'd done for the world before they came to Asheville. "What are you doing *today?*" was her pat response.

"Hi, Fay," Arlene said, rolling her eyes at me. "No, we haven't eaten yet. Yes, as a matter of fact, it is late to be starting supper. Gritz is standing right here."

She handed me the phone.

"All the doctors and lawyers down here have nice young Jewish wives, and you have to live with an old woman? What does she cook, tofu chopped liver?"

"Hi, Aunt Fay. It's good to hear from you," I said, sidestepping her first salvo.

"I want to talk to you about your dad in a minute, but first, did you get it?"

"Your Paully stuff?" I said.

"No, the pope's bank statement. Of course, Paully's stuff. Big Fay is already bragging about how good her program is going to be. Says she has pictures of the Torah that some *schlep* from Spain brought over in fourteen ninety-two or something like that. Big deal!"

"You're going to like this, Aunt Fay. Moses still has the actual wanted poster of Paully. Says he took it off a telephone pole himself. I'm going to take it to Kinko's and make you a copy."

"That's my nephew! Listen, I hate to mention this to you, but your dad is heading for big trouble."

"Didn't he go to his cardiologist like I told him?"

"Bigger trouble than that Roto-Rooter can think up. Henrietta Block saw him holding hands with a young woman, not more than sixty-five, blond, wearing enough makeup to sink this condo into the deep blue sea. She says the *shiksa* is from Iowa or some other godforsaken place."

"There are plenty of Jews in Iowa, Aunt Fay."

"Like how many, twenty-four? Trust me, this girl wouldn't know the difference between a Jew and a Martian."

"There's a difference?" I said.

"Hush, don't even say things like that. I saw on Oprah last week that if you want something to happen, all you have to do is say it aloud eight times. Why aren't you ever on Oprah? You could make a lot more *gelt* than that *goyish* hospital pays you. Listen to your aunt Fay. Call Oprah."

77

"You're right, you're right," I surrendered. Agreeing with everything she said was the only way to get her to agree to anything I said, and sometimes even that didn't work. "Is Dad around?"

"He's in the kitchen. I'll call him. You talk to him, for the peace of your mother," she said. "Solly, pick up the phone. The phone," she repeated. "A man who can't hear needs a *shiksa* from Iowa, don't you think, Gritz?"

I didn't even try to answer.

"Gritz, Fay is driving me *meshuga*," Dad said before even a hello.

"She says you have a romantic interest."

"Romantic, shmomantic. At my age, it's just a woman. Send me a prescription for that Niagara stuff, okay?"

"You want spray starch?"

"I spend a couple hundred thousand to make you a doctor, and I get a comedian. You know what I mean."

"Sure, Dad." I could talk stocks with Dad, but erections were something else. I looked up to see T walking back into the kitchen. "Dad, guess who's visiting me tonight for supper."

"Not my brother Carl, I hope. He's gotten his last dollar from me. Don't give him a cent."

"Not Uncle Carl. T Royal."

"Really? Where's he been?" Dad said it like T had just gone to lunch and was late coming back for work at Goldberg's.

"He's moved back from Charlotte. Back to the Battery Park."

"Tell him to look up Polly. Tell her I said hello."

"Dad, it's not a hotel anymore. Besides, Polly was a lot older than you. She'd probably be over a hundred now."

"So just because I was stupid enough to retire, does that mean she had to?"

"Want to talk to T?" I asked.

"The boys are waiting to start our pinochle game. I've got to go. Get T a prescription of that stuff you're going to send me. I'll pay. I tell you, there's an epidemic of insurrection down here. Like when your kindergarten got measles, all at one time. Terrible. Just terrible."

"Maybe it's the salt water," I said, proving that neurotic confusion can be acquired by a telephone call. There was no comment. I couldn't tell if Dad hadn't heard me or was analyzing how much ocean water he'd swallowed of late. "Dad, I went to see Moses Bloom for Aunt Fay. He mentioned that you and he played poker at the Battery Park. I never heard you talk about that."

"That was before you were born. I played for a couple of years, I think. Then Leo Finkel and I quit together."

"T told me how W. D. Paully made Leo so mad you both quit. I had no idea."

"Oh, I didn't leave just because of that. When you're Jewish in the South, you have to make compromises. The main reason was I knew with Leo gone, I'd never make any money at the game. Leo would get so nervous when he had a good hand he would shake all over, bite his cigar butt nearly off. Everybody knew to bail out of the pot when Leo had a good hand."

"Aunt Fay wants to know about Paully. Didn't she ask you anything? I bet you could give her a lot of information."

"God forbid, I don't talk to Fay any more than I have to. She cooks, I eat. She yaps, I leave."

"So you remember the New York girl getting murdered, too?"

"Who doesn't? They called me for the jury, but I got off. That case was bad for business. Everybody was talking, nobody was buying. How did you hear about the murder?"

"The subject popped up when I was visiting T. It's a very interesting story."

I looked over to T, who was talking to Arlene.

"Not that interesting. *Schwartza* killed her. They caught him."

"T says Mordecai Moore didn't do it."

"Your mother always thought the uncle had something to do with it. He was a real kook. One of Paully's devotees."

"You knew the uncle, too?"

"Oh yeah, I knew him. He played cards with us at the hotel when he was in town. Traveled for the college in Raleigh or something. He would play maybe once a month. Paully and the professor seemed awfully cozy. I don't know which one hated Roosevelt more. Always making some kind of statement about how FDR was going to get us into war with Hitler. The professor was a shrimp, maybe five feet tall. Thirty-eight short portly suit."

"Is that so?" I asked. "T told me FDR came to Asheville in thirty-nine on a campaign swing."

"Hell yes, he did. His campaign headquarters was at the Grove Park Inn. I was glad it wasn't the Battery. I mean, I don't think Paully really had much of a militia like he claimed he did, but he definitely wouldn't have minded seeing Roosevelt dead. Neither would Raby."

"Senator Bob?"

"You were always good at history, son. Yeah, he said he could run the country better than Roosevelt with his eyes closed."

"Paully?"

"No, Raby. He said he could get elected president himself if FDR wasn't on the scene. That he could keep the country out of the war. They hurried him out of town, though."

"Raby?"

"No, Roosevelt. He made it over to the Cherokee Indian Reservation and a couple of fund-raisers, but that girl was murdered at the Battery the same week, and I guess the president's people didn't think it was safe for him to be in Asheville with a murderer on the loose." Dad paused. "Everything else under control?"

When Dad asked if everything was under control, it meant he was done talking, whether you were or not. I assured him that everything was in perfect order in my life.

"Don't forget to mail me the you-know-what," he said. "Put Jews for Jesus as the return address. Your aunt Fay hates them worse than she does Republicans. She won't touch anything in the mail from them."

I hung up the phone more exhausted and tense than I ever was after psychotherapy sessions. I always envied my gentile friends. They seemed to be able to have fairly calm, normal conversations with their parents at least once in a while.

"Mr. G.'s doing well, I suppose," T said, sitting down at the table after seeing me hang up.

"Fine," I said. "He said to say hi. And to tell you he's glad you're back in town."

Arlene placed a long loaf of garlic bread on the table, followed by a big bowl of spaghetti.

"T, would you say grace for us tonight?" I said, surprising not only Arlene but also myself. We never said grace, but I hadn't had a day like this one in a long time either.

"Lord," he said, "we thank you for the food we are about to partake of, and for the goodness . . . for the goodness that you have let us see in our lives, even though we sure 'nough don't deserve it. Thank you for letting Gritz and me get together again. And if it don't matter to you, maybe you could let those special souls needing to get home get on home. I know you know who I mean. Amen."

"Amen," Arlene and I joined in.

"Do you believe in souls that can't get home?" T asked Arlene as she passed him the pasta.

"You mean, like ghosts?"

"People that ain't quite people, if you know what I mean."

"I'm not sure why they're among us, but yes, I definitely believe in the possibility of their existence."

I was surprised that T spoke so openly about Mordecai, but Arlene made people feel comfortable right off the bat—the total opposite of her daughter. I briefly filled her in on the story of Mordecai Moore and the murder at the Battery Park. And the afternoon's sighting.

"Seems to me this man wants the real murderer found out," she said. "You know, to clear his name so he can leave—that sort of thing."

"It's pretty late for me to try and straighten that mess out now, but I'd sure like to," T said. "Not that I plan on going home anytime soon, but when I go, I want to get gone for good. No sticking around, you know." He paused. "You think they got colored baseball in heaven? Maybe I could see Cool Papa Bell one more time. He used to throw so hard from deep in center field that people said he could break a catcher's hand if he caught it wrong."

"I think we ought to find out," Arlene said matter-of-factly.

"Find out what?" I said in a muffled tone, due to the bread in my mouth.

"Who did it. If T's friend didn't do it, who did? Then maybe the spirit—ghost, whatever—can depart and let T enjoy his retirement in Asheville," she said, smiling at our dinner guest.

"But the murder is sixty-five years old," I said.

"T, I think you and I need to show this ex-son-in-law of mine that sixty-five years isn't that long," she said, putting her hand on his forearm.

"Don't time fly like the wind?" T said, reaching for the shaker of Parmesan.

All three of us got quiet for a few minutes, savoring our meal. I was pleased that T and Arlene seemed to enjoy each other's company so quickly. He was a triple-twirler with the spaghetti. Arlene cut hers and then stabbed. I took a bite of bread, leaving the remainder as a semicircular lifting and soaking aid. Three different people, three ways, one reason.

"So, where would we start?" I finally said.

"There's no better place to start than at the beginning," Arlene said. "Hey, I like that. I should make that into stitchery."

"And the beginning is?" T asked.

"What about your friend Talmadge?" Arlene said to me. "Why don't you talk to the chief about finding those old files? There have to be court records somewhere. And T, you and I can go down to the library tomorrow and research the microfilm they have of old *Citizen* newspapers. I mean, if you want to."

"Sure, but let's not forget Pete Reid either," T said. "He wrote about the whole thing for the paper. That man can lie like a dog when he wants to, but usually that only pertains to rainbow trout and women. I was going to see about going fishing with him anyway. I could give him a call."

"I don't know how the two of you feel about this, but I was talking to Perrier Skyhawk about Mordecai, and she thought we could try and reach out to him," I said. "Let her be a channel, or whatever it's called. I mean, I've never really believed in that sort of thing, but I'm open to giving it a try if y'all are."

"I watched a show the other day about somebody trying to do that," T said. "Looked like the real thing to me."

"Perrier told me about going to Oklahoma with Arnie, and about his grandmother showing them how to use those kinds of powers," Arlene added. "Maybe she can even reach Gabe. He was supposed to leave me a pile of untaxed money he'd hidden all the years we were married, but he died before he told me where it was."

In my practice, I always tried to dissuade people from straining too hard to get back to a time long gone, but was that choice really ours to make in this case? One thing was clear. Two special people—one alive, one dead but still active—needed to know what happened that night in September 1939. And if I could help, why not?

CHAPTER TEN

"Ven a ganef kisht darf men zich di tsein ibertseilen."
"When a thief kisses you, count your teeth."

The next morning, I woke early with a pounding headache thinking about how much I didn't want to see Bobby Raby. More than that, I didn't want to deal with those talking-head lawyers from Trinity with their classic bow ties, pinstriped seersucker suits, and matching stiff attitudes. I hoped Talmadge could meet me for lunch at Possum's. He'd sent me an electronic page saying, "Got court records." I'd need to have Essie alert Possum. He might want to camouflage the cockfighting pit behind the restaurant.

We had only one bathroom on the second floor of *Kleina Shmahta*. Arlene and I shared the floor and knew who had dibs on the shower. When the water was turned on, the pipes gave off loud whining sounds. It was quiet that morning, so I grabbed a towel and headed down the hall. I opened the door to the bathroom to find one old African-American in an untied, obviously borrowed lavender terry-cloth bathrobe and plaid boxer shorts standing at the commode.

"Oh, excuse me, T. I didn't know you . . . stayed over."

Arlene, T, and I had been watching *Seinfeld* reruns after supper when the pasta got the best of me and I found myself in a losing fight with sleep. Arlene noticed and quickly volunteered to drive T back to the Battery Park. I'd excused myself and gone upstairs to bed.

"When peeing becomes a full-time job, you realize God's got to have one heck of a sense of humor," T said.

I replied with a nervous laugh and tried backing out but bounced off the open door.

"It's all yours. Arlene said it would be okay if I slept over," T said, flushing the commode.

I think it was the first time in our long history we'd ever avoided eye contact.

"No problem," I answered, looking at my toes. Toe four was trying to dig its way to China through the old hardwood floor.

T brushed by me, and I reentered the bathroom and closed the door. I battled a strong urge to peek before it was completely shut to watch where T went. The only sleeping accommodations on the second floor besides my room and Arlene's was a tiny reading nook over the stairway where we had a loveseat wedged in. T could have camped out there. The adult in me won out, deciding it was none of my business. I locked the door and turned on the hot water, but I felt a strong need to finish quickly and get to work before I ran into T again, or Arlene.

I hurriedly dressed and left for the office without breakfast. Essie was always good for at least one bear claw. She brought in leftover pastries from her many church functions. Adolf, of course, was already on duty, alerting the Luftwaffe that a Jew was escaping. I really needed to get out to the pound and find a housebroken American mastiff and train it to take care of that piece of constant yap.

When I got to the hospital, it was so early Ophelia Walton had not even pulled out her vacuum for the day. The sad, neglected alcoholic wives from Atlanta and Charlotte who made Von Ruck home were already out of their rooms, dressed to the nines but slumped on the sofas and in the armchairs staring at nothing intently.

"Good morning, ladies," I called out as I climbed the front stairway.

No one answered, but Sophie Watkins whistled.

I was surprised to see Bobby Raby already sitting outside my office. He was clutching what seemed to be a rolled-up carpet remnant like Linus did his security blanket. When he saw me, he stood up with it like he was ready to follow me into my office.

"It'll be just a few minutes, Bobby," I said, more to establish authority than anything else. "You're really early."

He grimaced, pulled at his crotch like a pitcher adjusting his jockstrap, and sat back down, mumbling something that sounded like "bastard." For my own security, I didn't like letting patients in my office without Essie being outside, though what protection she could offer was questionable. I also wanted a sugar fix and a cup of coffee before taking on my least favorite patient.

I found a pink slip stuck on my door: "Dr. G., Please call me at O'Henry when you get in. Jesus McFarland."

I unlocked the double doors and went into my office. I picked up the phone and called Jesus first thing. He was head orderly at the hospital. He rarely called, but when he did, something big was usually going down. Quiet, strong, and trustworthy, Jesus would have made a great chief of staff, but Dink had the credentials and connections. All Jesus had was a G.E.D., five kids, and bad teeth, but I had no doubt who could run the hospital better than anyone else.

"Jesus? Dr. G. here. How can I help you?"

"It's Bobby Raby. I was doing a routine room check and came across this rug stuck under his bed. I didn't think you'd allow him to have it. It has one of those German symbols on it."

"A swastika?"

"Yeah. He got really mad about me confiscating it. Came in shouting that he was going to have his lawyer sue us and crap like that. He said he could get me fired with one phone call. I thought maybe he could, with his family connections and stuff, so I gave him back the rug. I wanted you to know first thing. I can't afford to lose this job."

"Don't worry, Jesus. Thanks for letting me know, though."

"I'm sorry. Normally, a patient can't intimidate me, but Bobby, he's different. You know what I mean?"

"I know exactly what you mean," I said.

"He's what Reverend Smith calls 'a product of the devil's workshop,' " Jesus said.

Now, that was one indisputable diagnosis.

I hung up just as Essie buzzed me that she was in. Ready or not, it was time to take on Bobby.

Trinity had sent a recent memorandum that we were not to order our patients in but to get off our duffs, open our doors ourselves, and greet them with a firm handshake. It always felt more like a photo op when two corporations were going to announce a merger than the beginning of a breakthrough therapy session. I did what I was supposed to, but Bobby made no attempt to shake my hand. Of course, with what looked like a small battering ram under his arm, it wouldn't have been easy to do.

As Bobby passed, Essie called softly, "Missed you at the revival."

"Would you have a bear claw handy?"

"No, but I have two fresh cinnamon rolls and one slightly stale prune Danish."

"The Danish would be great," I said.

"Large or small coffee?"

"Giant," I said, glancing at Bobby.

While Essie gathered my breakfast, I watched from the corner of my eye as Bobby took a seat, crossed his legs, and kicked the upper one back and forth like he'd just put a quarter in a vibrating chair.

"It would be a blessing if you could come tonight," Essie whispered, handing me the Danish and coffee, then closing the doors for me as I headed to my desk.

Like a game of chicken, there were a few seconds when we struggled silently over who would go first.

"This may be a mental hospital, but it's still America."

I looked at him but said nothing. That was one cool thing about my occupation. I was expected to, even paid to, keep my mouth shut most of the time. When a patient was intent on getting something really troubling off his chest, I practiced the healing art of displaying that special look that said, *Yes, tell me more.*

Bobby took the bait like the crawfish he was.

"That dumb-ass orderly at O'Henry violated my constitutional rights. I want him fired."

I wrote down *Dumb-ass*, then crossed it out. What really caught my attention at that moment was that I'd forgotten to flip the hourglass to start the session. I wanted to spend no more time with Bobby than required.

"I'm going to take this fucking hospital to court. I want this harassment to stop."

It was time for the aging sage to speak at least a word or two. "We try to respect each other at Highland, Bobby."

"That's a joke. Montague had my roommate pulled out of bed yesterday at five in the morning for those damn shock treatments. Stuck a rubber plate in his mouth, and away he goes. When he came back, he didn't remember who I was."

"Let's not discuss your roommate right now."

"I didn't think you'd support me on this. I mean, you being a Jew and all. All you people can do is moan about Holocaust this and Holocaust that. I give you credit for one thing. You've done a good job hoodwinking the whole damn world."

I bit hard into my prune Danish. I'd sworn to myself the last time Bobby started his Holocaust-denial routine that, doctor or no doctor, I wouldn't let him get away with it. Still, this was supposed to be therapy, not a historical debate.

"Bobby, I have rules to follow in this hospital, and so do you."

"And what do your rules tell you?" Bobby said. "Screw the patients every chance you get?"

"You can't provoke fellow patients."

"And how many fellow patients are living under my bed?"

He was winning round one.

I slurped a big swallow of coffee. It was hot, and it hurt going down. I needed the punishment for ever agreeing to treat Bobby Raby.

"Bobby, how about we keep the rug here, in my office? I'll lay it right beside that window over there until we can talk some more about this issue."

"You want to keep my rug in your office?"

I nodded. I figured I could hide it in my closet when Bobby left.

"Why in God's name would you want to do that?"

"We need to talk about why this rug means so much to you. What's behind these feelings?"

"My granddaddy left me this rug. Hitler gave it to him personally when he went over there to visit. Why is that so hard to understand?"

Good ol' Senator Bob. Nothing like a swastika office rug to make you feel warm and fuzzy.

"Your family means the world to you, doesn't it, Bobby?"

"Doesn't yours?" he said.

Bobby was in top form. Yes, my immediate family meant the world, but Aunt Fay usually meant indigestion.

"Speaking of family, Mother called me last night. Said she's coming up from Tarboro and would like a joint conference with us."

"What about your dad?"

"I told you, Dad's dead. What do you write down in that little book of yours?"

I looked down at three doodles and a grocery list but didn't see the need to tell him.

Bobby had no wife or children. Maybe God had decided to keep future Rabys from marring our landscape. Bobby had told me he'd never met a woman who appreciated the Raby heritage like she should.

Once in a while, a shrink gets to play King Solomon instead of Mel Brooks. It's one of our few perks.

"Bobby, why don't we wait till next time to discuss the rug? It will be safe right here. Maybe we can include your mother in our next session. Isn't she coming up?"

"That's what I just said, if you listened to a goddamn thing!" Bobby bellowed. "When I told her who my doctor was, she said she knows you. Went to Asheville High with you. Whitaker was her maiden name. Emma Whitaker."

I fought the sudden urge to regurgitate stale prunes and coffee. Yes, I knew his mother. Intimately, as a matter of fact. If circumstances had been just a tad different thirty-five years prior, I might have been looking at my son instead of a patient. I slapped the cover of my notepad shut. Two thoughts occurred to me: I needed to chase this overgrown weed out of my office as soon as possible, and maybe I should get to Essie's big tent before it folded.

"I had no idea your mother was Emma Whitaker," I said, trying to disengage myself from the flood of memories.

"Yeah, she married Daddy right after high school, and, bingo, they had me."

Bingo wasn't the word that came to my mind.

"I thought I'd mentioned all that, but hey, I probably did and you weren't listening, as usual. Anyway, the rug, when can I get it back?"

"We'll discuss it. Just leave it with me for now."

"Okay, but I'm holding you responsible," Bobby said, standing up.

When Bobby left, I unrolled the black piece of carpet and wiped me feet on it as hard as I could.

I saw three more patients before lunch. All were what I categorized as legal pharmacological addicts—patients who were determined to obtain the newest FDA-approved drug, convinced it was the magic formula to cure or at least block out what ailed them. I tried various forms of nondrug treatment with such patients, from biofeedback to gestalt therapy, but in the end, I usually acquiesced to prescribing them what they had their hearts set on. I tried to convince myself that antidepressants did help some people. And besides, it was hard not to appreciate Eli Lilly's annual golf soiree in Pinehurst, with its tons of free golf balls with *Prozac* brightly stamped across the dimples.

Just as I was ending the last session, I heard Pearlie's horn outside. Two beeps were the first warning. Three beeps meant, "Get the hell out here or we won't get to Possum's at twelve twenty-three."

"Don't forget to be back at one-thirty," Essie said without looking up.

I allowed her to watch a minuscule television at her desk. When *One Life to Live* was on, I knew not to expect eye contact. In the South, soap operas seem to be exempt from conflicts with the Christian faith. Essie watched virile husbands and barely clad wives and girlfriends hop from bed to bed, never missing a minute but always shaking her head judgmentally.

When we got to Possum's, I was surprised to see two vehicles in addition to Talmadge's police car. I couldn't imagine why the place would be so busy. One of the cars, an old army-green Subaru Brat—part car, part truck—sat in the alley between the restaurant and the three motel rooms. I saw one large, naked foot, pink flesh on the bottom, chocolate skin on the top, sticking out the rolled-down passenger window like a human stop sign.

"Everything okay in there?" I felt the need to ask as I walked by.

"Go away," a man's voice replied. All five toes stretched a moment, then went back to resting position.

As I entered the restaurant, Possum came bounding out the red swinging kitchen door. "I told the chief you'd be here momentarily," he said, two plates of food on one arm and two on the other. "Sorry your usual plate's not waiting on you. Been as busy as Mickey D's today. Don't know what's going on."

"Good for you," I said.

"Good if it don't kill me," Possum said. "One day, I'm closing early to go bowling, and the next, I need to hire help."

Talmadge, at the bar, swiveled around. "I went ahead and started," he said. "Never can tell when I'll be called away."

"Thanks for meeting me," I said. "Have you eaten here before?"

"Seems like I've passed this place a thousand times, but I've never stopped."

Possum is just as happy you haven't, I thought.

"Sorry, Gritz, but I run out of fried okra," Possum said as he passed again. "If business keeps up like this, I'm going to have to start going to Ingles twice a week. Even had to hire a dishwasher this morning. Said he just got into town, needed a few minutes of sleep and then he'd help me clean up."

"Guess the word's gotten out. About your barbecue," Talmadge said.

"God's always trying to get your attention, ain't he? I mean, after all these years in the restaurant business, now I'm ready to kick the bucket, and the word finally gets traveling," he mumbled as he pushed his shoulder into the door.

For such a big man, Talmadge ate in small bites. He wiped his mouth with a napkin and said, "Your friend piqued my curiosity the other day. I asked about those court records, and I was told they were probably waterlogged and buried down on River Road in one of those abandoned tobacco barns the city rents as warehouses. I wouldn't attempt to find anything down there— those places smell like the flood of nineteen ten is still sloshing around. I faxed the clerk of the North Carolina Supreme Court, figuring a death-penalty case must have been appealed even back then. They got right on it, and here it is, every word of that trial and the appeal."

"Fascinating," I said as he handed me a manila envelope.

"I just skimmed it, but I'm going to tell you what we'll likely find is that fellow really did do it. I know Royal thinks otherwise, but we're right more than we're wrong."

"But T said he was with him all night."

"From what he said, they also consumed a few bottles of whiskey. What puts one man to sleep makes another man do things he never intended to do. I see it all the time."

I nodded in agreement but knew it had to be otherwise. If T was sure, I was sure. I'd stake my life on it. I wanted to tell him about Mary Mag's encounter but decided it might not add to my credibility to talk about it right then.

A couple dressed in matching medical scrubs brought their check to the bar near where Talmadge and I sat.

Possum came out of the kitchen with two dishtowels, one on each shoulder. "Everything good enough?" he asked, ringing the ticket on a manual cash register almost as large as the bar itself.

The skinny, young male reached for a toothpick and nodded slight approval. The girl looked around the place as if she didn't like the décor as much as Bojangles'. She didn't acknowledge Possum at all. Civility was obviously something they hadn't studied in school.

"I bet they won't eat for a week, Possum," I said.

The young man looked at me like he knew he'd been corrected but didn't know for what—and didn't like it either.

"Y'all come back, now," Possum said, giving him his change.

Turning to leave, he slapped his lunch partner on the butt, and both giggled as they left, letting the door slam behind them.

"Possum, you must remember Mordecai Moore and that murder at the Battery Park," I said.

"Poor son of a bitch. That boy got fried, and somebody got off scot-free, no doubt about it. But I always figured the good Lord would get his whack sooner or later. That was way before you were born, son," Possum said, looking half at Talmadge, half at me.

I explained to Possum about T moving home and about Mordecai's haint.

"Jennie Mae thinks she sees her dead mother sometimes. And wouldn't you know it, it's always when she's about to get naked and crawl into bed. Great timing for your mother-in-law to show up, huh?"

Talmadge's beeper went off. "I need to check this," he said, reaching into his pocket and pulling out a money clip.

"Put it on my tab, Possum," I said.

"You ain't got no tab, Gritz," Possum answered. "Business has been good. I'm going to treat the both of you. This ain't no bribe, now, chief."

"I'll sure be back," Talmadge said, turning to leave. "You cook barbecue the way I remember it. Lexington-style."

Possum seemed to straighten.

As Talmadge reached the door, a very large black man was walking in. From the size of his feet, I figured it was the man who'd been sleeping in the Brat. He looked at Talmadge but didn't hold the door for him as they brushed by each other. Talmadge gave the man's orange jumpsuit a good look but didn't stop to chat.

"Gritz, I want you to meet Arson Allison, my new head of kitchen maintenance."

I held out my hand to the man, but he didn't take it. One arm was normal length, but the other seemed like it just erupted out of his shoulder, giving birth to a full-sized hand. The man was a fifty-six extra tall if he was an inch. He appeared to be about forty years old and had rough beard stubble with just a touch of gray in it. When he turned slightly, I could see that his short-sleeved jumpsuit wasn't a fashion statement. The back read *Inmate*.

"Arson, Gritz here is one of Asheville's finest doctors."

Arson looked at me like I was the biggest wuss he'd ever run into.

"I didn't want to mention it to the chief, but Arson here just got out of the brig. Needed some part-time work. He's going to swap part of his pay for one of my rooms out back."

Finally, Arson spoke. "They never gave me nothing for my sore ankle down at Central. I think I sprained it kicking the fool out of that damn cafeteria worker." He held his left ankle in the air toward me.

"I'm a psychiatrist, but I guess I'd soak it in hot water."

I saw him look at the sudsy water in the sink behind the bar.

"Oh, I thought you was a real doctor," he said, walking into the kitchen.

"He ain't got much personality, but I figure he's experienced enough for what I need him for," Possum whispered.

My watch said lunch was over, though I wished I had more time before heading back to the salt mine. When I got outside to look for Pearlie, Talmadge was still in his car, talking on the radio. He motioned me over.

"Tell them we don't have a damn SWAT team. Get Searcy and Penland over there. I'm on my way," he said, then turned to me.

"Get in."

"Pearlie's on his way," I said.

"Can't wait. We've got a hostage situation. At the hospital. At Highland."

"Jesus Christ! Who?"

"We think one of your orderlies is being held hostage by a patient."

As I got in the car, Possum hurried outside, waving a portable phone in his hand. "It's the hospital. They said your beeper must be turned off. Some kind of emergency."

"Tell them I know. I'm on the way with Talmadge."

As we cut across traffic, Talmadge flipped on his siren just as I heard Pearlie's go off behind us at the restaurant. Talmadge heard it but had more important things on his mind. I looked at Possum, standing in the doorway of his café watching us drive off. Arson was leaning against the doorframe behind him. He appeared to be rubbing his ankle with his normal hand.

If only I'd become a chiropodist instead of a shrink.

CHAPTER ELEVEN

"Vos ken vern fun di shof az der volf iz der richter?"
"What will become of the sheep if the wolf is the judge?"

The hospital buildings had already been evacuated by the time
we arrived. I could see a gaggle of orderlies corralling patients
onto the volleyball courts. In front of the O'Henry dorm, I saw
several cops crouched behind their cars. On the side of the building
that had no windows, I saw Dink, Essie, and four seersuckered
legal eagles standing behind a large elm. A massive black rain
hovered over the scene. It reminded me of what William Sydney
Porter, the writer for whom the dorm under siege was named,
remarked about Asheville. He married a local gal and later moved
into her family compound but wrote precious little while he was
in our town. "A terrible dark malaise came over me while I was in
Asheville," he was quoted as saying after he returned to New York.

I was quickly informed that Bobby Raby and Cage Blevins were holding Jesus McFarland hostage in the dorm's television room. That was not a small task, since Jesus was strong as a bull. He had taken many an angry patient to seclusion when needed. I felt like Tevye complaining to God in *Fiddler on the Roof*: "Why *my* patients, God? Why not Dink's?" As with Tevye, God was silent to my pleas.

Talmadge handed me a metal bullhorn like the one Governor Wallace used on the doorstep to the University of Alabama so JFK would be sure and hear him in Washington. Just as I took it, hardly knowing which side of the instrument to speak into, another cop car screeched into the hospital grounds and pulled up where we were hunkered down. The passenger door flew open, and Mayor Bloom jumped out.

"Goldberg, what the hell's going on here?"

"I'm not sure," I said. His smell hit me like a load of dung.

"WLIS and the *Citizen-Times* called my office saying one of your lunatics wants to make a statement, and he evidently wants to make it directly to the mayor. Give me that thing," he said, jerking the bullhorn out of my hands.

Looking first to see where the television cameras were aimed, Shel turned in their direction, not seeming to care that it put his back to the dorm and the supposed recipient of his wise words.

"This is your mayor. We will not submit to extortion in Asheville."

There was no answer from Bobby or anyone else. Shel looked surprised and dejected.

"Let me try," I said.

The mayor readily handed me the horn, and I took a few steps toward the front of O'Henry but stayed well behind the police cars.

"Bobby, this is Dr. G. I'm here to talk this out."

No response.

"Bobby, what's this all about?"

"Duck!" somebody yelled.

We all hit the ground.

"Nobody shoot!" Talmadge shouted.

A rock with a rubber band around it bounced off the top of one of the cop cars and landed by me. It had a piece of notebook paper bound on it. As I unwrapped it, Shel crawled over on his knees and demanded to see it. He read the note and then looked again for a camera. When he saw WLIS anchor Angel Davis, he motioned her over to put the camera back on him.

It says, "Call me at 227-7786," the mayor announced proudly.

"Great," Talmadge said. "Now, every nut in Asheville will start dialing."

Shel looked shocked that the police chief would make such a comment.

This time, I jerked a cell phone from the mayor's hand. It was a fancy model that had the Dow Jones average currently on the crystal. I dialed the number, and Bobby picked up.

"Dr .G., I want to make a statement. On television. I want that blond chick and the mayor standing by my side at the front door right now."

"Bobby, listen to me. You need to let Jesus go first. This could turn dangerous for everybody."

"I'm getting out of this place. I want Dr. Montague's Mercedes with a full tank of gas parked at the front door."

"What do you want from the mayor?"

"I heard Bloom is going to announce for the Senate at the justice center dedication next week. That's all we need in Washington, another Jew. If he runs, he might just win, and I want him committed to opposing even the discussion of black reparations. I want him to promise to restore America to its roots. I've been planning this for a while. I'm going to announce the formation of a local chapter of the Free American White Nationalists—the FAWNS. I guess it's going to take another Raby to restore this country's heritage."

If only it was deer-hunting season.

Bobby had potential as a politician—namely, an evil background and family money. But starting a political career by taking a hostage showed poor planning.

"Okay, Bobby. Let me arrange for you to talk to the media, but only after you let Jesus go."

Bobby must have inherited his media savvy from his grandfather. My favorite story about Senator Raby concerned the time he hit a pedestrian with his car in New York City, then bravely carried the girl to the hospital in his arms and married her a week later on the site of the accident.

I motioned for Angel Davis to come toward me. Though her face was fashionably anorexic, her double-breasted red raincoat beefed her up to a size three.

"Could you set up a camera on the front entrance of the O'Henry dorm?"

"Sure," Angel said like a woman who sniffed a six o'clock scoop. "Can you give me their names? Why they're here, in the hospital?"

I smiled and went back to talking to Bobby.

"Bobby, I'll have the Mercedes at the front door in a few minutes, and you can make your speech to Angel, but first you need to let Jesus go."

Actually, I was getting some pleasure out of this, too. I couldn't wait to order Dink to hand over the keys to his treasured car.

Shel motioned for me to give him the phone. He put his hand over the mouthpiece so the microphones wouldn't pick up what he said.

"Listen here, you little nut case. I am the mayor of this shitty city. I demand you give up right now."

Talmadge didn't seem happy with my idea of how to end the situation. "Gritz, we can't give him a getaway car!"

"Trust me on this, Talmadge," I said. "Dink's got a navigational tracking system on that German tank."

What worried me was that the longer this thing lasted, the better the chance for a full-fledged riot. Few residents of Highland actually wanted to be there. Given the chance to yell and scream and run . . . well, it might be too tempting for some.

Talmadge went over to inform Dink we needed his car. I could tell he wasn't happy with me by the way he waved with his middle finger.

A police officer suddenly emerged from the crowd escorting a well-dressed, tall, leggy woman. She had blond hair obviously aided by Clairol; it was pulled back in a sexy old-time bun held tightly by a tortoise-shell clip. She wore a leopard-print silk blazer over a solid black dress that draped down to mid-calf, accentuated by matching leopard pumps with spike heels. My eyes fell to her left ankle, which displayed a small tattoo of a purple butterfly on a white lily.

My heart started pounding furiously at the sight of Emma Whitaker, just as it had right after high-school graduation when a muscled, frustrated artist in Myrtle Beach burned that butterfly into her delicate, white, pure skin while I stood watching in my bathing suit, dripping Atlantic Ocean and lust. The years had stolen her young face, but just the sight of her—my Emma Blossom, as I used to call her—within five feet of my nearly extinguished, almost vacant soul gave me hope there was a living God who hadn't totally given up on one nearly lost Southern Jewish psychiatrist.

And just like decades earlier, I didn't know what to say or do in her presence. *Smitten*. That was the word I'd finally decided upon after years of trying to get a handle on the depth of her effect on me.

As she approached me, just the smell of her made me realize I was not yet among the walking dead, as I usually felt. Something other than a hostage situation was jump-starting my heart. My whole body felt like it was going to explode.

"Let me have that phone, Gritz."

Bobby's mother's voice was still as sexy as a red silk nightgown about to be tossed off. In a split second, it was like I was sixteen and at the Rexall lunch counter hoping for an Emma sighting. This time, that silly awkwardness felt great, though.

"Emma." It was all I could say without losing my breath.

She didn't respond to me but talked into the phone. "Bobby Rice Raby the Third, what do you think you're doing? Let that man go, you hear me? Right now, let him go. Do you hear me, Bobby?"

I'd seen her that mad only once before, when I had to turn her down for the Sadie Hawkins dance. Those were the days when, in my family, dating *shiksas* was comparable to supporting Hitler's SS. Though I thought it was the greatest thing that ever happened to me when Emma walked over and asked me to the dance, I was afraid for my life. If Aunt Fay ever got wind of it, I knew she would fly down in a second and emasculate me in front of a dance floor full of *goyim*.

Emma stood waiting for Bobby to cave in. Tall and proper, she always projected elegance. It could have been a blessed event, her showing up back in my life out of the blue, if it weren't for the situation that brought her to me.

God bless mothers. Thirty-three or eighty-three, sons of any kind, shape, or description will crumble at the mere thought that their mom might be in the vicinity. Within fifteen seconds, Jesus came walking out the front door. Spanish words—expletives, I presume—shot out of his mouth like rounds of machine-gun ammo.

"Bobby, I'm coming in!" Emma yelled, this time without mechanical aid.

No SWAT team could have done better. Soon, Cage fled, his guitar held high in surrender. In another couple of minutes, just after Emma went in, Bobby emerged with his mother by his side. His body language said, *Just shoot me now.* Talmadge directed his men to apprehend "the dumb shit." Shel quickly confiscated Bobby's promised air time to give Angel a tantalizing teaser about how there just might be a big political announcement coming soon. He also explained how singlehandedly defusing this terrorist incident was all in a day's work for him.

Off camera, Shel glared at Emma, then me. She had more of a history with him than I did, but he didn't act like he was glad to see her in the least. His grimace seemed to say, *Why you? Why now?* His jaws were so tight I could almost hear his teeth grinding. How Emma could have left me for Shel was right up there with understanding the Big Bang, Jesus moving that stone off his grave, and how eating pork in a Chinese restaurant was somehow deleted from the Torah commandments.

Aunt Fay never called Emma by name. To her, she was always "the little *nafka*." I was ordered to watch out for girls like her. But to me, there were no other girls like her. Shel and I watched out, all right—for Emma's every move. Now, I stood together again with Shel, my lifelong nemesis, and Emma, my lifelong siren. It felt like a personal play of mine was being performed—just a new scene, but without a script to go by, as always.

The orderlies herded the patients back to their comfortable stalls. Emma and her butterfly floated toward me.

"Gritz, you look good, really good," she said. "You know, I've never forgotten us. We did some crazy things together."

"Me neither, Emma," I said, glancing downward.

"Remember getting this for me?" Emma said, turning her ankle. "I think this was his first tattoo, by the way he acted. I'm glad I got it. Every time I take a bath, I think of it, of us."

If God was playing a joke on me, if I was going to wake up and find out this was a dream, I was going to be really ticked this time.

It was a perfect time to come up with the words I'd never been able to say decades earlier. But time had not been a good teacher. No perfect words were forthcoming. All I could say was, "We were supposed to meet with Bobby tomorrow, weren't we?"

"That's why I'm in town. I just happened to hear the radio and called the police. Somehow, I just knew it was Bobby." Her fingertips touched my elbow. "I'm really sorry for all this. I don't know why he turned out this way."

The thought of Emma and me behind closed doors together made me tremble like the day when I first laid eyes on her. I didn't know it then, but first love is not erasable, not with age, not with reason. At sixteen, I didn't have much to barter with, but I remember negotiating with God that morning I saw her in homeroom. I pledged to never let a fried dead pig part touch my lips again if the Almighty would authorize my plunge into interfaith dating. God didn't say yes but didn't say no either, I kept telling myself.

"I didn't know you'd become a doctor until Bobby mentioned your name. I figured you would end up running Goldberg's. You'd be good at that, too," she said. Emma always said the right things at the right time.

"Wal-Mart took care of that career," I said, immediately worrying if that was too flippant.

"I'd better get down to the jail," Emma said. She turned to leave, then paused. "I still love you, you know."

I wanted to say, "I still love you, too," but I didn't. One of those ridiculous moronic smiles that used to make my cheeks ache for a week was all I could muster.

After Emma left to go with Bobby, I checked on Jesus. He was fine. I called around to all the halls to see if the incident had sent my patients into a contagious flurry of quirks. It had. I ordered them an extra round of antipsychotic medication for the night.

I saw Essie urgently waving at me as she walked carefully across the mole-inhabited hospital grounds.

"Dr. Montague wants you in his office, pronto," she said, handing me a couple of phone slips.

"I'm on my way, Essie."

She turned, walked a step or two, and looked over her shoulder.

"Honest, Essie, I'm going."

Dink and the Trinity contingent were waiting for me. They didn't nod or say hello or anything else when I walked in. They did look at me with deeply educated sneers, and then they started talking to each other like I wasn't even there. Scorn filled the room as thickly as the mold that lived happily in Highland's old buildings.

Dink began his rant, known by those of us close to him as "Dr. Dink's Dishin'."

"We must minimize what this will look like on the evening news. Our patients—so far, at least—seem to have taken this display of anger and criminal activity in stride. This never should have happened," he said, looking directly at me, "but since it has, let's make the most of it. Let's show the world that we can handle these things calmly and properly."

Anger and outrage are pretty much part of a mental hospital's regimen, though most of the time they tend to smolder instead of burn.

"I want to make sure we're all on the same page," Dink said, his wide tie rolling up and down over his big belly with each breath. "This was just an aberration," he continued, looking at the four stooges from Durham.

I agreed. Highland was pretty darn boring.

"We talk to no one. We have no comment to the media, period. The police will take care of Raby and Blevins. I heard CNN already has a scroll about the uprising. Hopefully, they'll forget about us by six."

I slowly pulled out the two pink slips Essie had handed me and held them under the table, trying to read them. Dink, of course, noticed.

"Dr. Goldberg, the Raby boy was your client, correct?"

"I would hardly call this an uprising," I said. Some situations just beg for a smart-ass reply.

Dink was not amused. His tie rolled up higher on his stomach.

"Bobby Raby is a very angry young man, but he showed absolutely no signs of outright violence, if that's what you're getting at."

The four bow ties wiggled at me.

"We need to be careful of the liability the university could be exposed to. In the future, I recommend more stringent analysis of our clients," the stiffest of the four lawyers said acerbically.

After several more cover-our-butts comments, Dink closed the meeting. However, he motioned me to stay.

"Gritz, this is it. One more time and I'll have to file formal dismissal charges against you. I won't put up with any more of your intransigence."

I looked at him for a moment and said, "Heard any good CDs lately?"

Dink's face turned red as cherry pie filling as I stalked off.

Being a glutton for punishment, I pulled out my cell phone and called Aunt Fay, one of the names on Essie's pink slips.

"Bobbie Batista just interrupted *Talk Back Live* with your *mishugunahs*. Are you okay?"

"Everything's over. Everybody's okay."

Thanks to technology, a hostage situation in a mental hospital might make live national news for fifteen seconds on an otherwise slow day.

"You've got to get a better class of patients, dear. What are you dealing with Nazis for anyway? Give them to the *goy* doctors."

I silently prayed that CNN wouldn't give much time to the news report, particularly to any pictures of Emma Whitaker. When Aunt Fay first learned I wanted to date Emma, she'd threatened to quit sending her fresh apricot *hamantaschen* pastries every *Purim*. Withholding high-fat or sweet food from a Jew is the ultimate bludgeon. Any Jew worth his weight in cholesterol would cave in to a demand like that. Aunt Fay knew how to use such weapons only too well.

CHAPTER TWELVE

"An alter freint iz besser vi nei'eh tsvai."
  "One old friend is better than two new ones."

Soon after I got out of Dink's inquisition, I headed home. I found Arlene and T sitting at the kitchen table perusing stacks of what appeared to be photocopies of old *Citizen* papers. Arlene looked enthused. T looked exhausted.

I gave them a quick summary of my afternoon.

"Wouldn't you know, Fay heard about it down in Florida while T and I missed the whole thing buried in microfilm in the basement of the library. Are you sure you're okay? How about I get you a Dewar's on the rocks?" Arlene asked, standing up.

"No, thanks. I think I'll take a shower and try and sleep it off."

"Why would Raby do something so stupid?" Arlene said, shaking her head. "What could he gain by putting on a show like that?"

"There's some new right-wing nut group he wants to promote, or something like that."

T looked like his mind had drifted off. He finally said, "Gritz, do you remember when that traveling hypnotist put old man Dillard to sleep in the window of Massie Furniture? I bet half the town came by to see that man sleeping like a baby right there at the red light on Main Street. Old lady Massie said she sold more mattresses that week than she ever had in the history of the store."

"It's publicity no matter how you get it, I guess," I said. "On top of everything else, guess who turns out to be Bobby Raby's mother? Emma Whitaker. I had no idea she married Senator Raby's son, did you?"

"I lost track after you and her . . . after you went to college. She was quite the beauty, I remember that."

In the sixties, intermarriages between Jews and gentiles were considered a *shanda*, a shame. When Shel, Emma, and I were in high school, our friend Maury Cohen ran off with Edna Brown, who was not only not Jewish but the Methodist preacher's daughter. Maury's grandfather, an Orthodox Jew, vowed never to speak to him again and had Wilson's Funeral Home deliver a casket to the cemetery. The plain wooden box holding every childhood picture of Maury—every memento his grandfather possessed of the boy—was lowered into a grave. In my day, the only way to date a girl who wasn't Jewish was to act like the whole thing was platonic—study at her house, go to the library together, that sort of thing. Shel, never to be outdone, found a slicker way to get around the unspoken law. Officially, he went steady with Laura Lerner, a lesbian girl who otherwise met community requirements of being an M.O.T.—Member of the Tribe. He bragged that he paid Lennie weekly to show up with him in public, and that he and Emma would sneak away and go kayaking at Lake

Chatuge or dancing in Charlotte. I never understood what Emma saw in Shel, but maybe she got tired of stolen smooches with me in the psychology section of the library. There's something about Freud and Jung looking over your shoulder that takes away from the moment.

"Find anything helpful at the library?" I said.

"That murder was front-page news every day for a month," Arlene said. "It was the hottest summer and fall on record that year. Pete Reid did a good job reporting the crime—very dramatic writing."

"We made extra copies for you," T said.

"Show Gritz that article about Moses Bloom," Arlene said, walking to the sink. "He could use a good laugh about now."

T flipped through about fifty sheets before he found the right one. "Small article at the bottom of the page," he said, handing it to me.

The paper, dated October 2, 1939, had an article on the upcoming trial of Mordecai Moore. Given that the murder occurred in early September, it was obvious that the court system of yesteryear didn't have the backlog problems of today. I saw a smaller article circled with a pen. "Local Businessman Surprised in Jury Room," the header read. "Asheville businessman Moses Bloom was dismissed from active jury duty yesterday in the civil trial of *Henry Vanderbilt v. Bank of Asheville*. After a short lunch break, George Gossett, jury foreman, unlocked the courthouse room in which the jury had been deliberating to find Bloom and a female fellow juror in what he termed 'a very compromising position.' When pressed for more details, Gossett would only say, 'It was an amorous embrace.' Neither Bloom nor the unidentified woman could be reached for comment, but a mistrial was declared."

"Everybody knew it. That man chased skirts like my beagle treed squirrels. They weren't real particular, neither my dog nor Moses," T said.

"I haven't run across that article stuck away in one of his albums," I said. T and Arlene looked confused. "Moses lent me his lifelong collection of clippings and pictures the other day. Three albums' worth."

"There's another article you've got to see, Gritz," Arlene said, drying her hands on a towel. "About a mystery writer, no less."

Once again, T pulled out a piece of their library bounty.

"Mystery Writer Asked Opinion on Murder," it read. "Mystery writer Abigail Dunbar of Palmsdale, Florida, was contacted late yesterday by her aunt, local resident Mary Alice Casey, for her opinion on how she would go about solving the Sardano murder. It has been ten days since the New York coed was tragically found shot in her room, blood soaking her robin's egg blue silk pajamas. Mrs. Dunbar, known nationally for her Father Killjoy mystery series, said in a phone interview yesterday that she thinks whoever committed this horrible crime must have had possession of the 13th passkey. Sheriff Hurt Bailey said at his September 18 news conference that there were 13 passkeys to the rooms of the Battery Park Hotel held by hotel employees for the purposes of cleaning and maintenance, and that 12 keys had been accounted for, with one still missing. Hotel manager Chunk Hill said the keys were not assigned but just 'out there,' and he had no idea who might have gotten hold of one. He further stated that a full review of hotel security has been put into action, and that the Battery Park is 'as safe as a battleship now.' Mrs. Dunbar said that she would not comment further, but that she hoped the missing key to the murder would turn up, and the real-life mystery soon be solved."

I looked at T. "Did Mordecai have access to a key?"

"I doubt it. Those keys were not given to hall boys like us. The maids all had one. The night watchmen—there were three, I think, that alternated nights—they all had one. Of course, Chunk had one. I'm not sure who else might have."

"So the lock on the girl's door wasn't jimmied?"

"Not only that, but the girl's uncle said when he knocked on her door for breakfast and didn't get an answer, he tried turning the knob to her room, and it was definitely locked. Everybody figured it weren't real likely the girl got up and locked the door after being shot."

"But why would the killer lock back up? Or could he have left out a window?"

"Not unless he was Spider-Man. If you look, there aren't many ledges or balconies or nothing out those windows. Besides, there was that insurance man from Tennessee that said he saw the killer locking back up as he left."

"What insurance man?" I said.

"He was staying in the room directly across from the girl. He said about one in the morning, he heard something that sounded like a gunshot. At first, he said he thought it had to be lightning from a storm that was going on that night, but after the power went out, he heard somebody moving in the hallway outside his room. He said he cracked the door just enough to peek out. Since it was pitch black, he couldn't make out who it was, but somebody was definitely leaving the girl's room. He said he asked the man if he heard the loud sound, too, and if it sounded like a gunshot to him. The man answered that it sounded like a gun to him, but he guessed it was just the storm."

"And the sheriff determined the man leaving was Mordecai?" Arlene asked.

"I suppose so, but I don't much see how. The insurance man said he couldn't see the other man's face, but the man spoke with an accent, like he was from Germany or somewhere like that. You think a colored boy from Greer, South Carolina, is going to be speaking like that?"

"So how could a jury convict Moore on such weak testimony?" I asked.

"Wasn't hard. They never heard it. Pete Reid wrote about it in the Citizen—it's right here in these papers—but once the trial began, there was no insurance man to be seen. I always wondered how Pete settled that in his gut," T said in a soft voice. "We kept going fishing after that, but neither of us ever brought it up."

"One of those pink elephants," I said.

"Say what?"

"Something everybody sees but nobody wants to acknowledge."

"It was that, all right," T said. "And more."

The real question that begged to be answered, though, was not how it happened but why. If the girl wasn't robbed or raped, why would Mordecai or anyone else kill her?

A sound like a motorcycle erupted outside. I looked to see Adolf running in circles, barking like he'd just discovered another inferior race. I saw two teenagers riding into my driveway on a bright orange ATV with four giant, mud-eating tires. The six-foot blond boy halted the motorized annoyance and pulled off his helmet. Nate Goldberg waved. So did his second-in-command, four-foot-ten Stef Goldberg.

"I hope you don't mind, Gritz. You know I promised them a Honda if they both made the headmaster's list three times in a row," Arlene said a little sheepishly, but proudly, too. "And they made Nate technical director of that school-access cable show. I'm so proud of those guys."

"Dad, are you okay?" Stef said, bounding into the kitchen. "We just heard about it over at the park."

"Nobody got hurt. It's okay," I said.

Nona and I hadn't made a great couple, but we made great children.

"Let me take you for a ride," Nate said. "It'll take your mind off things."

I preferred a large dose of antacid, a Valium, and a long shower. "That's okay. Give Arlene and T a whirl," I said half seriously.

"I'd love a ride," Arlene said.

Stef took off her helmet and handed it over.

I picked up the stack of *Citizen* copies and headed upstairs, where I looked forward to a feather bed and my extra-long and fluffy buddy pillow, even though I knew the world was going to find me again much too soon.

Dreams are what my profession idolizes, but snakes symbolizing penises and stampeding elephants representing domineering fathers have never intrigued me like real-life foot fetishes and debilitating obsessions. I must admit, though, that the dream I had after my shower that late afternoon almost sent me scrambling for my Jung primer.

It seems Shel Bloom was still mayor, but I was his son and Emma my mother. Willard Paully, Solly Goldberg, and Senator Raby all had some kind of business venture going—tire recapping, I think. President Franklin Roosevelt rode into town on an orange ATV, saying he needed my help in solving a murder, and that if I was successful, he would arrange for Emma to become my wife, and that he could even work it out for Aunt Fay to accept her with open arms and double apricot *hamantaschen* pastries. T had this enormous old key poking out of his pocket, but he couldn't remember who it belonged to or what it opened. Pete Reid and

Mary Mag were having sex in a Battery Park room when Mordecai Moore, attired in leather-fringed rodeo apparel, broke down the locked door and shot T, who was hiding under the bed in blue silk pajamas.

"Gritz, wake up, wake up," Arlene said, shaking my shoulder. "You're screaming."

A bad dream can make reality so much more tolerable.

CHAPTER THIRTEEN

"Der man iz der balebos—az di veib zaine lozt."
"The husband is the boss—if the wife allows."

It was always her toes. Slender and bare, without the slightest hint of stubbiness. Her perfectly trimmed and painted toenails were scarlet usually blended with a touch of sienna, skillfully applied with the skill of a master—no smears, even on the pinkies. Her arches, particularly when assisted by high-heel pumps, reached regally skyward, but without pretentiousness. Her skin, not overly exposed to the sun but never innocently pale either, politely flirted for a gentle caressing of one or both feet. Some things in life, thank the Almighty, just never change.

Emma sat opposite me, legs crossed, scant sandals displaying feet bare as my office's snack pantry, rocking back and forth gently within inches of my boring brown gabardine-covered shins. I'd approached the day's meeting with the taut emotions of a high-school boy helplessly in love. Was I was still that boy? Always that boy? Had age dimmed the spark, smothered the fire?

We were there to talk about Bobby's condition and a solution to his problems. How could I say there was little anyone could do to cure recurring asshole syndrome? How could I tell that to his mother, my resurrected goddess? I really didn't want to talk at all. The slightest slip in diction or minutest change in the manner Emma flipped her hair back could destroy the precious mental script I'd clung to almost all my adult life. Would a sculptor melt down his masterpiece on purpose? Would a writer shred his fine-tuned novel just for fun? This was a huge, overpowering, life-directing obsession I had cherished territorially over many years. I wanted to slip off her white sandals and knead her while she purred.

"When I heard you were Bobby's shrink, I almost laughed out loud," she said.

Things were not beginning well.

"That didn't sound right. I just meant it's ironic how our lives intertwine—not just yours and mine, but everybody's."

The last few days were making serendipity feel like one of life's sureties, rather than a wishful little thought. The recurring cast of characters was so clear, the plot so murky.

"I thought Bobby was making progress, but obviously I was wrong," I finally said.

"Bobby has always been angry. He doesn't respect anyone except maybe Senator Raby. He idolizes that man," Emma said.

"I had no idea that you married into the Raby family. He speaks fondly of his grandfather."

It was difficult to accept Emma's having a thirty-three-year-old son, even harder to acknowledge thirty-five years had passed since she and I were a couple. Maybe our brains really did start shrinking at thirteen, as some studies declared. That would explain why everything from our twenties to our fifties seems so much less memorable than our teenage years.

She looked at me and then down at her lap. After a long, uncomfortable silence, she spoke. "Gritz, I need to be honest with you. Whatever-I-say-never-leaves-the-room kind of stuff."

"Certainly," I answered. I could feel my pulse throbbing in my left ear. I hoped she couldn't hear it.

"Gritz, after we split up senior year, you knew Shel Bloom and I dated for quite a while."

Yes, I most certainly remembered the two worst years of my life. The thought of losing Emma was bad enough. Losing her to Shel Bloom seemed a terminal wound. I did what any psychologically inept human might have done—turned anger on myself and ended up a patient in a mental facility dealing with raging depression and OCD symptoms.

"Shel went on to Chapel Hill. I went to Asheville-Biltmore College. He started dating some Jewish sorority girl, Marsha something or other, for appearances, like he did with Laura Lerner, but I would go down to visit him at school. During our freshman year, I got pregnant. Moses pitched a big one when Shel told him about us. He said fooling around with a *shiksa* was one thing, but marrying her was another. Right in front of me, I heard him tell Shel to marry Marsha right away and keep me on the side. Shel offered to pay for an abortion, which was illegal at the time, of course. I told him absolutely not. He did get Moses to fork over money for me to quietly disappear into the Crittenden Home in Charlotte, for unwed mothers. I told him I wasn't going to do that either. I decided I could stay with an aunt in California when I started to show. Just as I was packing to leave, Junior called. He asked me to the movies, of all things—*Love with a Proper Stranger*, with Natalie Wood and Steve McQueen. I figured what the hell and went out with him that night. Then he called right after that for another date. You can figure out the rest of the story."

"I'm not sure I understand. Junior who?"

"Bobby's dad. Robert Raby, Jr. We got married three weeks after he first called me for that movie."

"So Bobby's natural father is Shel Bloom. That was a really nice thing for Raby to do for you."

I was starting to see where Bobby got his personality, and to understand how the apple hadn't fallen far from Shel's tree either.

"Junior never knew," Emma said quietly. "I started to confess it all to him when he was lying in the hospital after he had that last heart attack. They said he wouldn't make it through the night, but I still couldn't do it. I mean, what would be the point?"

I stroked my goatee with my right hand, a nifty movement I performed when a patient expected a comment from me and I had no idea what to say.

"Nobody knows except Shel and me, and now you, but I think somehow, I don't know how, it still has had an effect on Bobby. I just thought you ought to know. Maybe it will help."

Sure, help. Now, I was treating not only a certified criminal but also a bastard's bastard.

"Has Bobby always harbored so much hate?"

"Always. It's like he was born with it. You will continue to be his doctor?"

"Taking a hostage is not like lifting a pack of gum. I doubt they're going to let him out of jail anytime soon, Emma."

Tears streaked her face. I pulled a wad of tissues from the stash that Essie kept refilled on my desk. I wanted to move my rolling chair closer to her to dab her tears, but it was too much of a risk. My hands might shake and give me away. Instead, I pushed the tissues into Emma's hand, receiving the slightest graze of her long, slim fingers over my knuckles. As if thirty-five years had been a mere thirty-five minutes, that same inescapable longing I'd tried desperately to forget rose like a phoenix from the ashes.

After an awkward minute or so, I said, "What about Shel? Has he done anything for you or Bobby over all these years?"

"Not at first, but then after he went into politics, every so often he would send me a package. The box had no return address, but I knew his handwriting. It was usually a shoebox filled with cash. One time, it was these weird, old gold coins. I took them to a coin dealer. He said they were solid gold, German. He paid me a few thousand for them. Strange, huh?"

"Maybe Shel really has a heart."

"I always figured it was more hush money than support. Insurance. My husband made good money as a lawyer. Shel knew I didn't really need it financially, but news of an illegitimate son wouldn't have done a whole lot for his political career."

I told Emma I'd do what I could for Bobby. I was acutely aware of the time that might be involved for one divorced shrink and one prime-of-life widow to get together. The more serious complication of my possibly becoming a stepdad to an avowed racist if things worked out didn't interfere with my initial analysis of the situation.

Emma uncrossed her luscious legs and stood. Her long, straight neck was just as graceful as it always had been, like a swan's. I stood, too, but somehow the wheels of my chair rolled funny, catching the tips of Emma's left toes.

"Oh, my God," I said, bending down. "I'm so sorry, Emma. Do you need a Band-Aid?"

I gently lifted her second toe between my thumb and middle finger and lightly tried to rub away the boo-boo. The toe had a narrow silver ring around it. It was such a crazy thing, slipping off that ring into the palm of my hand. Juvenile, too. But having *Dr.* in front of your name doesn't guarantee either good sense or maturity. I looked up to see if Emma noticed. If she did, she didn't give any sign of it. Emma's toe ring was mine!

"It's okay, Gritz, really."

I knew I had to let go of her precious digit, but it was really hard.

"I'll go downtown later and see if they'll let me talk to Bobby," I said finally.

"Bless you, Gritz. I am most appreciative."

She looked like she wanted to say something more but turned and reached for the doorknob. I rushed to get it for her, her hand just beating mine, my hand covering her fingers, my heart gushing like an uncontrolled well of buried feelings. And then she was gone.

I tried not to look at Essie, but she knew instantly.

"Tough session?" she said. "I've got a extra bear claw."

"I need a few minutes before my next patient to return a call or two," I said, still not looking at her.

I felt sweat about to run off my forehead onto my wire-rim glasses. I had no calls. She knew it, and I knew it. I took the pastry and went back into my office.

I knew God had more important items on his to-do list than listening to my petty annoyances, but every now and then, I felt the need to ring up the head honcho anyway. I stepped outside onto my tiny balcony.

"God, I know I don't make Friday-night services very often—okay, almost never—and I complain about frivolous stuff like being bored and those two age spots that popped up on my forehead last fall. I know you were too busy to help me sink that putt a few weeks ago, even though I would have won the tournament. But could you please give me just a hint of what you're doing with my life right now? I mean, I blink and T's back, and then Emma's back, and then there's Mordecai Moore, who never left. I have old feelings of love that feel fresh, and I have new feelings of old hate. I'd like to ask for the first time in about three decades that things slow down just a bit." I paused for breath and then added, "Amen."

God didn't answer, but a sparrow did fly over the balcony and poop on my glasses.

I asked Essie to arrange with Talmadge for me to see Bobby. I really thought a jail cell could do more for the boy than we could at Highland, but seeing him would give me an excuse to set up another session with Emma, maybe even a dinner. I was throwing ethics to the wind. After all, this was Emma Blossom I was obsessing over.

Asheville might have been short on shelters for the homeless and computers for every classroom, but it voted overwhelmingly to fund the finest jail cells in North Carolina. The Raby Justice Center was to be dedicated soon, but that day I found Bobby housed in the old jail, which sat on the top three floors of the crumbling Art Deco courthouse downtown. Talmadge was out on an emergency, so a stooped, limping man who resembled a disabled Woody Allen led me down the dark hallway. I guessed this was the same jail where Mordecai had received his rubber-hose beatings. And downstairs was where he'd sat for his trial.

Bobby was in the next-to-last cell, wearing an orange jumpsuit just like Arson's. He seemed to fit better in jail than at the hospital.

"Dr. G., you're a sight for sore eyes."

Likewise, I thought, but I said, "Hello, Bobby."

"Have you come to get me?"

"That's not going to be so easy this time. You did a pretty stupid thing yesterday." I was surprised at my candor.

"I was just sitting outside O'Henry, trying to figure out a way to get some publicity for the FAWNS, and that S.O.B. Jesus McFarland walked by. It was a situation that called for quick thinking on your feet."

More like thinking with your feet, I thought. "It doesn't make any difference who it was, Bobby. You held another human hostage. You know you can't get away with that."

"Lincoln did. Do you know how many Confederates died while in captivity? Did anyone put *their* captors in jail?"

In my business, rationalizations are as common as car horns blaring at south Florida intersections.

"Who are these FAWNS, Bobby?"

"We're going to take this country back, I tell you!"

"Back from whom?"

"The Third World Order. Even Bush, he acts like a blue blood, but then he lets his daughter go steady with a Jew from Austin."

Maybe it was good Emma hadn't told Bobby of his heritage. I couldn't see Bobby giving a good bar mitzvah speech. Emma had never exhibited racist or prejudiced feelings when I was around her. Bobby's hate must have come from the Raby side of the family. I never knew Emma's husband growing up. I think he went to military school in Georgia.

"The FAWNS have a national headquarters in Montana. We started our den here last fall. We meet down by the river in an abandoned garage. We have a shooting range down there. Plenty of rats to aim for," Bobby said with one of his smart-ass smirks.

"Bobby, where did you hear about this Third World Order stuff?"

"Here it comes! You're going to try and tell me there's no

such thing, that it's all lies. Well, I know what I know. Your people run the whole damn show. Bet you're going to tell me you haven't attended meetings either."

Picturing Aunt Fay as the chief executive in charge of world political power didn't ring true, but the next time I attended one of our giant strategy sessions, I'd be on the lookout.

"Granddaddy was quoted as saying that if this country had elected Willard Paully president, everything would be different. You do know about Commander Paully, don't you? Roosevelt kept him off the ballot except in the state of Washington. He operated right here out of Asheville."

"I've heard of him," I said. *Too much lately*, I thought.

"Dad said Senator Bob and Paully were tight as a sailor's knot. I wish I could've been around back then."

I could see how he would have fit in just fine.

"Bobby, you can't keep going around breaking the law whenever you feel like it."

"I live by my own laws."

One of Bobby's neighbors flushed a commode, and stink drifted our way. Even using the visit as leverage to see Emma again had its limits. Fortunately, I heard the sweet sound of Pearlie's horn outside. It was nearly noon. That left twenty-three minutes to get to Possum's, and it would take at least five minutes to march back out of the jail.

"I've got to go, Bobby. Do you need your medications increased while you're here?" I felt I needed to ask for Emma's sake.

"All I need is to get the hell out," he said. "Is Mom pissed?"

I didn't like anybody talking that way about my Emma Blossom. Besides, my goddess would urinate, never piss.

"I'm ready!" I yelled to the jailer.

A squeaky door down the hall opened. If the jailer walked any slower, he would have gone backwards. I didn't want to be Bobby's doctor. I didn't want to be anybody's doctor. As I exited the cell, I happened to look up. Crudely carved into the wooden framing above the bars was, "All ye who enter, abandon all hope."

CHAPTER FOURTEEN

"Arein iz di tir brait, un arois iz zi shmol."

"The door to evil-doing is wide, but the return gate is narrow."

"You've had three calls from the same woman. She wouldn't say who she was or what it was about." Essie sighed. "Where are you? I can barely hear you."

It was difficult to use a cell phone in Asheville, signals bouncing indiscriminately from one mountain peak to another like Uncle Carl going from brother to sister at family reunions asking for loans that everybody knew he'd never pay back. Of course, Pearlie's cab didn't help either.

"Did it sound like Marsha Bloom?"

"No, it definitely wasn't her. Oh, Dr. Montague said Trinity was all over him this morning to tighten security. He said to tell you they don't want Bobby Raby back here under any circumstances."

I'd have to figure a way to stall the university hierarchy, at least until Emma and I had a couple of sessions about Bobby. Not for him, for me.

I heard the theme song of *The Young and the Restless* in the background.

"Gotta go, Dr. G."

"Go right ahead, Essie. I'll be back after lunch."

Just as Pearlie rounded the corner onto Maple, I heard a siren blaring. Pearlie always cut that corner too sharply, but we'd never been stopped before. I looked behind us and saw a maroon Mustang with no markings. But the flashing blue light on the dash gave it all the authority it needed.

"Might be those renegades, Gritz. I'm not going down this time."

"It's Talmadge Livingston, the chief of police. It's okay."

Pearlie looked at me like he wasn't sure if it was kosher or if I'd been a ploy of his enemies all along. Luckily, he didn't act like he was going to pull a hidden gun.

Talmadge strode over with a professional swagger I hadn't noticed before. Maybe his shoes hurt.

"Didn't mean to surprise you, Gritz, but I've been reading more of those court transcripts. Something about this case interests me, not sure why. Anyway, I came across something I thought you'd like to know."

Pearlie sat erect, looking straight ahead, like his commanding officer had just come by to check the spit shine on his boots.

"Notice who was Moore's defense attorney," Talmadge said, handing me a sheet of paper with his thumb at a sentence in the middle of the page.

"Culpepper Bailey?"

"The sheriff's brother," Talmadge said. "Bootlegger, from what the old-timers say."

"I'll ask T and Moses. One of them said the sheriff's brother played at that poker club. Got time for a repeat at Possum's?"

"Wish I could. Between T and Possum, I've gained three pounds in the last week. I've got to be at Bobby Raby's arraignment in about an hour. I'll grab a hot dog at the courthouse. Did you meet with the kid?"

"Yeah, but he doesn't think he did anything wrong."

"Most don't," Talmadge smiled.

"Any chance of bail?"

"Not unless you want to take him and lock him up at your place," Talmadge answered, rising from the door and turning to go back to his car.

"Trinity says no way on that," I said. "I'll be meeting with his mom later."

"We'll keep him. I really want to know a little more about that FAWNS group anyway. I mean, are they a real subversive group or just a few rednecks looking for trouble?"

At the mention of *subversive*, I saw Pearlie's head lean back to hear more.

"I don't know. He'd never mentioned them to me before," I said.

"Check you later," Talmadge said.

I looked at my watch. It was 12:20.

"Pearlie, we've got to get moving."

He knew what I meant. Even before Talmadge pulled away, Pearlie jerked the cab into gear and did a couple of wheelies down Maple. I wasn't sure what would happen if I got to Possum's at 12:24, but I remembered what Dr. Baines used to say in my obsessive-compulsive seminar at Tulane: "You can count on death, taxes, and obsessive-compulsive behavior." Then he'd pull out a Windex bottle filled with blue Kool-Aid and chug it down to shake the new students from their malaise.

My plate of Q and fried vegetables—it was supposed to be okra, but sometimes fried batter was all you were sure you were eating—sat on top of the tiny bar waiting for me. A couple of flies were battling over which one would get to land on my sweet tea. The neon in the Pabst Blue Ribbon sign above the Campanella photo flashed off and on hysterically. I didn't see anybody in the whole place until I sat down and stabbed the vegetables. From the corner of my eye, I saw a large brown head covered with unkempt black, curly hair slowly rise from behind the bar, a bright yellow garbage tie hanging perilously to one sprig of growth protruding over a massive ear.

"Hi, Arson. Didn't see you there."

Arson looked at me and then rubbed his nose with a red-and-white-checked dishtowel.

"Nice day," I said.

"Suppose," he answered, then squatted again behind the bar.

"Bless the Lord, Gritz! I saw all that stuff on television yesterday. Shame that white boy had to ruin your lunch like that," Possum yelled from the kitchen.

"I hope I don't have a repeat today," I said.

"I doubt it. The devil never works two days in a row. Haven't you ever heard that?"

"Can't say that I have," I answered after swallowing a mouthful of tea.

"I have," Arson said in a muffled voice from down under.

"It wasn't all bad. The boy's mother turned out to be an old flame of mine."

"Can't be that good," Possum said. "I saw an old flame at Ingles just the other day, and all I got was a kick in the shin and a dose of acid reflux."

At the sound of tires screeching, I was first out the door, then

Possum, then Arson. We didn't see a wreck or even a near miss. We saw an old, tiny red Triumph convertible a hundred yards past the restaurant backing toward us, going the wrong way down Maple. The young blond woman driving wore a red-and-white bandanna around her head and a matching scarf wrapped around her small but perky breasts. Her skinny, bare arms displayed at least a million freckles. Five or six cars swerved around the beat-up convertible before she finally backed into the parking lot.

"Dr. G.!" Candy exclaimed, putting the car into park and bopping out like a female jack-in-the-box. She pulled down her red short shorts so they could at least attempt to cover something.

Arson pulled up his pants and adjusted his twist ties.

Possum stood as straight as his scoliosis allowed.

"Hi, Candy," I said cautiously.

"I saw what they tried to do to you on television," she blurted, putting her arms around my neck, then dropping them quickly, realizing she might have been just a touch forward. "I've never known anybody as famous as you. My dream has always been that somebody like Ray Charles or James Brown would retire to Happy Valley, but I never dreamed I'd know someone who was on CNN."

"I'm okay, Candy. I'd like you to meet a couple of friends of mine, Possum Jenkins and Arson Allison."

Candy shook hands with them both. "Any friend of Dr. Goldtooth is a friend of mine."

"Let me fix you something to eat, little bit," Possum said.

"Just a beer will be fine," she answered.

He looked at me. I nodded that she was old enough. I could be wrong, but I thought I saw Arson scratch his beard with his short hand, trying to defeat a smile.

"Can I grab your ear for a minute?" Candy said. "I tried to call you all morning."

"Sure," I said glancing to the sky just in case that sparrow with the runs was tracking me.

We went inside, and I picked up my plate and took it to the table where Candy had seated herself.

"Gritz . . . Is it all right if I call you Gritz?"

"Everybody else does," I smiled. It was a simple solution, since my last name was obviously more than she could handle.

"I love the man to pieces, but . . . ," she said, looking at me and then focusing on the salt shaker on the table. "Mr. Moses called me into his room this morning and asked if I'd do him a little favor. He said that he'd pay well for it."

It surprised me how shy she looked, since I'd assumed Candy did favors for the male residents of Happy Valley all the time.

"Mr. Moses asked if I could assist someone to die. At first, I thought he was joking, and I said, 'Mr. Moses, you've got plenty of good years left.' He said he wasn't asking for himself. He was wondering if I could just give Estelle Levitz 'a little push toward meeting her maker,' as he put it. He said it would be a blessing to help the poor woman out of her misery. I said, 'Mr. Moses, I can't do that.' I said it was against the law for me to do it and for him to even ask. His face got red as a beet, and then he suddenly dismissed the whole thing, said he was just joking. What's up with all that, Gritz? Everybody knows Estelle and Moses aren't bosom buddies, but I'd never believe he'd go as far as murder."

"Me neither. That's bizarre," I said. "Is he on new meds?"

"Same stuff. I don't want to lose my job, Gritz. If I tell my supervisor, I'm sure Moses will deny ever saying it. I thought about talking to that rabbi man with the goody-goody smile, but he gives me the willies, so I thought I'd ask you. I'll be glad to pay you. That *is* what you do for a living, isn't it, give advice?" I thought I felt Candy's toe pushing down one of my socks, but when I moved my leg, I saw a giant fly buzz off to Possum's kitchen from under the table.

"You can't pay me anything, but you might want to talk this over with a lawyer. Is there any reason you can think of that Moses would harm Estelle?"

"Not really. I used to love to talk to her, and to hear the stories she told."

"I didn't think she could talk."

"Not since last year. But before her stroke, she was quite a chatterbox. Did you know she was invited to the White House by President Roosevelt, but she refused? She told me the president knew what Hitler was doing to her people and just let it happen."

"Why was she invited in the first place?"

"Estelle told me that when she was in her twenties, she helped the government get the goods on some Nazi kook right here in town."

"Paully? Willard Dudley Paully?"

"I think that was his name. She told me all about it, more than once. That little lady climbed through the window of his office and stole a bunch of files that the government later used to put him in jail. She said all the men in Asheville were too chicken to break in, but she put on a pair of her husband's pants and got it done."

"It's hard to picture her doing that after seeing what shape she's in now."

"She also told me she and her husband had one of the largest salvage businesses in the South. Sold everything from fur pelts to all kinds of scrap metal. Sounded like she was the glue that kept the whole business together. She told me they shipped stuff all over the world. Said I'd be surprised at what they sold. Even after her stroke, she can use a computer faster than anyone in the building. The stroke affected her speech, but not her hands or her mind. She just started using e-mail instead of talking. She's nobody's fool, let me tell you that."

"The lady seems like a ball of fire under that paralysis," I said. "She stopped me in the hall after I left Moses' room and handed me a tiny piece of paper. It had the word for *liar* on it. About Moses."

Candy reached under the front of her shorts. "They don't put pockets on these things anymore," she smiled. "Another thing that got me thinking this was getting out of hand was this," she said, also handing me a slip of paper. "Estelle sent me this e-mail just before I left to see you."

I read the note out loud: " 'The secret dies with me. It's in the bag.' "

"What does she mean by that, do you think?" Candy asked.

"She's got something that somebody else wants," said a voice behind us. Arson's voice. He was drying some shot glasses with the same towel he'd used to wipe his nose. "She's takin' it to the grave. That's what she's saying."

"Moses wants something Estelle has?" I addressed the question to Candy but really hoped to get a response from Arson.

"Sure, he does," Arson mumbled, wiping the bar with his shirttail.

"You know what else is odd?" Candy said. "I just happened to notice Estelle's account with Happy Valley posted on the computer the other day. It had a note on it to send the bill each month to Mr. Moses' accountant. It's not cheap at Happy Valley. Why would Moses pay Estelle's bill if he hates her so much?"

"Well, Estelle is family," I said.

"Sure, but would you pay your sister-in-law's bills?" Candy asked.

She had a point, but things that normally made sense had gotten murky in the last week. At Tulane, we were taught that only serial killers and psychopaths were confident of everything they did. That was reassuring, because that day I wasn't confident of a damn thing.

"I'd say she's got something on the old fart," Arson said, walking into the kitchen. "No telling what a man will do if he needs something bad enough."

Candy and I didn't say much else. She downed one Bud and asked for another. I finished my plate and got up to leave.

On the way out, I asked, "How did you know I was here?"

"The mayor told me you eat here all the time," she said.

"You talked to Shel Bloom about this? How does he know where I eat?"

"I didn't say anything about Miss Estelle. I just told him I was looking for you."

"He didn't ask why?"

"Yeah, he asked, but I told him just because I give him . . . I told him it wasn't any of his business. I thought we were, you know, friends. You know what he told me this morning? Said he'd just run into the woman of his dreams, and that he wasn't going to let her get away this time. Why tell *me*?"

I wanted to tell Candy those words were not exactly a gift from heaven to me either. Did things ever really change? Thirty-five years later, and here I was frustrated over the same woman, the same man, the same situation. Asheville was growing by leaps and bounds. Folks from all over the world were discovering our little mecca. I used to know just about everybody in town. Now, I hardly knew a soul. Everybody was a new arrival, and still here I was, in the same town I'd been born in, in the same job, still jousting with the same people over the same things I had at sixteen. The year 2004 felt much like 1966, but with cell phones.

I wondered if people who lived in 1939 felt nothing much had changed for them either. I was sure the soul who lived in the shadows at the Battery Park would agree with me. It seemed fate had picked a few of us to stay in those shadows. At least until we could shed some light on the subject.

CHAPTER FIFTEEN

"Klaineh ganovim hengt men; groisseh shenkt men."
"Petty thieves are hanged; big thieves are pardoned."

I got back to the hospital about two, in plenty of time to prepare for my afternoon patients but too late for Dink's conference with the worrisome bunch of lobbyists. I didn't like passive-aggressive behavior in others, but I myself did an excellent job of either arriving late or not at all to most staff meetings. I've found that if you can put a title to a behavior, it's much more likely you can get away with it.

"Dr. Montague said to tell you he is not a happy analyst, Gritz. He also said to remind you that you've used up your excuses."

"I'll take care of it, Essie." I'd never met a happy analyst in my entire career. I needed to warn Dink about having too-high expectations. "Any other messages?"

"Pete Reid at the *Citizen-Times* has called twice. He says he'd like for you to come by his house at soon as possible. Didn't say what it's about."

"Call him and ask if I can run by sometime after five. Buzz me when Mrs. Watkins gets here." That really wouldn't be necessary. Her whistling would be all that was needed.

"Will do," Essie said. "Only one more day for the tent revival, Dr. G."

"It's been a busy week, Essie, but I'm going to try."

"It's going to be good tonight. I heard Reverend Love preaches right off the back of a big flatbed truck he drives right onto the stage, never missing a beat of the Lord's word."

"Uh-huh," I said, fumbling to get my double doors unlocked.

I told myself I was trying to get away from Essie, not God.

My desk was becoming quite the repository for Mordecai Moore articles. Since I had a few minutes before my sessions began, I flipped through some of the material and spotted an interaction between District Attorney Sammy Dills and Moore.

"Son, are you sitting here with a straight face and a clean heart telling these God-fearing jurors that your confession was not a confession? That you disavow your statement to Sheriff Hurt and his deputies about ordering that sweet Yankee college girl who had her whole life ahead of her to either quiet down or you were, let me quote you now, you were 'going to have to pull this here trigger'? Is that what you want these fine citizens to believe?"

"Yes, sir, that's what I'm saying. That Lieutenant Goodson from New York City came into my cell with a piece of black rubber pipe and he hit me, hit me hard, so hard I wanted to die. That's when I said what he wanted me to say."

"Now, listen here, boy, these jurors have given up their precious time with family and job to judge what went on in the

Battery Park Hotel that sad, sad night, and they don't need to sit here and listen to bald-face lies. Did Dr. Daniel David not check you over and find no signs whatsoever of any beating? Is that not God's truth? You tell these fine, upstanding citizens the truth, now."

"Dr. David did come by a few days after I was beat up, but those rubber pipes don't leave much marks."

"Lord, have mercy. I've heard it all, Your Honor. I won't ask these upstanding citizens to hear any more rubbish like that. The prosecution rests."

Essie buzzed. "Mrs. Bloom is standing here. She's insistent on seeing you right away. Cage is refusing to come out of seclusion for his appointment, and Mrs. Watkins can't be found. Pete Reid said five this afternoon will be fine."

Scheduling changes might rattle some, but not my Essie.

"Send Mrs. Bloom on in."

I flipped the court transcripts over and stood, but Marsha was in no mood for polite greetings. She brushed right by me. She wore a solid gray workout outfit of running bra and matching spandex pants, the kind generally sported by women with more-than-ample tushes that were better kept hidden than focused upon, the hope being that the magic of fabric constriction might make cellulite disappear. She stepped on Bobby Raby's swastika carpet, which I'd neglected to hide in my closet.

"What in God's name is that?" she said. She didn't wait for an answer, walking right over to her usual seat and plopping into it, causing the cushion to breathe out loudly in defeat. "I've had it. The mayor and I are done, kaput, finished."

Hurrah! That was what I'd been waiting for months to hear. There were days when I wanted to tell Marsha to leave the big shit so badly it hurt, but I desperately clung to yet another axiom of my mentor, Dr. Baines: "You've got to help your patients own their decisions, not make their decisions for them."

With a great deal of contained joy, I said, "What happened?"

"When he came home last night, I had his favorite meal cooked. I mean, after all, he did have a horrible day with those rednecks."

As Marsha crossed her legs, I thought, *What about me? My day wasn't a walk in the park either.* But I said nothing. Her Nike training shoes hid my favorite part of her anatomy—feet that showed expensive maintenance, not the mall variety of foot care distinguished by smeared pinkie toes, but high-dollar buffing and waxing. On her sandal days, listening to her whining was so much more bearable. But I stayed with her story that day as best I could.

"He ate everything I fixed, and I mean everything. I'm a very good cook. Everybody says so. Then he wiped that funny-shaped mouth of his with one of our good linen napkins and said, 'Marsha, I want a divorce.' I tell you, I could have *plotzed*. I know you've warned me about my anger building up, but let me tell you, I've got a lot less today. I picked up the gravy bowl—my best china, too—and threw it at him as hard as I could."

This story was starting to interest me. I wanted to give her a standing ovation, but I sat tight.

"It hit him smack on the forehead and busted, gravy flying everywhere. You know what he did? Nothing. He just sat there, gravy dripping down his face. The *schmuck* just sat there. Then in a minute or two, he says, 'I know this is sudden, but just today I ran into the woman I've always loved, and on the drive home, I decided we should be together. I picked up my cell phone and called the police station.' And then I said, 'Police station! Is she a hooker or what?' And he says, 'It's a long story, but they got in touch with her for me, and once I heard her voice, I knew I had to be free to be me.' "

I understood Marsha's shock completely, but if she thought she was going to *plotz*, it was nothing compared to my own state of mind. It was a moment of instant internal meltdown. I felt like I'd been tossed onto one of those flaming Indian pyres, except I was still alive. Could Emma do this to me twice? Of course, Shel said only that he talked to her. He didn't say what she said. Marsha thought she was dealing with uncontainable anger. What about mine? *Breathe deeply*, I told myself. I still had a patient to deal with.

I stood, walked to the balcony door, and looked out. It was another gray day in Asheville. Using my sports-coat sleeve to wipe the sweat that had beaded on my forehead, I said, "Continue, Marsha. Don't stop."

"I don't know who the woman is, but can you believe that after all these years, he leaves me at just the sight of an old flame? Wait till she sees how he makes love!"

As I focused on two humping squirrels in a giant elm, I thought, *She has, and wait till you hear what she got for it.* I wanted to scream, *Woman, I hear your roar, and I understand! That fucking husband of yours is not going to get my Emma this time!* But I remained outwardly stoic, using all the strength I could muster to keep my clenched left fist from busting through the glass pane of my balcony door.

Marsha started crying. "I *loved* him!"

Zelda's sweet scent filled the room like a sudden fog. *That's a lie*, I wanted to say. *I know it and Zelda knows it. Come on, Marsha, I* yearned to yell, *you never loved Shelburne Bloom, and he never loved you. Come to terms with it!*

"Well, I think I loved him. I used to, anyway. It's just that if anyone was going to leave this marriage, I wanted it to be me!"

Now, the truth was beginning to emerge. My long-deceased flapper took her vapors and left the room.

"Does that realization make you angry?" I said in my best public-radio voice.

"What do you think? Hell yes, it makes me angry!"

"Did you confront him with your feelings? I mean, besides the gravy bowl."

"No, but I'm going to."

Marsha opened her small purse and turned it on its side to show me its contents. I found myself staring at a petite silver-gray pistol.

"Marsha, that's no way to deal with your problem!"

Without a thought, I snatched the pocketbook from her. She didn't fight me for it, but simply put her hands over her face.

Guns have always been strange objects for Jews. Well, American Jews. Israelis seemed quite comfortable with them. For some reason, we just don't go for artillery like gentiles. So when Marsha showed me the gun, it was quite a shock. I let her continue to sob as I reached inside her pocketbook and pulled out the deathly cold weapon. I nervously placed it inside one of my desk drawers. With Bobby's swastika rug staring at me, my office was starting to look like quite a violent place. I wasn't sure what to do with the gun, but I knew that in Marsha's state, she sure didn't need to have it.

Marsha stopped crying. "What do I do now?" she asked.

"Has he moved out already?"

"He wants a signed separation agreement first."

"Do you have a lawyer?"

"Hell no. It just happened last night," she said, recrossing her legs.

"I tell people, Marsha, that when they're in a turbulent period it's like being on a sailboat in a storm. Just hold onto the mast as tight as you can until the wind eases."

"And I pay you for advice like that?" she said, standing to leave.

Good, I thought. Sarcastic humor is much safer than bullets.

"Keep the gun. I don't even know how to use it," she said. "Shel kept it in his sock drawer. For what, I don't know. It took him five years to figure out how to use a condom."

"I'll give it back when things settle down, how about that?"

Marsha didn't answer. With her hand on the doorknob, she turned and said, "By the way, my S.O.B. husband had the nerve to leave me a note to ask you to give me some kind of albums that his father lent you. Can you believe that?"

"I don't have them here, but I'll take them back to Moses myself in a couple of days. I just need to copy a picture for my aunt in Florida."

"He won't be happy, but what do I care if he's happy?" She stared my way but seemed not to see me. Then she said, "Why did he ever marry me?"

I knew, but I wasn't telling.

Cage was waiting when I stepped outside my office. Somehow, he'd convinced Talmadge that he was just an innocent bystander who got caught up in the fray with Bobby, but I didn't buy it for a minute. Essie was trying to get him to play some gospel tune. He seemed less angry than I'd ever seen him, and at least he was playing the damn instrument.

"Dr. G., do you think Cage could come to the revival tonight? I'd make sure he, you know, got back by curfew."

"Let me discuss that with Cage," I said, smiling at Essie and motioning him into my office.

We had an abbreviated session. He told me that Essie had been giving him religious materials, and that he was reading them. He did seem much more mellow. I was glad somebody was getting help from someone at Highland, even if my secretary seemed to be doing the doctoring.

I had another patient to see and some dictation to catch up on before I could get free to go over to Pete Reid's. I had Essie get T on the phone for me while I worked.

"I'm glad you called Pete for me," I said. "He wants to see me at five at his house."

"I didn't call the man yet," T said. "I was going to, but Arlene and I went shopping for a picture to hang over my couch, and it took longer than we thought."

"That's weird. Why would he call me out of the blue if you didn't call him?"

"Maybe Talmadge called him."

"Maybe, but I don't think so. Anyway, I'm on my way over to Pete's place. Want to come?"

"Sure, I'd love to see the old coot," the eighty-eight-year-old said.

"Can you bring a bag?" I said.

"Just took a batch out of the oven. Arlene suggested I add a touch of cayenne. What do you think?"

Cajun nomnom seemed a bit trendy to me.

T and I pulled up to 13 Parris Lane in Pearlie's cab.

"This place kind of looks like a hideout," Pearlie said as we got out.

He had a point. Pete's humble abode sat at the end of a short gravel road lined with heavy oak trees not pruned in many years. With some grooming, the place could have felt like a pleasant, secluded nook. You could tell the house was a log cabin, but the enormous overgrowth of kudzu made it appear green. It looked like Hansel and Gretel might pop out—or worse, a wolf.

Pete and my dad had a long history together. Pete hung around Goldberg's to shoot the bull and occasionally to buy something.

Dad said he was a brilliant writer but a lousy customer. The latter, of course, outweighed the former.

"Pete seems to have a knack for raising poison ivy," T said as we walked down a short path to the front door.

"I guess it's good for keeping the Fuller Brush man away."

I pressed what looked like a doorbell but heard no sound. Then I knocked loudly. Still, no one came. When I looked in the front bay window, I saw enormous stacks of newspapers in the middle of the floor acting like giant pillars holding up the ceiling, but I didn't see the writer himself. I didn't want to invade Pete's privacy, but he had asked to see me. I tapped on the front door again.

"Just a damn minute," Pete called out from somewhere behind the newspaper piles.

When the front door finally opened, Pete was dressed in a red-and-black plaid shirt, washed-out denim pants, and brown hiking boots, his trademark outfit in all the photos that ran with his columns in the *Citizen-Times*. He looked at me and then at T.

"Theloneous Royal. I'll be damned. Thought you were dead."

"Not dead enough to keep me from going fishing one day soon. That hole below the dam is calling me bad."

"City made that off-limits about ten years ago. Besides, I don't fish anymore. When I want to cast a line, my shoulder wants to take a nap."

"Getting old is a pain in the ass, ain't it?" T said.

"Come in, come in, boys. *Mi casa es su casa*, or some shit like that."

Pete's décor fell somewhere between a car salesman's office and a trip to the 1950s. A formal couch was juxtaposed with a metal folding chair and a plastic coffee table. A rather sickly elephant ear plant sat in a split plastic pot gasping quietly for water near the entrance to the kitchen.

"Your name has been mentioned to me more than once lately, Mr. Reid."

"I know, I know. Everybody reads my column, everybody."

"Actually, this concerns something you wrote about a long time ago," I said. "The Battery Park murder."

Pete's age-spotted, fat countenance stared at me, then at T. His left hand started to shake as if he had Parkinson's. He quickly put both hands in his pockets.

"I was planning on calling you when you called me," I said, trying to act like I hadn't seen his tremors.

"Want something to drink? Pimple-ass doctors want me to drink only water. Can you imagine?" Pete frowned.

"My mama always used to say it's okay to drink like a fish, as long as you drink what a fish drinks," T said. " 'Course, Mama's dead. I'll take a shot of whatever you got."

"I'll go with the water," I said.

Pete frowned again.

He walked over to a small bar that stood in the corner of the living room and poured two drinks, which he brought over to where we were standing. He handed one to T. His hands weren't shaking so much now.

"*Salud*," he said, evidently not remembering my request for water, or not wanting to acknowledge water as a real drink. "I called you, Gritz, because I heard you've been asking a lot of questions to the likes of Moses Bloom." He stared me dead in the eye, then T. "I'm an old man. T, you're maybe what, a year or two older?"

T nodded.

"Yeah, well, lots of things have happened in my eighty-some-odd years, not all of them real pretty. About that Battery Park thing, just don't go there. Isn't that what the kids say nowadays? Just don't go there, I'm telling you for your own good."

I didn't know how to respond. It wasn't as if I woke up one morning and asked to be involved in a sixty-five-year-old, long-closed murder case. Evidently, Moses hadn't liked my questions and called Pete. But Moses acted like he hadn't even known Pete was still alive. I was starting to feel that asking about an old murder that was supposedly solved was like poking a corpse that was supposed to be dead but wasn't. A little wiggle might mean a whole different outcome.

T looked at Pete with a deadpan expression. "Pete, with all those stories you wrote about mountain superstitions and legends, surely you musta run into a ghost or two."

Pete looked at T, a little confused, then went back to the bar. He poured himself a shot and held up the bottle toward T, ignoring me again.

"No thanks," T said.

Pete swallowed the new drink and poured a third. "I've been told probably a thousand ghost stories. What about them?"

"Believe it or not, that's the only reason Gritz and I been sniffing around about Mordecai. I swear, I seen his ghost at the apartments. Ever since I came back to the Battery, he's been showing himself around the place. Almost seems like he's the one making us ask these questions. Feels almost like we don't have much of a choice in the matter."

Pete walked back over to where T and I stood. "I don't know about that. All I know is some things are better left lying where you found them."

I thought about the Sardano family, and Mordecai's, too.

"Well, Mordecai ain't exactly a talkative soul," T said. "He just shows up now and then, and I'm not real happy about him wanting to share with me, you know what I mean?"

"Gritz, how did you get into this? You a fan of the supernatural?" Pete said in a sarcastic tone.

"I'm not sure what I believe. I just want to help T settle back in town. But I've always been interested in Asheville history."

"It would scare the shit out of you if you knew it like I do," Pete barked back.

He walked away from T and me and stared out his bay window at the misty blue Balsam Mountains in the distance. The silence seemed like an hour but probably amounted to a minute. Finally, Pete turned around and grimaced, his forehead wrinkled like a pug's but without the cuddly quality. I wished Mordecai would suddenly appear and order us all to have a drink and forget the whole thing.

"I've interviewed lots of criminals in my lifetime," Pete said. "One guy particularly stands out in my mind. A loner from over in Nantahala. He told me that crime is a young man's game. Retribution is nothing more than a fool's fantasy and a victim's dream. I guess I know as much about that hotel murder as anybody alive. I covered it from day one, but I'm here to tell you that you or nobody else needs be sticking their nose back into that mess. Listen to this old man. More times than not, a person loses that game of retribution. Why can't you leave it to the Almighty to settle up scores?"

I wasn't sure if what I'd heard was a veiled threat or well-meant advice. "He didn't do it, did he?" I couldn't believe the words coming out of my mouth. It wasn't like me to push a subject beyond its welcome. It wasn't in the constitution of a shrink to be straightforward, but it felt mighty good for a change.

"I can honestly say that I don't know who did it," Pete said, grabbing his left hand with a slightly less-shaking right. "I guess it's highly unlikely that Mordecai did it, if that night on death row meant a damn thing."

"What night on death row?" I asked.

"Pete interviewed Mordecai the night before he was executed. Didn't you, Pete? I read that piece in the paper over and over, more than I should have, I guess." T looked at his shoes, then took his shirt sleeve and wiped his eyes really quick.

"I went to elementary school with Hissy Cunningham," Pete said. "He became the warden at Central Prison in Raleigh. The paper sent me to cover the execution, and I called Hissy and reminded him I needed a favor. I saved that boy's ass a hundred times in school. Every time the little shit didn't get his way, he pitched one damn fit. We gave him his nickname in about the third grade, I think. I got Hissy to let me stay in the cell next to Moore the last night the boy was alive. It was a journalistic first. After I wrote the story, some dumb-ass in the legislature blocked journalists from being able to do anything like that again. It wasn't the prison or even the execution that was so memorable. It was that singing. Those goddamn hymns."

"Oh, Lord, yes," T chimed in quickly, like he was in a congregation listening to the preacher. "Some spirituals grab your soul and hold on for high heaven, don't they, Pete? I remember you writing about them singing."

"I made a career out of writing about traditions," Pete continued, looking at me like he sensed my confusion. "But that damn night beat anything I ever wrote about. There were about seven cells on death row at that time. The men moved up a cell each time another convict was taken into that room where they did it. When you got to the last cell, you knew you didn't have much time left. After midnight the night of an execution, the men on death row had a tradition of singing spirituals—the same ones each time, slow and low. 'Dear Lord, your sinful child is coming home. Open your door wide, your sinful child is coming home,' they'd sing. Moore just sat in his cell with his head hanging almost between his legs. Then he lifted up and said, 'Mr. Pete, you know I didn't do it, don't you?' And I said, 'I don't know nothing of the kind, son.' He says, 'Yes, you do, you got to, but I don't blame you for not saying so. There ain't a thing you could do about it. You just tell them in that article of yours that I am right with my God, okay? And tell my mama that I'm going to be just fine. I'll be waiting over there to give her a big hug when it's her time to come. God knows who really killed that girl, but I'm ready to take the punishment. Jesus had to, and I'm ready, too. I'm just about give out, but God knows the truth, and I think you do, too, Mr. Pete.' "

Pete gave me a look like I'd better listen, and listen well.

"I've been within five feet of some of the most powerful people that ever lived, Gritz. I interviewed Winston Churchill when I covered World War II for AP. I once smelled the stink of General MacArthur's breath. But I tell you, I never felt more helpless than that night lying on a dirty mattress in the cell next to a man who was about to be executed for a crime he said he didn't do. I swore to myself that when I rose the next morning, if I ever fell asleep at all, I was done talking and writing about Moore. I filed my report and mentioned the singing, but not what Moore said. Maybe I was wrong, but at my age, I'm not about to start analyzing something I did more than a half-century ago. It's too late to save a dead man, don't you see that?"

"What about justice?" I said in a high voice.

T put his hand on my shoulder.

"Boys, I don't mete out justice. That's not my job. It's not yours either."

The quiet was that of two sides that had shot their last rounds, and it was deafening.

"What about that missing key?" I said in a much lower voice.

"The uncle said the door was locked when he tried to get his niece for breakfast, and then unlocked when he came back fifteen minutes later."

"That damn thirteenth key," Pete said. "I'd almost forgotten about that."

"Whoever had it was probably involved, wouldn't you say?"

"Not necessarily. It could have been lost, then found. Hell, lots of things."

"You knew her uncle?" I kept on.

T looked like he was getting uncomfortable with my volley of questions.

"Sure, he played cards with us every time he was in town. He traveled North Carolina talking to farmers—dairy farmers, I think—for his job at the college. I didn't want to have anything else to do with him, if you know what I mean. Queer as a three-dollar bill."

"You mean odd?" I said.

"No, I mean queer, homosexual, alternative lifestyle. He and Paully were awfully close. They were like twins politically. They hated Roosevelt with an equal passion. The uncle always tried to impress Paully by quoting something Paully had published in that fruitcake paper of his. Paully claimed he had over a million followers with that rag. Of course, only a professor with a name like Hieronymous would try and cozy up to a man like Paully."

"Do you think her uncle could have killed her?"

"Could have, but I doubt it. I think he may have known who did, though. He and Hurt had this big conference at the jail a couple of weeks into the investigation. Some people thought the uncle was going to be charged after that meeting. He came in from Raleigh one afternoon at the sheriff's request, and the next thing I knew, the paper told me to get over to Moore's house with our photographer, that they were searching an outhouse for the murder weapon."

"Was Mordecai gay? Could the uncle and he have had a connection of some kind?" I asked, looking at T.

"He never tried to kiss me." T laughed awkwardly, like he knew it wasn't funny. "I never thought about it. He was shy around women, but he told me that he and Fanny were courting pretty heavy."

"So if the uncle didn't do it, and Mordecai didn't do it, who did?"

"Did you not hear what I just said?" Pete erupted. "The two of you need to forget this. It's too late to start worrying over this now. And if you know what's good for you, you won't."

"Moses Bloom told me the same thing," I said.

"Well," Pete said, giving me a condescending look.

T motioned with his eyes that it was time to end the discussion.

"I guess we better go," I said.

"Guess you better," Pete said. "Do everyone a big favor, you hear? T, you learn to live with a damn ghost if you have to. Call the local priest. Maybe he can do one of those Catholic exorcisings or something. And Gritz, you stick to doctoring. Forget about trying to drag up old stories. That's what writers do. You're a damn doctor, for God's sake."

He went back to his bar and poured himself his fourth shot in fifteen minutes. We saw ourselves out.

"Uh-oh," T said as he walked out Pete's front door. "I think I rubbed against that damn poison ivy. I bet I'm going to regret what just happened."

Ditto, I thought. And I hadn't come near the plants.

CHAPTER SIXTEEN

"Di klensteh nekomeh farsamt di neshomeh."
"The smallest vengeance poisons the soul."

I should have followed my personal discipline of never answering a phone call from Florida when in the middle of a massage, but I figured if someone tracked me down at Perrier's place, it must be important.

"Did you mail Paully's poster yet?" Aunt Fay asked.

"Not yet, but I will soon." Another bad judgment call. Never deny Aunt Fay anything. "Can I talk to Dad just a minute?" I asked.

"He got some package from you, and you'd think he just made a big suit sale or something. I've never seen him so giddy."

"Candyman here," Dad said as he got on the phone.

"You got the package."

"I'm the most popular man in Century City. I tell them my son the doctor sent me a little gift."

"Dad, don't share those pills. They could kill certain people."

"Dangerous, shmangerous. Most of my friends live full-time on banana peels. How dangerous can a tiny blue pill be? Morris Siegel got an erection looking at your aunt Fay. Can you imagine?"

"Dad, did you call Pete Reid for me?" I asked as Perrier massaged my soles. I'd called her for emergency kneading after my encounter with Pete.

"Why would I call Pete? I'm out of business. After he brought back that worn pair of linen pants for a refund, I didn't have much use for the man, writer or no writer. The pants stunk!"

"I just wondered. He called me out of the blue to tell me to quit asking questions about the Battery Park murder."

"Don't make an old man repeat himself. I don't have that much oxygen to spare."

So it was Moses who must have called Pete.

Dad reeled off his and his friends' latest health problems. "They found a lump in Izzy's groin last week."

"Too bad," I said.

"He says he's not going to do anything about it. He always wanted bigger balls."

"Dad, be careful giving out those pills, now. I could get sued."

"You worry too much. You're making old men smile. Who needs money when you can make love?"

I felt a familiar, sharp pain in my pelvis. This, I'd learned from Perrier, could mean only one thing: my subconscious longing for parental approval had blocked my pleasure meridians, forcing my purple chakras into gridlock. I told Dad to tell Aunt Fay I'd send her poster real soon, then hung up.

"Another rough day, Gritz?" Perrier asked as I dropped the phone to the floor.

My taut muscles felt instantly better from the touch of her warm hands. "Remember me telling you about Mordecai Moore?"

"Of course," she said, putting her left elbow into a muscle pocket that felt more like an endless pit of pain.

"It seems there are a lot of people who don't want to remember that whole incident."

"Meaning?"

The woman's skill at pulling out a story was as sharp as the pain in my sacroiliac.

"Seems like I say the name Mordecai Moore and people start getting nervous. I've just come from a meeting with the man who covered the whole story for the *Citizen*. He probably knows more about the case than the judge and jury did. He practically ordered me to forget about the whole incident. Sixty-five years later and people act like it happened yesterday."

"Time doesn't always heal. Sometimes, all it does is make a wound fester," Perrier said, pouring more coconut oil on me.

"Ever met Pete Reid?"

"I read his columns. He's pretty good when he doesn't get carried away with himself. He's the guy who covered the story for the paper?"

"Exactly. Moses Bloom must have called him after I mentioned the murder to him. Do you know Shel Bloom's father?"

"Oh, yes, I've dealt with that guy. Big grouch. Once, the synagogue sisterhood decided to make unleavened bread baskets for Passover and take them out to Happy Valley. He wouldn't take the basket. Said he'd had all the crackers he ever wanted. Said if the sisterhood wanted to really help, we'd bring him a BLT."

"What would upset an old man like that enough to call Pete?"

Perrier ran her hand up my calf, then up my inner thigh, stopping within millimeters of lewd-conduct charges.

"Gritz, people's histories cross in ways we have no clue about. *Bashert.* Isn't that what our religion calls it? No meeting is an accident."

It was no accident that Perrier's skilled hands had finished my left leg and were now traveling up my right. This lady, noted for making noodle *kugel* in Boca, had really upped her skills.

"The Cherokees say the same thing—though not in Yiddish, of course. One of my other customers told me that Moses Bloom was determined to get his son elected senator before he passed away. Digging up buried history can make just about anyone nervous, particularly politicians. Every family has something to hide."

"I suppose," I said as she covered my lower half with the sheet she'd pulled back, then headed again to my feet.

"I discussed with Arnie about trying to reach Mr. Moore. He said it was fine with him. We could try it anytime you want."

"You mean the séance?"

"We don't refer to them as séances anymore. The industry thinks *crossover reunions* is more fitting. We have tomorrow night free. It should be held in the Battery Park. Do you have any idea what time the actual murder occurred?"

"I just read it in the microfilm copies Arlene and T researched. The coroner said it was in the area of twelve-thirty in the morning."

"That's when we ought to do it then. Exactly at twelve-thirty."

"I don't know if I can stay up that late," I said. "I'm a morning person."

"I'll stop at Starbucks on the way. Espresso will wake the dead, no pun intended," she said, continuing to work on my muscular roadblocks, opening a few to at least a one-lane bypass.

From my vantage point lying on my stomach, I noticed that Perrier had repainted her toe scenery. The sunrise was gone, replaced by a night vista. A full moon filled most of her big toenail, beaming over a dark purple cityscape, a lightning bolt crossing the sky right under the moon. Her feet weren't the youngest, but nobody created a mural like Perrier.

As Pearlie let me out of the cab in front of my house, I didn't notice any sign of life. Even Adolf was nowhere to be seen or heard.

I'd almost reached the kitchen door when I heard him.

"Gritz, I need Daddy's albums back. You've kept me waiting for over an hour."

It was a weak-pitched sound within a loud voice, something you knew came from a person with greasy, slicked-back hair that hung over fat ears that resembled giant flaps. The voice came from high in the throat of an obvious spineless coward.

"Well, if it isn't Mayor Bloom," I said, turning toward the smell.

Dusk did wonders for the appearance of the man. I didn't reach to shake his hand, nor did he reach for mine. I cringed at the thought that this jerk of all jerks had even spoken to my Emma again.

"I told Marsha to bring home those albums."

"I haven't looked through them all. I told her to tell you I'd deliver them back to your dad in another day or so."

"I want them now."

"Okay, then. Come on in," I said. "I'll round them up for you."

"I'll just wait out here. I like this time of night."

I went upstairs and found the three albums. There was one I hadn't examined yet. Even though His Dishonor was waiting, I took a couple of minutes to flip through it, trying not to tear any of the brittle black construction-paper pages. I wondered what was so darn important that Shel would come to my house at night to retrieve them. All I saw were more pictures of Moses giving away checks to more charities, one photo of Moses' wife giving out a check, and one of Moses holding the keys to a brand-new Tucker automobile; the caption said it was one of only sixty-five ever to roll off the assembly line. There were several articles and photos of Shel as he climbed the political ladder. A photo of him as chairman of the elections board showed him shaking hands with a young Bill Clinton. Another showed Moses and Shel standing with Governor Hill as Shel was elected vice chairman of the Democratic Party of Buncombe County.

"Gritz, I can't wait around all night! I'm an important person," Shel yelled from outside.

I slammed the album cover shut. A piece of paper blew out of the book and onto the floor. As I picked it up, I noticed it had a business letterhead and was addressed to Willard Paully. *Another relic for Aunt Fay's sisterhood program*, I thought, and put it in my pocket. I figured the Blooms would never notice it gone.

"I'm still waiting!" Shel called, this time sounding like he'd decided to stick his head in the kitchen door.

When I got downstairs, I heard the door shut. I looked outside and saw Shel leaning against Stef's Commando. I promised myself that, out of respect to the car, I'd get it washed as soon as possible.

As I approached him, he lurched for the albums, pulling them from my hands the way he used to steal comic books from me during study hall. I was too old this time not to retaliate.

"You're not getting her, you know. Emma. Not this time."

"Just watch me," he snapped, tucking the albums under his arm and turning to walk toward his car.

I watched him in the shadows of the moonlight, his bent posture reflecting a man who didn't have his own plan about life and had no energy to do anything but continue like he was. He got into what appeared to be a brand-new steel-gray government car and drove off. The odor began to clear as the taillights receded down Montford.

Remembering the letter in my pocket. I pulled it out and read it. The letterhead had the name of Kripp Industrials, Berlin, Germany. It was addressed to Willard Dudley Paully, Asheville, N.C., U.S.A.

"Dear Commander," it read, "I wanted to personally thank you for your beneficent efforts in helping the cause we both cherish. What you and your associates have achieved is truly remarkable, and with time and the benefits of history I think we will see even more how important a contribution you will have made. Carboloy will undoubtedly make or break our effort and the efforts of our enemies, and with the access we now have and the resulting costs to our foes from this arrangement, we are certainly on our way to a great victory. Yours truly, Gustav Kripp."

I'd never heard of carboloy, and I wondered why Moses would have a letter about it addressed to Paully. I'd have Nate Google it on the computer when he got home.

The combination of a body doused with coconut oil, a visit from the mayor, and now a letter to Commander Paully made me want a long, hot shower. Outside, Adolf's yelps filled the otherwise still and humid night. I looked outside and saw that he'd actually made it under the hedge—at least half of him had. I went back in, picked up my half-full drink can, opened the kitchen door, and tossed it. Bull's-eye! To my surprise, his barking became a growl, then a whimper. Evidently, Herr German Shepherd had accepted that his latest attempt to rid the world of one more Jew had failed. Things were looking up.

CHAPTER SEVENTEEN

"Ganaiden un gehenem ken men baideh oif der velt."
"Heaven and hell can both be had in this world."

When I awoke, daylight was struggling to filter through my half-closed blinds. I fiddled with a lump around my neck until I discovered that my necktie was still loosely tied there. Trying to shake my left hand back to life, I noticed my palm was covered with black ink obviously rubbed off the crumpled microfilm copies of the *Citizen* newspapers I pulled from under my body. Various photojournalistic snapshots of Mordecai Moore stared sadly, helplessly up at me. My ceiling fan was going full blast, whistling as it clung weakly to the ancient plank above. I didn't move for a couple of minutes, imagining the obit if the fan detached and fell: "Dr. David 'Gritz' Goldberg was unexpectedly beheaded this morning at his home."

Arlene poked cautiously around my cracked door. She was

dressed in denim from head to foot. Blue cowboy hat, blue jumper, blue-and-white-checked gingham blouse, and blue boots with red rhinestones. A retiree with assets can be a dangerous thing.

"T and I are going gem mining in Franklin. I've always wanted to do that. Can you get away?"

"Wish I could. When will you be back?"

"Late this afternoon, I'd expect."

"Perrier suggested we hold a séance for Mordecai. She says it should be at the time of the murder, half-past midnight, at T's place. I was thinking about trying to do that tonight."

"I'm sure T will be interested. Of course, we'll need to get back and get to bed for a few hours if we're going to do that this evening." She cut off her speech like a child who'd just blurted out how much candy she'd consumed when nobody was looking. "I mean, we'll both want to take a nap, since it'll be a full day. Gritz, this is okay with you, isn't it? I've never done anything like this."

"Sure, I took the kids gem mining one time. It was a lot of fun."

"Not gem mining. You know, T and me. It may be cliché, but I feel like a kid again."

I rubbed my goatee to stall a reply. There were no mannerism classes for shrinks, but you picked up certain little aids like that.

"It just happened. I love being with the man. I—"

"Arlene, don't apologize to me. I think it's great."

"Remember 'Send in the Clowns'? Just when you think you've got it all figured out, life throws in a curve you never expected."

I smiled. I didn't mind the curves. It was life's cloverleaf intersections that got so complicated.

I showered, downed orange juice and a bagel, and grabbed

my *Citizen* reprints. I thought there might be time that day for more reading. Fall is a slow time for nervous breakdowns. You'd think the leaves dying and falling off would make people depressed, but it seemed that cold, gray weather cranked up most of the neuroses. From Thanksgiving to Christmas, it was like holiday sale time at Goldberg's Department Store. Sometimes, we had to turn away clients, prompting Trinity to order yet another study of how to get more beds into the same tiny holes at Highland, which in turn caused doctors and staff to struggle against their own depression.

When I got to the office, I found Essie sitting stiffly at her desk. Once a year, she valiantly tried to break her soap-opera addiction. During revival week, she unplugged her five-inch television and put it under her desk. I knew it wouldn't stay there long after the Reverend Love left town, but I put it in the category of fasting for Yom Kippur. Most of my brethren and I fast for a day and try to feel pious. In reality, all that changes for most of us is that we get a short-lived headache from lack of food and water. Then we go back to screwing up things just like we had before the fast.

"Reverend Love was wonderful last night, Gritz. He told us how he came to know the Lord, and his tears flowed like the River Jordan. I wish you could have been there. He's staying an extra couple of nights, since the response was so good. How about tonight?"

Saying that her revival conflicted with my séance didn't seem appropriate. "I'll do my best," I told her.

She and I both knew my best wouldn't be good enough to get me to the front lines of the Reverend Love's assault on evil. Every year, I danced around her church's revival, and I suspect Essie played along. I didn't mind entertaining alternate ways of worship. It was the horrible nightmares that made me cringe. The

163

threatening fingers pointed in my face, the scalding-hot branding irons charring my chest—not by Protestants but by Aunt Fay, who was scarier than a pyromaniac with a matchbook collection.

All was quiet that morning among the patients. Many went home after Labor Day and didn't come back for a while. There was an enormous packet of material from Trinity sitting on my desk, but I knew better than to get into that can of worms. I kicked off my brogans, put on my Wal-Mart reading glasses, and got down to some serious perusing.

I decided it would be helpful if I put the *Citizen* reprints in order by date. You could immediately tell by the size of the headlines that the 1939 murder was a big happening in Asheville. It wasn't that no one had ever been shot in town. Ever since I was a kid, Saturday-night shootings and assaults were almost as regular as Sunday-morning Bible school. I never considered western North Carolinians especially violent people, but there was a fine line in us sons and daughters of the Old North State between what annoyed us and what angered us enough to kill.

The first headline was from September 16, 1939: "New York Coed Found Dead at Battery Park." Pete Reid had done a thorough job of getting firsthand interviews. He talked with several women on a sightseeing bus tour who had evidently been housed on the floor above where Evangeline Sardano was killed. One lady from New Hampshire said she thought she heard a man and woman arguing, and then a scream and a shot, but when she looked out her window, she guessed it was some 'goings-on at the bar across the alley' and put her earplugs in and went to sleep. Pete quoted Sheriff Hurt Bailey as saying he was going to talk to Elbert Stubbs, the night watchman. Apparently, Stubbs was to have made rounds on each floor every hour of his shift, marking a crude time sheet as he went. But for some reason, during the midnight hour, the fourth floor—Evangeline's floor—had not been checked, or at least not been checked off on the time sheet.

The papers from the first three or four days after the murder mainly gave a scenario of panic and confusion, but Hurt was constantly quoted as saying, "I have a handle on the situation and expect imminent arrests." The girl's uncle, Professor Hieronymous Sardano, was said to be trying to contact her parents, his brother and sister-in-law, Antonio and Mary Sardano of Fishkill, New York. "When I went to see if she would like to join me for breakfast, I saw my poor niece lying there, on the floor, in a pool of blood. This is such a tragedy," he told Pete by phone. Every day that no one was arrested, the town's hysteria increased. One photo showed a crowd of at least fifty people hanging around outside the paper's offices waiting for any news of the murder.

Many men were brought in for questioning, and three were held, even though no charges were filed.

Two neighbors of Heinrich Mueller, a violin teacher, evidently called the sheriff to tell him they'd seen Heinrich climbing through his boardinghouse window early the morning after the murder. At first, he seemed like a promising candidate for arrest. A bartender claimed Mueller had left his establishment sometime before midnight the night of the murder, saying he had to see a girl he'd met that day at the Battery Park. Mueller was released after two days. He said he'd just been bragging to the bartender of a nonexistent tryst, and that he'd actually spent most of the night in the arms of his lover—rumored, Pete wrote, to be the daughter of the owner of Mueller's boardinghouse. His alibi was later confirmed by "an anonymous but trustworthy woman" and announced by Sheriff Bailey.

Another bellboy besides Mordecai was also detained. He'd been arrested but not convicted of a prior felony—breaking and entering—and had worked that night. His alibi evidently checked out because, with no comment whatsoever, he was pictured walking out of the jail on the fourth day after his arrest.

The night watchman was finally located and detained the longest, six days. The *Citizen* ran a picture of Elbert Stubbs's wife bringing him food from home. "I'm afraid El's not going to make it. He won't eat a thing," Alicia Stubbs was quoted as saying. Sheriff Hurt finally declared that "Mr. Stubbs could not have killed the girl or in fact known anything about the murder because he left his duties for a couple of hours around midnight and went home due to an intestinal distress" from eating a bad piece of fish at an unnamed downtown restaurant. Two others who dined at the restaurant verified that they, too, had fought the very same battle with "dastardly diarrhea."

Essie buzzed. "Gritz, can you take a call from Moses Bloom?"

I picked up the phone.

Moses was already talking before I said hello. "Listen here, Gritz Goldberg. I was at your *bris*. One little snip and you cried like a baby. You have some nerve encouraging my daughter-in-law to leave my son. And Shel pays you for this kind of outcome? He's standing here by my deathbed right now. The boy is heartbroken, and it's all your fault."

The mayor couldn't even ask for his own divorce without blaming it on somebody else! Of course, I'd wondered how he was going to announce the breakup to the citizens of Asheville this close to declaring for the Senate. Now, I knew. He'd blame the shrink. I'd never gotten used to that hazard of my occupation.

"Mr. Bloom, Marsha is my patient. I can't discuss this with you."

"The hell you can't! You're career is finished. We'll ruin you."

I heard some fumbling with the phone, like Moses was about to hang up on me. Then he said, "Tell your dad hello," and did hang up.

Though I saw no real chance of Mordecai Moore making an appearance, the anticipation of the séance still made me edgy and impatient all afternoon. Fortunately, I was blessed with a nervous breakdown in the afternoon—not mine, but a new patient's. Starting sessions with a new "client" offered the prospect of an interesting new neurosis, maybe even odd symptoms I might need to research and improvise a treatment for. Unfortunately, the patient usually ended up telling a story similar to that of the person who'd just left my office. Nevertheless, I was glad Mary Louise Guthrie showed up that afternoon.

"Ms. Guthrie, how long have you battled alcoholism?"

"I don't remember. I think it started during high school. We all hung out on Folly Beach in the summer. Everybody called me Gidget."

I looked at my new patient, her hair desperately in need of a good shampoo, her skin sagging off her body like that of a gray rhino. No matter how hard I tried, I couldn't look at Mary Louise and think Sandra Dee.

"How old are you, Ms. Guthrie?"

"Fifty-nine."

You've got to be kidding, I thought as I scribbled in my memo pad. "Have you ever broken your addiction for a time—I mean, stayed off alcohol for a period before you went back?"

"No, I stay drunk on extract almost all the time."

"Extract?"

"Vanilla extract. That's what I drink. I get it at Food Lion, where nobody asks questions."

"How much do you drink?"

"The whole bottle. They aren't very big, you know."

"How many bottles a day?"

"Four or five, depending."

"And you've come to Highland to quit?"

"Hell, no. My husband put me in here. My new husband. Henry never would have done anything like this. We were married for thirty-nine marvelous years—well, maybe not marvelous, but good years. I wouldn't get out of the house for months after he died. Then I met Julio at a ballroom-dancing competition about a year ago, and we were married three months later. I knew he married me for the money, but I thought he'd at least wait until I died. There's a pretty big age difference. Thirty years."

"Julio is twenty-nine?"

"Twenty-eight and three-quarters, I think."

"What would you like me to do, Ms. Guthrie?"

"I want you to send me home so I can divorce Julio and go back to living my life the way I always have. I might be an alcoholic, but I'm quite content."

"What do you want for the rest of your life?"

"I want to die in a single bed with a bottle of vanilla on my nightstand and a good romance book in my hands."

I thought about what she said. It made a whole lot of sense. It may not have been the healthiest lifestyle, but I'd heard a whole lot worse.

"Gidget, you're on," I said. "You can pack up and go home." I wrote up a discharge slip and handed it to her to take to her charge nurse. I wanted to pull out a bottle of McCormick's best and suggest a toast. *Fuck you, Julio!* I wanted to shout.

"Thank you so much, doctor. I didn't think you'd understand."

The rest of the workday was nowhere near as fun. Nobody ever seemed to appreciate me like those I set free.

Since I knew that Arlene wouldn't have time to prepare supper that night, I'd arranged to meet Stef and Nate at The Hot Dog Castle on Lexington. Restaurants are perfect places for the furthering of good relationships. Even if the conversation goes dead, you have food to satisfy the soul. I'd discovered early in my marriage that there was nothing so fine as bonding with your kids at a cheap eatery, downing disguised animal organs in deep red casings covered with mounds of sauerkraut and lots of mustard. Maybe it was the nitrate overdose that made everybody talk so much.

Pearlie dropped me off a block before the restaurant. Nate had made it clear I'd embarrassed him in front of his friends the last time I'd shown up in the cab.

"Gritz, I have to go pick up Hattie Whitcomb and take her to the doctor. It might be a little while before I get back."

"Do you want me to bring you back a Chicago Dog?"

"Better not. I think I saw one of those towelheads working in there. Homeland Security, you know."

There were some things you let pass with Pearlie. I got out and went into the restaurant.

"Dad, I'm thinking about becoming a vegan," Stef said, her mouth full of the number six, the Brooklyn Barker.

"Really," I said.

"Yeah. I think I need to honor my body more."

"Nobody else is going to, that's for sure," Nate said.

"Shut up."

"We don't say shut up in this family, you know that," I said.

"Cram it then, Nate."

"That's better." It was a good time to change the subject. "Do you believe in communicating with the dead?" I asked.

"Random, Dad. Really random," Nate said, dipping a fry into a sea of ketchup.

"My friend T thinks that an old buddy of his is still at the Battery Park, although he died in nineteen thirty-nine."

"Why not?" Stef said. "I mean, if there is an afterlife, then it seems not only possible but probable that those we call dead would be among us, just in another form."

"Heavy, man, heavy," Nate smirked.

"Dork," Stef snorted.

"Your grandmother's friend Perrier is going to try and communicate with the dead man tonight. We need some information that only he might be able to give us. I don't know how I feel about it, but I told her it's worth a try."

"Sure, it's worth it. I'd like to be there," Stef said. "Can I?"

"It's going to be late, and you have school."

"Yeah, Stef, you might need a diploma one day. I mean, if your vegetables run out."

Stef threw her napkin at him.

When we left The Hot Dog Castle, we all headed in different directions. The kids recommended an antique bookstore not far away. I needed a Western dime novel, and I wouldn't find it at Barnes & Noble.

"Oh, Nate," I called as he headed down the street. "Do me a favor."

"I loaned you money last week, and you never paid me back," he said.

"I'll pay you back tonight, and I'll add twenty for this. I need you to look up somebody on the internet. See what the computer pulls up on Gustav Kripp." I spelled both names for him. "And find out what the heck carboloy—c-a-r-b-o-l-o-y—is."

"I'll find it," he said. "Make it thirty and I'll tell you why Stef's getting a D in physics."

"Just carboloy, Nate," I said.

CHAPTER EIGHTEEN

"Der vos farshtait zein narishkeit iz a kluger."
"He who is aware of his folly is wise."

Pearlie dropped me off at the Battery Park after eleven-thirty. T and Arlene were waiting. All was quiet at the old hotel. The assistant with the teased hair and her tiny dog were waiting at the elevator as we approached.

"I asked Bitsy if she'd join us," T said. "She doesn't remember Mordecai, but she knows the Battery Park like the back of her hand."

"Is that right? So she's always worked here?" I asked, slightly out of breath again from the steps. I felt fat. The thought briefly occurred to me that maybe I ought to stop using restaurants as meeting places.

Bitsy overheard us and answered the question herself. "I worked here and the Grove Park Inn, mainly," she said. Her face was like a miniature doll's head, her skin pulled tight under her chin from multiple facelifts. Her makeup was somewhere between a clown's and an opera diva's. "You might say my office was over there," she said, pointing to the Grove Arcade across the street. "By the way, I'm Bitsy Baker. Pleased to make your acquaintance."

I think I told her my name, but I was confused by what she'd just said. I turned and looked toward the arcade.

"Not in the arcade, just outside it," Bitsy said, looking at FuFu but explaining to me. "Let's just say you could usually find me next to one of those gargoyles at the lobby entrance."

"Oh," I said like I understood this time.

"Let's get on upstairs," T said.

Arlene took me by the arm as T and Bitsy entered the elevator. "*Nafka*, Gritz. She must have been a hooker."

When we got to T's apartment, Arnie and Perrier were already there. And much to my surprise, so was Pete Reid. He looked at me and said, "I owed T this one." He gruffly said hello to Bitsy as if he were greeting an old acquaintance, but one he didn't care to remember.

"I want all of us to take off our shoes and socks and sit cross-legged in a circle," Perrier announced as soon as the greetings were over. "We want to be actively involved in this process when twelve-thirty arrives. It's very important we release any and all negativity. Let's all get comfortable."

"I'm not going to sit Indian-style in my bare feet," Pete grumbled. "Not for a dead man nor a live one."

Arnie's face grew blood-red, and he stared at Pete with his dark eyes. Then he took his left hand and rubbed his thick head of black hair and took his right and started fiddling with a knife in a sheath hanging off his beaded belt.

Pete immediately took off his boots but not his socks and sat down.

When Bitsy removed her shoes, I saw she had a copper ring on each of her tiny, bony toes. She also had a tattoo on her shin, a heart with an arrow through it. The inscription *LOVE* was in red block letters.

We looked like a seniors' yoga class getting ready to stretch our little hearts out.

"Sorry I'm late," Mary Mag announced loudly to all of us as she let herself in T's unlocked door. "I was soaking my corns when I remembered about this . . . gathering."

T introduced her to the group. Bitsy, of course, knew Mary Mag. FuFu, on the other hand, snapped at her.

"FuFu, you stop it or Mummy's going to have to take you and put you in your cup for the night, silly goose."

I could tell by the way he was constantly adjusting his position that Pete wasn't going to stay long if we didn't get started. Besides, his feet smelled.

"Could someone cut the lights?" Perrier said, pulling out eight fat candles from her shopping-bag-sized pocketbook.

"As office manager of this facility, I'm not supposed to let you light candles," Bitsy said. "But I guess I can let it go this one time, can't I?" she said into FuFu's slobbering mouth.

Perrier lit the candles and passed them out. "I'm feeling resistance. Please let go of any doubts you have. Everybody take a deep breath and blow out their resistance, okay? On three. One. Two. Three."

We all took deep breaths and blew.

"That's much better, much better," Perrier said. "I did a little research and am passing out a few historical happenings of nineteen thirty-nine. I want each of us to read one item. Mr. Moore will be more comfortable revealing himself to us if we know something about the time in which he lived."

"And died," T added.

"Exactly," Perrier said. "Take a minute and decide on one. If someone uses it before you, just pick another." She glanced at her watch. "We have about ten minutes before twelve-thirty. I think if Mr. Moore wants to reveal himself to us, it will be at precisely that time."

"All right, let's get started," Pete said.

"Enrico Fermi announced the successful splitting of the atom," Arnie read.

"Italians are such great lovers," Bitsy said wistfully.

"*Dust Be My Destiny* with John Garfield was a hit movie," Arlene read.

"So were *Goodbye, Mr. Chips* and *Gone With the Wind*," Bitsy added.

"Okay, I'll go next," Mary Mag said. "Joe Louis was the heavyweight champ."

"Roberta Flack was born, and so was Dick Smothers," T added.

"The average cost of a loaf of bread was eight cents, and a new car cost seven hundred dollars," Pete said. "I was rollin' in dough back then. The *Citizen* and AP both paid me for the same article a few times. All I did was change a few words."

"The average life expectancy was a little over fifty-nine years," I said.

"Lord," T said. "I wouldn't call that the good ol' days."

"Okay," Perrier concluded. "Now, all that ought to make Mr. Moore a little more comfortable. Let's all hold hands and be very, very still and ask Mordecai Moore to come out, to join us."

I took Pete's hand. It was hard to hold onto because it was so sweaty.

"Mordecai Moore, it is twelve twenty-six in the morning. We know your pain, and we know your misfortune. We want to do what you would have us do, but we need your participation. Would you please make your presence known to us? Give us a sign, any sign."

There was darkness, foot odor, and heat in T's apartment, but no sign whatsoever that Mordecai was anywhere near.

"Please, Mr. Moore, we want to help you cross over. We know you're stuck in a very uncomfortable place here on earth," Perrier said. "Mordecai Moore, we mean no harm. Please let us help to free you from this place."

"Hey, let's not get personal about the Battery Park," Bitsy broke in. "I get a raise at Christmas if our tenant survey shows a hundred percent satisfaction."

"Shut up, Bitsy. The damn ghost isn't going to vote, now, is he?" Pete said.

"Pete Reid, you shut the hell up yourself," Bitsy shot back. "I had enough of you about a half-century ago. Yours wasn't any bigger than Fitzgerald's," she said, holding up her pinkie finger.

"Please, please, everybody. No negativity. Not right now. A spirit trapped in between will not communicate with the living if there is any negativity. Ghosts are very sensitive," Perrier said.

If Mordecai Moore was among us, he was very, very quiet.

"Listen hear, fellow," Mary Mag said. "You already scared the living daylights out of me the other day. I'm paying good money to spend the rest of my days here at this place, and I don't intend to have them ruined by some soul stuck in between. Mr. Moore, if you know what's half good for you, you'll get your skinny butt in here right now. You hear? Right now!"

"I'm getting out of here before anybody finds out I was here in the first place," Pete said, trying to get to his knees. "Who the hell is pushing down on my shoulders? Let me up!"

Pete was sitting between Perrier and me. Both of us claimed innocence.

"This ain't no joke, now. I got a bad back."

"I think Mordecai wants you to stay, Mr. Reid. He wants us to continue," Perrier said firmly.

Pete looked at her with a frown but didn't get up. I saw him pull out a wrinkled brown-and-orange-plaid handkerchief and wipe his forehead.

"We acknowledge your presence, Mr. Moore. We thank you for coming. What can we do for your plight? Please tell us. Feel free to speak through me. I will speak for you," Perrier said.

I don't know if everyone needed to go to the bathroom as badly as I did, but during the next few moments, each person adjusted the way they were sitting. FuFu, who snapped and barked, was the only one to actually speak.

Finally, T said, "Mordecai, you know I love you like a brother. I've fretted my whole life over how they killed you and I didn't raise a finger to protest. But this is getting ridiculous. You need to get out of this place. Let Mary and me and Bitsy and the rest just sleep and eat till it's our time to go. We want to do it in peace. You hear me, Mordecai? Now, do something. Do something right damn now to let us know you're real. If it's you, let us know."

It hadn't rained in western North Carolina for weeks. The *Citizen-Times* reported in the next day's paper that there was absolutely no explanation of how, at exactly twelve-thirty that night, a short but powerful storm erupted over downtown Asheville, dumping an inch of rain in a fifteen-minute period. Thunder and lightning rumbled through, mostly in the vicinity of the Battery Park, the paper said. Dust blew up into clouds so thick that all traffic on I-240 halted. In the deserts of North Africa and

Arabia, such occurrences are called haboobs, but since they never happen in the South, there is no accepted name by which to describe what we witnessed. "It was like somebody really mad had a direct line to the powers that be and pitched one hissy fit," Mayor Shelburne Bloom was quoted as saying.

There were eight people huddled together tighter than Aunt Fay's dentures as that storm hit. For those fifteen minutes, an Indian, two blacks, a retired hooker, two Jews, a massage therapist, and a writer all hugged each other. Then the thunder and lightning stopped as quickly as they'd begun.

We'd all screamed at one point or another during the preceding minutes, but it was Bitsy who gave voice as soon as the lights came on. "FuFu's gone! Where's my FuFu?" She got to her knees in a panic and starting crawling around the apartment looking for the tiny white dog.

"Goddammit, I'm bleeding," Pete said, getting all the way up this time. He pulled out of his back pocket a second very wrinkled handkerchief and used it under his nose, which oozed blood. "This is damn crazy. I'm getting the hell out of here."

"FuFu, my baby, come to Mummy."

Arnie and Perrier continued to hug each other, looking surprised that they'd succeeded in reaching Mordecai Moore. We were all like car-crash survivors, not knowing exactly what had hit us but glad it was over. None of us heard him speak, but it appeared a mad haint was trying to get our attention.

T and Arlene crawled around the apartment with Bitsy right behind, looking under T's couch and bed.

My cell phone vibrated in my pants pocket, telling me I had voice mail.

"I must reach you. Call Shlomo immediately. Don't worry about the time. This is urgent," was message number one.

"I need you to call headquarters as soon as you get this," Talmadge said in a deep, serious voice.

"Gritz, this is Candy. I'm scared. I'm on duty all night. Call me."

When a Jewish shrink gets messages from a rabbi, a police chief, and a nubile *shiksa* nurse, it can't be good news.

CHAPTER NINETEEN

"Mit ein hintn zitst men nit oif tsvei ferd."
    "You can't sit on two horses with one behind."

The way my phone was set up, it automatically redialed my callers in the order the messages arrived. Shlomo was first.

"Hello, Gritz?" he said, a tad short of breath.

What did we do before caller ID?

"What's the matter?" I asked. My lowly status at Beth Augudus didn't make me an important person to contact for anything, so I assumed the call had to be about Moses Bloom.

"Everybody on the committee is out of town. I was hoping you could fill in. I can't find anyone else available."

"Shlomo, I don't understand. You know I don't belong to any committee at the synagogue."

"The *Chevra Kaddisha* Committee! You do know that in our religion someone has to sit with the body until it's buried, don't you?" Shlomo sounded like he was instructing a mentally challenged Chosen One.

"When did Moses pass away?"

"Not Moses. Estelle Levitz."

"No joke?" I said. "Estelle?"

"Gritz, a rabbi doesn't joke about these things."

How could I forget that *rabbi* meant *teacher*? There are some parts of Judaism that seem more superstition than faith. One is the tradition of watching a dead body until burial—something about keeping the devil away until God's angel can come claim the soul. I never could understand how the frail old Jewish congregants who normally volunteered for such a task could be strong enough to do any good against the troops of the Evil One, but I guess that was the difference between those of faith and those faithfully cynical. At a minimum, it was a nice idea.

"Everyone I called is either on vacation or sick. I'm sitting on the floor by Estelle's casket right now, but I have to go to Charlotte in a few hours for a conference on rabbinical rights. I was hoping you could relieve me. I've arranged for Herman Jarvis to relieve you. Estelle died at about nine last night, so she has to be in the ground by nine tonight. I'll rush back from Charlotte to do the actual funeral. No rest for the weary."

"I didn't know Herman was Jewish." Herman Jarvis was the landscape maintenance man at Beth Augudus.

"He's not, but he says he's circumcised. God allows for compromise in desperate situations."

I wasn't sure the situation qualified as desperate.

"It seems like Estelle left us rather suddenly, doesn't it?" I said.

"I didn't know she was alive until yesterday. God works in mysterious ways."

Oh, Lord, I thought. Shlomo was acclimating to western North

Carolina quicker than I thought. That Christian phrase was painted on several Asheville barn roofs.

"How soon do you need me?"

"As soon as you can get here. I'll go home and shower after you spring me, then hit the road. People don't realize what schedules rabbis have to keep. I was just explaining it to—"

"I'll be right there," I said, hanging up as quickly as possible.

Never give a young rabbi the sympathy he begs for.

FuFu was found cowering in T's broom closet. Bitsy picked the dust balls from its mouth and kissed the dog numerous times. Pete sneered at FuFu, who evidently had nipped him and caused the sudden nosebleed. He wiped blood from his mustache with his sleeve and headed out the door with no good-bye for anyone, muttering something about whores, ghosts, and deadlines. T and Arlene straightened up the apartment as Mary Mag, Perrier, and Arnie looked out the window to see what damage the storm had wrought. I explained to T about Estelle and asked if I could have Pearlie swing back by the hotel to take Arlene home after he dropped me off. T said Arlene would be fine right there at the apartment.

I wanted to catch Pete at the elevator, but he was already gone. While I waited for it to come back up, I returned call number two.

"Asheville Police Department."

"This is Gritz Goldberg. I had a message to call Chief Livingston."

"Hold," she said curtly.

It sounded like the call was transferred to a cell phone.

"Gritz, I got a call from Mayor Bloom a little while ago. He strongly recommended I look into the death of his aunt, Estelle

Levitz. You know her? Out at Happy Valley? She died suddenly, and he implied it may not have been from natural causes."

My mind reran what Candy had said Moses asked of her. But why would Shel alert the cops if his father had anything to do with it?

"I just met the woman the other day when I was out to see Moses," I answered.

"I'm told your religion doesn't allow autopsies, but I might have to order one. Would your rabbi have to okay that?"

"I guess so, but is it really necessary? I mean, the woman had to be ninety."

There was a brief silence. "When I got out to Happy Valley— I'm still here now—I found an empty vial of prescription medicine in the waste can in her room. Xanax," Talmadge said. "The mayor said he was visiting his father last night, and the little lady seemed fine to him. It seems the nurse on duty, Ms. Candace Kane, discovered the woman hadn't been at dinner, so she went to check and found her dead. No medical facility lets their patients administer their own medicines. Besides that, the empty bottle wasn't even from Happy Valley's pharmacy."

"Really," I said. I hated that I was giving one-word replies, but with my heart pounding into my esophagus, that was the best I could manage. My first thought was that Candy had been coerced, but if there was foul play, it wasn't too bright to toss the evidence into Estelle's own trash can. At her age, it wasn't unusual to die in your sleep.

"The bottle was from your hospital. From Highland," Talmadge said.

"What?"

"The empty vial in the waste can was from Highland Hospital."

I couldn't manage even a one-word response to that.

"Gritz, you still with me?"

"Yeah, Talmadge, I'm here."

"The bottle doesn't say who it was prescribed to, but it has your name as the doc that prescribed it. The cap has the name of Highland on it and the Trinity logo." Talmadge paused as if waiting for a reply. "Did you order some of that stuff for Mrs. Levitz?"

"Of course not, Talmadge. Why would I do that? She's not my patient."

I never understood why it was necessary to put the university mascot on every prescription, but I guess if you have a top basketball team, you want everyone to know, even those with panic attacks. Xanax was dispensed like Pez around Highland. Who at a mental hospital didn't have anxiety problems? I ordered regular rounds of the medication for Marsha Bloom, Bobby Raby, Cage Blevins, and several others, but the vial would have had their name on it. The only Xanax prescription I'd requisitioned with no name was that bottle for T the day we met on the rooftop. Since T was not a Highland patient, I'd just ordered a week's dose to save him the eighty dollars it would have cost him. Most of the doctors themselves occasionally popped a Xanax in lieu of a martini or a game of golf to settle down after particularly crazy days. Trinity didn't like for us to order prescriptions for ourselves, but all of us did.

"I'll check it out," I said to Talmadge. "That is very odd."

"Yes, it is." For the first time in our entire relationship, Talmadge sounded a little strained with me. I guess he was thinking the same about me.

I still needed to return Candy's call, but I wanted to track down T's prescription first. If that was his bottle, how did it get out to Happy Valley?

"Where are you now?" Talmadge asked.

"Um, I'm on my way to the funeral home."

"I thought you said you hardly knew the woman." Talmadge sounded agitated.

I did what any rattled man would do: I lied.

"I'm close to the rabbi, and he needs me to help him out. It's complicated."

"Sounds like it," Talmadge said, hanging up.

Arnie, Perrier, and Mary Mag all arrived at the elevator before it came back up.

"It had to be him," Mary Mag said to Arnie. "Maybe he's gone for good now."

"I'd be surprised if he left that easy," Arnie said. "We really haven't done anything to clear his name, nor did he tell us how to help him. But it does seem like somebody was trying to get our attention, that's for sure."

"If he hasn't left in sixty-five years, I don't suppose he's in any particular hurry now," Perrier added.

"I forgot to ask T something," I said, turning back toward his apartment. "Thanks for doing this," I said to Perrier.

"See you Wednesday, Gritz?"

"Maybe sooner," I said, rotating my neck, trying to pop it on my own.

T and Arlene were standing face to face, their hands joined in front of them as if they were about to belt out a Broadway duet. When they saw me, they promptly disconnected.

"T, did you get around to using that Xanax prescription I got for you?"

"I'm sorry, Gritz. Actually, I never opened it. A hot toddy does pretty damn good for me, you know. I haven't seen that bottle in a day or two. I think I left it at your house when I came for supper. Probably still sitting in your kitchen somewhere."

"I saw it," Arlene said. "I left it sitting on the kitchen counter by the door."

"You can have it back," T said, as if he'd done something wrong.

"Don't worry about it. I just wondered if it helped."

I didn't feel good about lying to two of my friends in the last ten minutes, but as Shlomo might have put it, maybe God allowed a little slack now and then.

Pearlie wasn't outside yet, so I decided to take a little walk in the September night. I passed the Grove Arcade, now reopened as an office, apartment, and retail complex after many years of sitting deserted and being shit upon by hordes of pigeons. Dr. Edwin Grove had envisioned the ornate structure, which took up a whole city block, as the first shopping mall in the country, but he died before seeing its scaled-back completion. I wondered if he might be leaning up against a wall in one of the alleyways. I mean, if Mordecai wasn't satisfied to leave the Battery Park, if Zelda was still in my office, maybe Grove was still a resident of our fair city, too. Maybe the whole damn street was full of past residents.

I pulled out my cell phone as I meandered the dark streets.

"Candy, I'm sorry it's so late. You called?"

"Am I glad to hear your voice. I heard the chief tell the mayor he was going to call you. Do you think he knows we talked? I didn't do it, Gritz. I swear I didn't."

"I believe you, Candy."

That made three people I'd lied to in the last half-hour. I was getting used to it. Maybe I'd tell Aunt Fay that I was dating a nice

Jewish girl who knew how to cook *kasha varnickas*. That might keep her off my back for a few days.

"What do you know about all this?" I asked.

"Estelle seemed fine about five-thirty this afternoon. I mean yesterday. I mean, as fine as she got. Her doctor left instructions for us to try and let her roll herself to the cafeteria—to give her arms a little exercise, I guess, guiding the wheelchair. Anyway, we were short a couple of people in the serving line, so I had to pitch in and help, and things got so hectic that no one noticed Estelle hadn't been to supper at all. Shel came to eat with his dad, and then we . . . well, we took a real short walk during my break, the mayor and I." Candy paused. "About eight o'clock, during my regular rounds, I noticed Estelle was sound asleep in her wheelchair. I didn't try and move her, but at nine o'clock, I went back to try and get her in bed, and she was dead. Gritz, I didn't have a thing to do with it. I swear I didn't."

"Did you find the empty bottle of Xanax?"

"What empty bottle?"

"The police said there was an empty bottle of Xanax in Estelle's wastebasket."

"That's the first I've heard of it."

She didn't sound like she was lying.

"Did anybody else go into Estelle's room except you?"

"I don't think so, but of course just about anybody could have. We don't lock the patients' doors."

"What about Mayor Bloom? Was he with you all the time?"

"He was . . . I mean, after supper he was. We've become good friends. He says I give good advice," Candy said proudly.

"We all need a little advice every once in a while." I hadn't had any of her kind of advice in far too long. "How did Moses take the news?"

"You know Mr. Moses. He said he wasn't going to get dressed to go to any funeral, particularly not Estelle Levitz's. He said she should have died ten years ago anyway, that only meanness kept her alive."

"Just sit tight, Candy. Chief Livingston didn't mention your name to me at all. That medicine, I guess they think she overdosed on it. It came from my hospital. I may be the one that ought to worry."

"How could that have happened?"

"Good question. I don't know. Did you mention anything to the chief about that note Estelle gave you?"

"No, not yet. I did mention it to the mayor, though. He said he'd talk to the chief about it."

"I've got to do a favor for the rabbi, but I'll check with you later today, after we get some sleep. Call me if anything new develops."

"Gee, that makes me feel like Lois Lane," Candy said.

CHAPTER TWENTY

"Borgen macht zorgen."
"Loans will get you moans."

Even though it was the wee hours of the morning, a tall, lanky man who looked about my age, dressed in a black suit, white shirt, and solid black pencil-thin tie, greeted me as I entered Wilson's Funeral Home. His bright red hair went well with the green carpet, green walls, and green furniture. He seemed to be comfortable in his attire, never once playing with the tightness of his collar or checking his tie.

"Gritz Goldberg, Lord bless. I haven't seen you in a month of Sundays. So very sorry for your loss." His tone was somber but genuine.

Benjie Wilson, son of Benjamin Wilson, grandson of Benton Wilson, was a classmate of mine throughout middle school and high school. Much like children of preachers, children of funeral directors tended to be hell-raisers and giant pains in the ass for school administrators. I thought it justified, figuring they were out for all the fun they could get before they were sucked into the profitable but dreary family business. Benjie told great dead-body tales during recess. He described every detail of the process, from draining fluids and refilling the corpses with "longer-lasting juice" to the proper makeup techniques. We heard it all. He said that reconstructing an accident victim for viewing took the creativity of Picasso and the skill of a surgeon. Benjie was the first boy in our class to actually view firsthand the female private parts. His dad evidently let him watch the "restorative art" from head to toe. Once, Benjie described a woman's vagina in such detail that Shel puked all over his pants and had to go home. As the years progressed and each of us learned in our own ways about women, Benjie's funeral-home stories gradually lost their power over us. I went to Tulane and Benjie to the famous Nashville School of Interment. I never saw him except for that time we ducked each other coming out of the Adam and Eve Bookstore off Eagle Street.

"Long time, no see," I said, shaking his cold hand.

"I've never seen you here before—I mean, as part of the Beth Augudus committee," Benjie said seriously. "New recruit?"

"Just a pinch hitter," I said.

"Let me direct you to the last room down the hall. Your people usually request that space."

Though I'm proud to be Jewish, I hate it when practitioners of my faith are referred to as "your people." When Nona and I were first married, a backwoods preacher who'd known my family for years proudly introduced himself to her at a local restaurant. I thought I was going to have to wrestle Nona to the ground and bind her like a rodeo calf when the preacher, describing his recent visit to Israel, told her, "I've just visited your homeland."

"What part of Long Island did you see?" Nona growled back.

I followed Benjie's giant strides down the hall. We must have passed ten large viewing rooms, all with plush carpet, velour draperies, and Frank Lloyd Wright-influenced lighting fixtures. When we got to the last room, it had no elegant window treatments—no windows at all, in fact—and no dramatic floral wallpaper like the others. The whole room was dark except for one floor lamp that looked like it had been bought at a scratched-and-dented sidewalk sale. A lone gray metal folding chair with a stained watermelon-green cushion stood next to the plain wooden box that Estelle Levitz currently called home.

Seated in the shadows on the floor by the casket with his sandals off and his knees tucked up under his chin was Rabbi Shlomo Weiskopf. As I walked closer, I noticed his blue-and-white Hawaiian shirt, yellow Bermudas, and black socks, which made him look more like a bar mitzvah student waiting for his weekly Torah lesson than a meditating sage.

"Am I glad you're finally here!" Shlomo said, jumping to his feet, slipping on his Birks, and offering me his hand. Shlomo shook too strongly and continued too long, which all first-year psychiatric students learn often indicates an underlying lack of self-confidence and abundant character flaws. "There's nothing to do, really. You just stay with the body until Mr. Jarvis gets here. I think I can be back from Charlotte by seven or eight. We can bury her for sure by nine."

"No prayers to read or anything like that?" I asked.

"Nothing specific," Shlomo said, looking at Benjie and then shifting into a syrupy-sweet clergy voice. "Those of us who loved Estelle are obligated to protect her soul from the devil after she dies. Just physically being by her side is all that is necessary."

Benjie and Shlomo excused themselves and left the room,

leaving me alone with Estelle. I wondered if the devil could differentiate between a sleeping guard and a wakeful one. It had been a long day, and I was ready for some shuteye. I took off my golf jacket and wadded it up, making a pillow. There's really no good place to nap in a funeral home. Benjie had closed the door behind him. I reopened it and made myself a nice, secure spot in the front corner of the room behind the open door and as far across the room from Estelle as I could get. At five in the morning, not a creature was stirring, not even a corpse. If Mordecai Moore's spirit walked the earth though his body was dead, I wondered if Estelle's essence wandered, too.

I fell asleep quickly. When I awoke, my watch indicated I'd been in slumber land only about thirty minutes, but it felt like a couple of centuries. A loud noise had disturbed my sleep. At first, I thought I'd dozed in my office and Ophelia was starting her morning rounds on the first floor. When I realized I wasn't at the office but in the village of the dead, I got up and wandered the halls. I knew I wasn't supposed to bail out on Estelle, but the devil surely couldn't have attained his position without being a pretty sly fallen angel. I rationalized that on any given night, he'd surely have easier targets than cantankerous Estelle Levitz.

I determined the sound, which was akin to an electric drill press, was coming from a lower floor. I found a stairway that led to a basement. About halfway down, I noticed the smell. By the time I got to the bottom of the steps, I felt nauseated. It made Shel's scent almost sweet. At the end of the hallway were two black, leather-covered swinging doors with portholes. They seemed out of place, more like doors to a cruise-ship kitchen. I peeked inside and saw a short, overweight, elderly man wearing a white lab coat and what looked like one of those heavy black Israeli gas masks, except that it had a large floodlight attached. His pants didn't quite fit the rest of his outfit. They were those baggy affairs that chefs wear, black with red lobsters all over them. His shoes were not of the medical ilk either, appearing to be well-worn black combat boots. He stood over a fat, naked male body laying on a rolling metal gurney that seemed to be struggling under the weight. Tubes flowed in and out of the body, making a convoluted pretzel design.

When he saw me looking, he pushed the mask onto the top of his head and motioned me in. "May I help you?" he said, picking up a half-eaten chocolate bar. The voice was scratchy and deep. A giant, ugly black mole on his cheek moved up and down as he spoke.

"I heard the noise and decided to see what was going on."

"Routine embalming procedure. Substituting the eternal high-test formula for this poor heart attack victim's body fluids." His snort indicated he thought he'd just made a joke. "We don't normally have live overnight guests at Wilson's," he continued, now looking at me minus his headgear, which he'd taken off and laid on the man's mountain of stomach.

"I'm sitting with . . . I mean, I'm here with Mrs. Levitz."

"*Chevra Kaddisha* Committee, huh?"

"That's right."

"Surprised you, didn't I? I can tell you how folks prepare their dead in about any religion in the whole wide world. Your way is the best. Plain casket, no embalming fluid, keep the dead company before interment. Of course, we in the business hope your way doesn't catch on." The mole bounced up this time and stayed there, like he was waiting for me to laugh before he released his facial tension.

"Have you been doing this long?" I said, trying to make small talk across the cadaver.

His thin, dark hair had a grocery-store-coloring tint to it, somewhere between a rusty nail and an overripe banana. The way he kept his shoulders stiffly upright and his arms close to his sides reminding me of a cross between Mr. Rogers and Ed Sullivan.

"Fifty-two, actually almost fifty-three years now. Benjamin Wilson hired me right out of high school. He used to say I was born to embalm. I do it very well, even if I do say so myself. I've been planning on taking a sabbatical, now that my wife retired from teaching. Maybe rent a motor home and go fishing in Wyoming for a month or two. But you know, folks just won't quit dying." He said this as if he felt slighted that a higher authority hadn't provided an opportunity for him to travel, for all his work well done.

"I'm sure not everybody is cut out for a job like this," I said.

"Those of us in the business call it an art."

"Oh, yes, an art," I said, backing ever so slightly toward the door. "Restorative artist," I said, surprising myself with my recall of Benjie's schoolyard terminology.

"Death is rarely a Kodak moment. Those left behind wish to remember their deceased as beautiful gifts from God, literally and figuratively speaking. That's when they call Mutt Pressley to the rescue." He stuck out a hand gloved in beige latex for me to shake. "Marvin Muttley Pressley. Nice talking with you. Most folks just call me Mutt. Short for my mama's maiden name."

I skipped the handshake and patted him on his upper arm. "Nice to meet you. I'm Dr. David Goldberg, but everybody calls me Gritz."

"Now, that's a funny name for a Jew," he said seriously. "Your friend upstairs was an easy setup. The committee bathes the body and slips on a plain cotton shroud, and away she goes. I did need to ask your rabbi about a little blue velour zipper bag she wanted to have buried with her. Last request. Do you have your final requests on file with us?"

"I guess I should, but I don't."

"It's a lot better than telling your brother-in-law what you want. We keep very strict files on that sort of thing. First thing we do when we pick up a body is check to see if he or she was prearranged. Estelle Levitz had one of the oldest files I've ever come upon. It was dated late nineteen-forties sometime. She must have been a young woman back then. Anyway, she requested the typical Jewish burial, except she deposited this little zipper bag for us to hold onto. Wanted it buried with her, said it belonged to her husband. Evidently, the guy went out for a pack of cigarettes one day and never came back. At least that's what Benjie said."

Mutt went to a shelf and pulled down a cheap, warped cardboard box like you use to store your tax records. From it, he took out a blue zipper bag.

"She called every year around the same time to make sure we still had the bag. We figured maybe it was the anniversary of when her husband vanished. It used to be a lot fatter—you know, like it was more full—but one year not that long ago, a cute little nurse from Happy Valley showed up with the old lady, and we let Mrs. Levitz be alone with the bag for a few minutes, like they do with a safe-deposit box at the bank. Then she gave us back the bag and left. It wasn't so full then. Ever seen anything like this?" Mutt held the bag like he'd just picked up an exotic fruit at the grocery store.

"That's what my people call a *tefillin* bag." Jesus, even I was calling us "my people."

Every boy who becomes bar mitzva gets a *tefillin* bag. It's pretty strange stuff if you're not Jewish, and darn strange at thirteen even if you are. It consists of leather straps, a little black box to tie across your forehead, and another for one forearm. It represents a lot of things—the word of God, freedom from Egyptian slavery. Usually, the new owner's name is embroidered on the bag in

English and Hebrew. This one had *Edward Levitz* stitched in bright yellow.

"Estelle wanted this bag to be in the casket with her?"

"That's what the file said," Mutt answered. "I thought Jewish law dictated that nothing but the body, the shroud, and, for the male, his prayer shawl were allowed in the casket. I didn't want the woman going to hell—or me either, for that matter—because of some little misdeed this late in the game, so I asked Rabbi Weiskopf earlier tonight. He said absolutely not, that the lady must not have been a very observant Jew or she would've known better. He said to give the bag to you until you could give it to her nephew, Mayor Bloom."

"It seems unusual for a woman to want a *tefillin* bag buried with her, but I don't imagine God would really care. Shlomo said to give it to me? He didn't say anything to me when I saw him."

"I told him I was planning to rendezvous with a rainbow trout or two when I got off. September is a slow month in the death trade. Mrs. Levitz will be buried by the time I get back. I guess he didn't want any chance of a foul-up or something."

I nodded.

"What does someone use that for anyway, the bag?"

"Ever see pictures of those religious guys at the Wailing Wall in Israel, praying and bowing? Ever notice the little black leather boxes on their forearm and forehead? It comes from Deuteronomy: 'Bind them as a sign on your hand, and let them serve as a symbol on your forehead.' " We ended each Sunday-school class by reciting that.

"My wife and I went over there for a convention last year. To Israel."

"The Orthodox carry a bag like this. Sort of a briefcase for Hasidim."

That seemed enough to satisfy Mutt. He picked up his mining

hat, placed it back on his head, and looked at the pudgy dead guy as if analyzing what a Picasso like himself would need to finish another day's tough job.

"I guess I'd better get this fellow ready for his big day. Nice talking to you."

As I pushed the swinging doors open, I saw his reflection in the porthole windows. It seemed he was having one fine conversation with the dead man.

I looked at my watch. I still had another couple hours of duty. Since Estelle was going nowhere, I decided to take a tour of some of the other viewing rooms as the longest night of my life continued. Earlier, I'd spent time trying to get a dead person to leave. Now, my assignment was to make sure another one didn't.

You could distinguish the non-Jewish occupants of the funeral home easily. They were surrounded by massive floral arrangements that would have made my uncle Carl cry. He was the florist in the family, and also the blackest of the black sheep. When he deserted the clothing business to buy a flower shop in Detroit, the family never forgave him. Aunt Fay accused her brother of being a self-hating Jew, going into a business that catered to *goyim*. Uncle Carl said it was no different from selling suits. If you couldn't sell clothes or flowers for a Jewish funeral, what exactly was the big deal? "No flowers, cotton burial gown, plain casket, that's it!" Uncle Carl spit at Aunt Fay during a Passover family feast. "There's nothing profitable about dying in our religion, and you know that." I never had the courage to tell him how proud I was of him that night. Very few have ever stood up to Aunt Fay and lived to tell the tale.

I made a bathroom stop before rejoining Estelle, tucking her hubby's velvet bag in my armpit. As I relieved myself at one of the three golden urinals, I got to thinking about how probably ninety-nine percent of the world's people had no idea what a *tefillin* bag was or even that it existed. And then it hit me. It wasn't the nostalgia or ritual of Eddie Levitz's bag that made Estelle want to take it with her to eternity. The bag was a safe place to hide something. But what was it she wanted to hide so badly? Stuck under my armpit must have been a mighty valuable possession, at least to Estelle, but it seemed sacrilegious even to a nonreligious person like myself to go tearing through the bag at a urinal. I decided to wait and open it in Estelle's presence, so to speak.

As I approached her room, I heard men's voices. I could see the back of one man sitting in a wheelchair. He wore a ratty plaid flannel robe over p.j.'s, along with corduroy bedroom shoes and a ten-gallon white cowboy hat. The other man was wearing an old pair of blue jeans and a yellow T-shirt with "I Got It In Asheville" on the back. The bald spot on the back of his head glimmered like a *yarmulke* in the dim light. But I knew the greasy shine was not a religious symbol, but rather a middle-aged token belonging to Shel Bloom.

"Good morning," I said, though it wasn't.

"Gritz, what are you doing here?" Shel said, slamming shut Estelle's casket and whirling to face me.

"On duty for Shlomo. Moses, it's nice of you to pay your respects," I said.

"What did Eddie see in that woman? Tell me, do you know?" Moses said.

"I've never done this before," I said. "Sitting with the deceased."

"Looks like you need practice," Moses said.

"Where is she, anyway?" Shel asked.

"What do you mean?" I said.

"Aunt Estelle. She's not in there," he said, pointing his middle finger at the casket.

"What's that under your arm?" Moses asked. "Don't worry about Estelle. Dead bodies have a way of turning up."

"Mr. Pressley downstairs asked me to take care of it," I said, still holding the *tefillin* bag tightly. I left off the part about saving it for the Blooms.

"Shel inherits everything. Give it to me." Moses held his hands high in the air, but there was no sea to part this time.

I really had no choice but to give them the bag. I wanted to see what Estelle had kept hidden for so many years, but I didn't want the Blooms to learn I knew anything about Estelle's e-mail to Candy. I didn't know what it meant yet, but I understood it was something I should follow up on. I reluctantly handed the bag to Moses.

"Let's get the hell out of here," Moses said to Shel. "At my age, funeral homes make me nervous."

"Oh, by the way, Gritz, my lawyer will be sending you a registered letter soon. You know, alienation of affection laws are still in effect in North Carolina. The money we're going to collect from you and Highland will come in handy for my campaign, don't you think?" Shel smiled. "Marsha's whole personality changed when she started seeing you. My constituents will understand a sick doctor ruining a perfectly good marriage."

Shrinks are taught to rein in their emotions, but Shel was doing a superlative job of making me lose control of mine. I'd come across some downright revolting humans in my time, but this faux cowboy and his senator wannabe son topped my list. I hoped Estelle wasn't able to see the precious bag she'd watched over all these years handed off to her hated brother-in-law and his son. No wonder I'd never been asked to be on the *Chevra Kaddisha* Committee before.

Mutt suddenly emerged from the stairwell, dressed more for a swift, cold stream than a lab of dead people. He wore heavy brown canvas overalls tucked into green rubber hip boots. His floppy khaki hat made his ears look like satellite dishes. He had a tackle box in one hand.

He nodded to the departing Blooms before turning to me. "It's been a most unusual night here. I usually don't see a soul. Well, not living ones, anyway." He adjusted the straps to his overalls.

"Where's Estelle?"

"Police just got her. The district attorney demanded an autopsy. Where were you?"

"Bathroom, I guess."

"I couldn't stop them," he said. "The rabbi's not going to be happy with me."

"Nor with me," I said, pulling out my cell phone to call Pearlie to pick me up. Living out of his car, Pearlie was always on call.

"Oh, by the way," Mutt said. "I must be getting old. I forgot to give this to the Blooms on their way out."

He reached into his giant chest pocket and pulled out another blue velvet bag, this one much smaller than the first. I recognized it as the inner bag of the larger *tefillin* bag. The smaller bag held the *phylacteries*—the two tiny boxes with Old Testament scrolls and attached leather straps. The larger, outer bag I'd just handed the Blooms held the *tallis*—the prayer shawl—the *yarmulke*, and the second bag.

"Somehow, over the years, these two bags must have gotten separated. Will you give it to the mayor and tell him I'm sorry for the error?"

"Sure, I will," I said, grabbing the bag. "Sure."

Waiting for Pearlie, I had a sharp pang in my gut. I knew it was time for a Cardiac Arrest. Not a heart attack, but my favorite breakfast special—a giant, five-egg Western omelet oozing with real creamery butter and loads of green peppers and sliced mushrooms, served at Asheville's newest twenty-four-hour purveyor of extreme cholesterol, The Hard Lox Café. Thanks to a burst of newly arrived Jewish retirees, Asheville was finally ready for a true Jewish deli. Sex, booze, drugs, and all the other things gentiles turn to for comfort in times of stress mean little to us. When things get tough for Jews, we eat. And times were getting pretty tough for this Jewish psychiatrist.

"Take me to The Hard Lox," I said to Pearlie as I got into the cab.

"Okay, but let somebody taste your eggs first," he said. "You never know."

CHAPTER TWENTY-ONE

"Oif drei zachen shtait di velt: oif gelt, oif gelt, un oif gelt."

"The world stands on three things: on money, on money, and on money."

When Frank Markowitz rolled into town from L.A. and opened The Hard Lox Café, the Jewish community was so thrilled it held a special Friday-night service of thanks. Frank, who had recently requested to be called François, introduced noshing to a community that had also just gotten its first taste of sushi. Aunt Fay claimed that Jewish deli food probably caused more deaths than Hitler. Rumor had it that our California gastronomic guru had abandoned a career in oncology and a family of six to skip cross-country and move in with Ruth Schwartz's son, Hesh. This didn't upset Ruth as much as you'd think. She'd always said she wanted a doctor in the family.

Frank had spent a ton of money remodeling an old boardinghouse into a class-A restaurant. I loved it that Asheville could have such a wide array of eating establishments. The Hard Lox was a lot farther from Possum's than just across town. But I did draw the line when Frank placed his salad bar in an antique claw-foot tub.

"You're up early," Frank said as I walked in the door. "Quite a storm during the night, huh?"

"Did it hit this side of town?" I asked.

"I live in those apartments around the corner from the Battery Park. It was like somebody made Mother Nature one mad woman, let me tell you."

I didn't think it was a woman who'd gotten mad. More like a skinny, wronged black man, but I didn't say it.

There was only one other person in the restaurant, at the counter. He glanced my way while slurping his coffee.

"Morning," Pete Reid said, only halfway looking around at me.

"Morning," I answered.

Like anonymous, awkward lovers who'd gone farther than they intended the night before, neither of us was in the mood to chat.

Frank's morning cook popped out from the kitchen. He looked like he'd lost his way to the shower. Once I spotted the hickey on his neck and saw his unwashed hair, I lost my desire for a gourmet omelet and simply ordered dry toast and coffee.

"It's a sin to come in here and just order toast, you know," Frank said.

"Please forgive me, Father," I said, smiling.

Pete inspected his cup of coffee like he was looking for a drowning fly, then said, "Damnedest thing I ever saw, Gritz. Wouldn't have believed a word of it if I hadn't been there."

"It got better after you left," I said

I outlined my extended night at the funeral home. When I got to the part about Estelle's burial request and her body being hauled off for autopsy, Pete's face got red and he stood up to leave.

"Didn't I tell you and T that if you kept sticking your necks out, they were going to get chopped off? Didn't I?"

"It's not like we're trying to. It's more like we're being led."

Pete looked at me like I was the dumbest asshole who'd ever graced Asheville's city limits.

"Here you go, Dr. G.," Frank said. "Sure I can't get you a real breakfast? The produce truck just brought in fresh onions and salsa."

Pete tossed a five-dollar bill on the counter. "I'll wait for you outside," he said.

It's not easy to get indigestion from toast, but I proved it could be done. Hastily downing the whole slice of bread in about two swallows, I pulled out my charge card to pay my bill—all $2.05 of it.

"Do you take outpatients?" Frank asked softly as he pushed my card away from him. "On the house," he said.

"Yes," I answered hesitantly.

"Hesh and I have been having some problems lately. Do you do couples counseling?"

"I do, but I don't have any openings at the moment. Trinity cut back on the number of people I can see." I was getting much too comfortable at telling lies. Trinity really wanted us to take every misguided soul who came our way, but the thought of Ruth Schwartz assaulting me if she lost the doctor in the family was too much for me to handle at that moment.

Pete was waiting for me, leaning against Pearlie's door. It looked like he wasn't quite done with my reprimand.

"Gritz, say what you want about that thing at the hotel last night, I still don't believe in spirits and all that crap. And even if it was a fact—I mean, even if Mordecai Moore's soul is trapped in that damn hotel—it just can't lead to anything good by stirring the whole thing up. No, it won't lead to one good thing, trust me."

It seemed like my night was never going to end. I wanted to crawl into my bed and wake up the week before, when I'd never heard of Mordecai Moore, never thought about Willard Dudley Paully, never cared about Pete Reid.

"You need to stop this whole thing," Pete said. "Now."

"What am I doing? What whole thing?"

"They say a cancer can be in your body for dozens of years and you never know it. Then one day, a lump pops up and your whole life turns inside out. Well, there are other things in life like that."

I nodded, though I didn't really understand.

"Executing Mordecai Moore didn't eradicate any cancer on this town. It didn't even come close. And the thing is, now that it's popped back up, it's liable to start spreading again."

"Why blame me, for God's sake?"

"It's not that you mean to, but people fall into stuff without even trying."

"Pete, you aren't telling me everything you know about the murder, are you?"

"The skinny around the paper was that Paully was planning something big to happen in Asheville. Something that would get national attention for his cause, for the Silver Shirts. Knowing him a little bit from the poker games, I worried that he might try something really stupid, like assassinating FDR when he visited town."

"Are you saying the girl's murder had something to do with an attempt to kill the president of the United States?"

"I don't know what I'm saying exactly. It was just more of a feeling I got at the time. I didn't have any facts to connect the two."

"But there was no assassination."

"Tell that to the Sardano family." The lines in Pete's face

deepened. "It wasn't just Paully. I got the sense that there was also some kind of business arrangement—you know, under-the-table stuff—between Paully and Senator Raby and maybe even Hurt Bailey. They were always yappin', winkin'—you know, joshin'—during our poker games. Even Moses Bloom and Eddie Levitz seemed to be in on it, I'm not sure how. It was just the way they talked. Levitz Salvage always advertised, 'If we can't get it, you don't need it.' Maybe Levitz got something the others needed. I just don't know."

"That's all fascinating, but what does it have to do with Mordecai?"

"Hell if I know. Maybe nothing. I'm just telling you some things that have been on my mind for what seems like my whole life. Can't you appreciate that?" Pete's warble indicated he was about to break down.

I nodded again. This time, I really did understand.

"Paully would have loved to help Hitler any way he could. It was already illegal to do business with Germany before we got into World War II, but if Roosevelt declared war, any business conducted would have been treason. Raby was a rabid isolationist. He was even entertained by the German government early on. They liked him, probably wanted him to be president some day. With Roosevelt alive, Raby would never be president, now, would he?"

I considered telling him there was a rug that Raby got from the Fuhrer sitting in my office at that moment, but I knew every man has his breaking point. I wasn't sure who was closer to it, Pete or me.

"But Moses and his brother-in-law wouldn't have any business dealings with the likes of Paully," I said. "I mean, a Nazi?"

"That's exactly what could make it work. If nobody believed

they would, then maybe they could. I mean, maybe it was the perfect cover."

"And what about the senator? I mean, a senator sleeping with the enemy?"

"You had to know Senator Bob. He was always a pain in the ass for FDR, and the same in reverse. Besides, he wouldn't have dealt with Germany directly, just indirectly. I don't know, maybe there was some kind of political pull he could offer. He could scream, 'Save America!' all day long and sell us out all night, and all the while convince himself it was good for the country. We do that in the South, you know. Talk ourselves into believing what we need to think."

"I know Raby was a real character, but treason?"

"Never underestimate a politician with aspirations."

"Ever hear the name Kripp?" I asked.

"Sure. They make kitchen mixers, don't they?"

"Yeah, now they do. I gather they were big supporters of Hitler, too. I found a letter Moses had in an old album from a Gustav Kripp. The letter was addressed to Paully. It thanked Paully for some kind of support, and I'm sure it wasn't for buying a food processor."

Pete coughed—a smoker's cough that sounded like death come calling. When he finally caught his breath, he looked up at me. "Gritz, the past is kind only to those who don't remember it like it really was. The problem is, my memory is too damn good."

He turned and walked slowly to his car.

Why people think of history in the past tense always confuses me. The only difference between what was and what is might be the skill we acquire in how quickly we forget.

CHAPTER TWENTY-TWO

"Shpeiz kocht men in top un koved krigt der teller."
"The food is cooked in a pot, but the plate gets the honor."

When Pearlie pulled up in front of my house, the sun was about to rise and I was about to collapse. I would have paid a month's salary for a hot, pulsating shower and fresh, warm towels out of the dryer. Instead, I found parked in wait a new Mercedes CLK convertible bearing a *#1 Shrink* personalized license plate.

It felt like the night was never going to end without some kind of supernatural assistance. I didn't need Dink waiting on me at the break of dawn. "God, I feel like I'm free-falling into an abyss," I said quietly.

Once again, the Most High chose not to answer. The only bottom I could see was a big fat one sliding out of a very expensive toy. Dink walked toward me in a gait that indicated he was on a mission, and that I was it. He was dressed in one of those skimpy nylon sets made infamous by Richard Simmons, and it looked just about as silly on him as it did on the diet guru. My hind leg twitched like a peeing contest was about to commence.

"Gritz, I've given you all the warnings I could." He pulled an envelope out of his pocket and thrust it at me. "You are officially suspended from the hospital. We'll send your personal things over later. Don't even try and enter your office."

"Why? For what?" I said. "I couldn't have known that Bobby Raby was going to pull a stunt like he did."

Dink didn't look me in the eye. His gaze was focused across my hedge, where Adolf's low growl was building in pitch. This was one time I wished the dog would get his prize.

"It's not just one thing, Gritz. You know that. Bobby Raby's outburst didn't help, but when the police showed up last night with a search warrant for your office and found that prissy-ass little gun with no license and a Nazi rug . . . Well, Gritz, what do you expect us to do?"

"Why were they searching my office?"

"You're damn lucky you're just suspended. They found meds from our pharmacy in the wastebasket of a dead woman at that Seventh-Day Adventist nursing home."

"I know all about that, but I had absolutely nothing to do with it. The death, I mean."

"I suppose our pharmacist put your name on the bottle just for kicks."

"I did requisition those meds, but it was for a friend of mine, not Estelle Levitz."

"Save the alibis for your defense." Dink turned toward his car.

"Thanks for your support, Dink."

He jerked back around. "And if all that wasn't enough, Mary Louise Guthrie checked herself out of Highland with your authorization. Her husband is furious. He had to cancel a ballroom-dancing competition, and he's threatening to sue. If you ask me, the best thing for you to do is to disappear for a while. Trinity has ordered everyone from the hospital to put a lid on anything that relates to you. No comments, no interviews. Any press is bad press in a mental institution, you know that."

Dink was obviously more concerned about Highland's reputation than about whether I'd actually murdered someone.

"I'm completely innocent. You do believe me, don't you?"

"Well, yeah, actually. I can't see you hurting a fly," he chuckled.

I felt like I could kill one particular physician at that moment, but I didn't think pressing the issue would help my cause. I detested it when people described someone that way. Usually, they meant the person didn't look like they could take on a fly and win.

"Mayor Bloom is behind this. He's got to be."

"The mayor?" he said. "Why the mayor? Why don't you just blame it all on Trinity? That's your normal MO. Maybe it's a conspiracy. Maybe the CIA and the FBI are involved, too." Dink punched his electronic key, and I heard his car doors unlock. The car radio came on, bursting out Rod Stewart singing "Tonight's the Night." Dink squeezed his belly under the steering wheel, slammed the door, and rolled the electric window down. "Gritz, let me know where you're going to be. Trinity might need to reach you. I won't tell the CIA, I promise."

"Titty pink," I mumbled.

"What?"

"Never mind," I said. "Just never mind."

I hated to admit it, but Dink was probably right about one thing. I needed to be inaccessible, if not totally missing, until I could clear up the suspicions that surrounded me. Trinity's brigade of lawyers would drop their kilts if they got too many questions from WLIS about one of their docs possibly being involved in murder, not to mention the breakup of Asheville's first family.

I'd run. Not far, but far enough to get away from inquiring minds.

Going into seclusion would mean gathering up all the trappings of my life, including my new Apple PowerBook, my electric flossing machine, my U-shaped pillow designed to alleviate neck pain, my night guard to stop my teeth from clenching, and most certainly my CD player and my collection of depressive melodies by Bread, Janis Ian, and Carole King. Holing up was starting to be attractive.

"Is he your sergeant?" Pearlie said, leaning out his window.

"No, he's head of the hospital."

I told him to wait on me, that it wouldn't take more than a few minutes.

I went into the house by the kitchen door. I didn't want to startle the kids so early in the morning, even to tell them good-bye. Thank God for Arlene. T would be around to help, too.

I did need to wake up Arlene and tell her what was happening, though. I knocked lightly, slowly turned the doorknob to her bedroom, and stuck my head in. "Arlene," I called in a low voice.

"Gritz, is that you?" The voice was not that of a female.

"Oh," I said. Dad always told me I needed to get over my fear of sleeping over at friends' houses. I never did, but T obviously had.

"Gritz?" came another voice from the bed.

"I'm really sorry to barge in like this, but I've got to disappear for a little while."

"Oh, Lord," T moaned. "What happened now?"

"I've been suspended from the hospital."

"Bobby Raby?" he asked.

"That and the fact that somebody, probably the mayor, is trying to frame me."

"For what?" Arlene said.

"Murder, among other things."

"Murder!" Arlene sat up straight, tugging the sheet to cover her chest. It was dark inside the room, but a touch of streetlight filtered through the blinds. Embarrassments go down better in the dark.

"The police think I provided the pills that helped Estelle Levitz make her final exit. Out at Happy Valley."

"She was your patient?" Arlene asked.

"No, and I met her only once. I think Shel took that bottle of Xanax I got for you, T. He must have taken it off the kitchen sink when he came to get those albums I borrowed from Moses."

"You think the mayor would kill his aunt? Why would he do that?" Arlene's voice strained with early-morning sinus drainage.

"I don't know that he did, but I know I didn't."

"Ol' Mordecai felt the same way," T said. Then, realizing that wasn't the most comforting reply, he quickly added, "Gritz, I feel like I'm the cause of all these things that are happening. I mean, if I hadn't come back from Charlotte and all . . ."

"Stop it, T. Stop it right now," Arlene said. "Gritz, running away from the problem won't help. It will make it look that much worse. What you need is a good lawyer."

"So far, I haven't been charged with anything, but I think Dink might be right this time. The media gets a sniff of this, and it's front page."

"Where would you go?" T asked.

"Not far. I was thinking of Possum's."

"Sure 'nough, that might be just the place," T chuckled. "I'd offer my apartment, but that's probably where Talmadge would look first."

"I'll call you with my phone number when I get over there. I won't use my cell right now. It's okay to tell the kids where I am. Tell them I needed to get away for a night or two to catch up on some overdue paperwork. I don't want them worrying."

"Gritz, let T and me help with this," Arlene said cautiously.

"Yeah, and don't let him have the last word either."

"Shel?" I said.

"No, the devil," T said. "My preacher says that every Sunday. 'Don't let the devil have the last word.' "

I backed out of Arlene's room, knocking a big stack of papers off the wicker chair near the door—probably her set of Mordecai's newspaper clips. I went to my room, turning on all the lights I could. I heard shuffling and the voices of T and Arlene next door as I hurriedly packed some underwear and spare clothes. My hands were trembling. Almost every day on the news, you heard about innocent people spending the rest of their lives in jail, but why would I be the mayor's target? I couldn't really see him being that upset over my therapy sessions with Marsha. He never loved her anyway. But why would Shel kill his aunt just before announcing for national office? That would be just plain crazy. Or maybe desperate.

I took the time to inspect the second *tefillin* bag. Nothing seemed out of the ordinary—I mean, if two little, black, leather-wrapped boxes filled with miniature scriptures were familiar to you. I felt like I was cutting up God's underwear, but I pulled out my pocketknife and ripped the white cotton lining of the bag, just in case something was in there, but there wasn't. I figured that the Blooms must have gotten the important bag.

The aroma of freshly roasted coffee crept up the stairs. I finished packing and went down.

Arlene already had a cup of java, heavily creamed and sugared as I liked it, on the kitchen counter for me. She was wearing a rather slinky purple nylon robe over a purple gown with matching furry slippers. This was not her usual attire in my household.

"T's in the shower. I need to ask you a favor," she said, looking away from me. "You know when you were talking to your dad the other day? And he asked for a prescription?"

"How could I forget?"

"T doesn't want to ask, but you know we're no spring chickens."

They weren't young, but they were making my own social life look pretty sick.

"Why don't I write you a prescription, and you get it filled for T?" I said, trying to sound professional. This time, I was the one not looking Arlene in the eye.

"Thanks, Gritz. We both feel silly about all this, but it just happened, you know what I mean?"

"I think it's great. Just don't have any kids real soon. Not until Stef and Nate go to college."

Arlene looked at me and smiled. "Gritz, I've been thinking. If Mordecai Moore's apparition, or whatever you want to call it, is somehow real, it's been sixty-five years since anybody claimed to see him. Why is he showing up now? I mean, Bitsy has been at the hotel all along, and I bet some others who lived there during the thirties are residents, too. I still don't really believe in ghosts, not exactly, but if this is somehow really happening, shouldn't there be a compelling reason for Mordecai to show up now?"

"It seems that way to me, too, Arlene. Let me tell you another odd thing I seem to have gotten in the middle of." I described the Blooms' sudden interest in Eddie Levitz's *tefillin* bag.

"And Estelle Levitz wanted it buried with her? That's odd in itself."

"The guy who embalms at the funeral home gave me the inner bag—you know, the little one that's kept inside the bigger bag. He said they got separated somehow."

"Where is it now?"

"I left it in my room. I checked it out. There's nothing valuable, except for sentimental reasons maybe. But her husband deserted her, so why would she want to keep something of his all these years? Everything seems to indicate it was a hiding place for something, but what? And where is it now, if it was?"

"That's why she'd take it with her to the grave, too," Arlene said.

"You never knew Eddie Levitz," T said, walking into the room. "Nobody could have loved a man like that—I mean, only his mother maybe. He was worse than Moses to cruise Stumptown on Saturday night. He'd pick up anything, and I mean anything. And then all of sudden, he was gone. Vanished. Nobody every heard from him again. I sort of figured he and Mordecai met the same fate, except Eddie wasn't done in by the law."

Pearlie beeped his horn.

"I guess I'd better get going," I said.

I gave Arlene a hug, and T, too. Leaving a comfortable, secure place has always been hard for me, and this time I was doing more than just leaving. I was running. I threw my bag into Pearlie's cab and looked around. I saw Adolf watching me under the hedge, but he was quiet as a church mouse. Maybe a Jew on the run was nothing for a good German shepherd to protest.

"Just one more minute, Pearlie," I said. I walked to the back-porch stoop. "T, I can't see how any of this relates, but could Mordecai have had any dealings with Moses or Eddie?"

"Not that I remember. He may have substituted for me a night or two—you know, taking care of the poker club or something. But I don't really remember even that. Well, now, wait a minute." T grinned. "Now that I think about it, there was that elephant."

Arlene and I looked at T like he might have lapsed into Alzheimer's.

"As I remember, Eddie and Moses got Mordecai and a couple of others to go by and feed an elephant they had down on the river near their business lot."

"An elephant?" I said.

"Yeah. One time, the salvage company loaned the owner of a traveling circus some money to get to the next town but kept his elephant as collateral. Mordecai would go feed it, but then Moses said it was eating everything in sight and had the circus come back and pick it up. I forgot all about that story, but that's the only connection I can think of that the two had."

"Okay, well, come see me, as they say."

"Gritz, keep the faith, now, you hear?"

"I'll do my best, T."

I got in the cab, and we backed out of the driveway.

"My sergeant used to say that faith was harder to hold onto than a rainbow. That you had to trust in yourself," Pearlie said. "I sort of figured it was a one-two punch. Trust in the good Lord, and then trust in yourself, too."

"I guess so, Pearlie. Just so long as it's not a knockout punch."

CHAPTER TWENTY-THREE

"Besser di t'no'im tsereissen aider di ketubeh."
"Better to break off an engagement than a marriage."

Pearlie pulled into Possum's no-tell motel, the perfect spot to ditch the suspect of a felony. He glided the cab under a cascading waterfall of kudzu that crept off the bank like the unruly hair of an outcast Greek goddess. I felt the need to tell Pearlie of my predicament. I knew that if anyone understood a conspiracy, he would. He said that the troops of the devil were everywhere, but that he was sure a guerilla uprising of the faithful would eventually prevail. He assured me he was ready, willing, and able and had been training quietly in his company's tiny office trailer between cab calls.

Though I knew it was too early for Possum to be up and around, I was about to surpass the sleepless record I'd set as a medical resident. I needed a dark room with a hard bed and a shower, and I needed it soon. I hoped the middle room of the three was available. It was the only one that appeared to have any hope of not sliding into the ravine behind it. Pearlie beeped his horn respectfully three times and not so politely five more before we saw any sign of life from the second floor of the café, where Possum and Jennie Mae resided.

The head of a large brown woman with black and gray hair poked out the back window. "We ain't open till eleven-thirty. You just get along now, you hear?"

"It's me, Gritz Goldberg. Sorry to bother you, but I need a room now, please."

"Possum, Gritz Goldberg's here!" Jennie Mae yelled behind her. "Says he needs a room. Yes, I said a room."

"Gritz, is that you?" Possum said, finally appearing shirtless next to his wife at the window.

"I'm sorry to bother you this early, but I need a place to hide . . . to stay for a while. Do you have a room?"

"Do I have a room? Jennie Mae, did you hear that? Gritz wants to know if we have available accommodations."

Jennie Mae cackled.

"I'll be right down. Takes a little time for my knees to get the signal from my brain to go ahead and move."

It did take a few minutes for Possum to arrive downstairs. When he came out the back door, he appeared to be quite naked under a gold silk robe and blue, fluffy Smurf bedroom shoes. His skinny, dark legs looked like overcooked char-broiled drumsticks. He was holding a large can of Lysol in one hand and a broom in the other.

"What in the world brings you here, Gritz? That ex-mother-in-law of yours get testy?"

"It's a lot worse than that. The chief may think I tried to murder someone."

"No shit! You, murder someone? Must be April Fool's."

"I could have murdered someone, I just didn't."

"Gritz, I'd more believe Hugh Hefner called for Jennie Mae to spread out nude for *Playboy* than you could kill a fly."

There it was again. The fly thing. I gave up. If only Talmadge would join the prevailing sentiment.

"We don't lock these rooms anymore, but I figured I better help you straighten up the place. Jennie Mae is looking for a clean set of sheets and a roll of toilet paper. You know, this ain't no Grove Park Inn, now, Gritz."

"It'll be fine, I'm sure, Possum," I said, picking up a couple of empty beer cans off the torn lawn chair sitting outside my room.

I opened the door for him to go in first. It swung into the room, barely missing the foot of the single bed. An orange plastic beanbag sat in the corner facing a tiny black-and-gold-trimmed television. The walls had water-stained green paneling that bowed like a frog's back. The carpet was rusty brown shag with beige bald spots. When I peeked into the bathroom, I saw a toilet bowl perfectly coordinated with the carpet.

"I know the place looks kinda questionable at the moment, but wait till Jennie Mae gets here. She'll get you as comfortable as a bug in a rug."

I looked down at the carpet and scratched my ankle. "I'll need complete privacy, Possum. Can I ask that of you?"

"You got to be kidding. When I became proprietor of this place, I learned real quick that there are two rules you never forget. Always get the money up front, and never remember who gave it to you."

"Oh, I brought my charge card."

"I don't mean you, I just mean in general. I'll bring you the portable phone from the restaurant. We don't have phones in the rooms, but we do have satellite television."

"Really?"

"See that big ol' dish up there on the bank?" he said, pointing out the window above the commode. "There's a group of them doctors, they've been trying to buy my land for the last ten years. I told them I might sell when I retire, if I retire. But in the meantime, I'd promise them first chance at the land if they would do a few favors for me. I wanted a satellite dish with all the sports channels, free yearly prostate checks, and an unlimited charge account at Lane Bryant for the missus. I kind of like being a land baron."

Jennie Mae walked in with a bucket of water, a mop, and a gallon container of some kind of strong-smelling cleaning stuff.

"I couldn't find sheets, but nobody's slept on the ones in here in about a year," she said. "You going to be with us awhile, Gritz?"

"Could be."

"American plan or European? With food or without?"

"With, please."

"Possum, check in the shed and see if we got enough lard. We haven't had a long-term guest since your brother came, and we had to run him off."

"Sweetheart, don't go around telling a Jew what we cook with, or we're liable to lose our best customer. You know they don't eat pig products. Gritz, come to think about it, how do you get away with all you eat?"

"When it comes to dietary laws, most of us make up our own rules. My brother, for example, loves kielbasa sausage. He just doesn't eat it in his kosher home."

"That's what's confusing about religion," Jennie Mae said, standing tall and looking up at the stained ceiling or heaven or both. "Everybody makes up their own rules. But one day, the Lord is going to explain it to us all."

"Amen," Possum chimed in.

Jennie Mae looked at me. "Just keep the music down, and if you use one of those late-night channels, please keep your drapes closed."

"Gritz don't want any publicity while he's here neither, Jennie Mae."

She looked at him and then at me and shook her head. She pulled a wet string mop out of the soapy bucket and squeezed between Possum and me, dripping water everywhere except on the bathroom floor, where it was needed.

"Jennie Mae, I'm going to get an early start to Ingles," Possum said. "Hurry with your cleaning, now. Gritz needs his beauty rest." Possum shook my hand and turned to leave. "Sorry for your troubles, but glad to have you."

"Thanks, Possum."

"When I start cleaning, Possum always remembers something he's got to do," Jennie Mae mumbled, kneeling, her bottom facing me out the bathroom door.

"Jennie Mae, do you remember that murder at the Battery Park a long time ago?"

She kept scrubbing. "Sure I do. That boy never done it. He was as sweet as my cornbread."

"Got any idea who did?"

"I always figured that Hitler lover did it, or had her done."

"Paully? What would he have to do with it?"

"Nobody seemed to care, but that old gun they said Mordecai used? That old pistol they found under his commode? They said in the *Citizen* it was a German-made antique-like gun, real valuable. Now, what would a skinny Southern colored boy be doing with a pistol like that?"

"I wonder why the D.A. didn't ask that."

"All the D.A. had in his sights was Mordecai's dead ass."

"How would Paully have known the murdered girl? She was traveling with her uncle on his regular rounds through western North Carolina, as I understand it. They just stopped off for the night."

"Paper said the girl's uncle always stayed at the Battery Park and played in that poker club when he was in town. T used to come in and tell us about those fellows, especially Paully. This here community was none too happy to have him show up in Asheville, let me tell you. He didn't like coloreds any more than he did Jews. Anyways, I figured that maybe the professor introduced his niece to Paully and the other poker guys. That gnarly piece of Nazi crap might have had a hankering for some young stuff that night. The girl probably had other ideas, and things could have gotten out of hand. Wouldn't be the first time something like that happened."

"But would Paully murder her? I mean, surely she wouldn't have been the first woman to say no to him."

"In my experience, nothing makes a man act more like a criminal than a woman who won't spread her legs, pardon the language." Jennie Mae stood and tossed her rag in the bucket. "I mean, most men just creep off and lick their wounds or go looking for a bottle of liquor, but once in a while, they just go flat-out nuts. Of course, the whole thing could have been just a matter of being in the wrong place at the right time. Heard something she shouldn't, saw something she wished she hadn't. That's happened to all of us, hasn't it?"

I listened to things I shouldn't hear for a living, but that was a whole other thing.

"The lock on the girl's room wasn't broken. She must have let the intruder in."

"Well, yeah, but with no air conditioning and those rooms so close together, the windows would have been open, and a person might hear something real easy. Or it could be it happened earlier in the day—you know, by accident, just by turning the wrong corner or opening the door at the wrong time. God, I sound like one of those detectives. Ever read Walter Mosley? I never had a lick of proof about any of my ideas. Matter of fact, you're the first person I ever told. Then again, you're the first one that ever asked."

It took about an hour, but Jennie Mae and I got my room spiffed up. I figured that as long as no bare body part directly contacted anything in the room, it was usable. I was so tired that the pencil-thin mattress looked like a giant feather bed at Grandmother's house. I thanked Jennie Mae for her hard work, locked the door behind her, and then popped open my suitcase. I dug out the four bath towels I'd brought with me. I wrapped myself like a mummy from my bald spot to the soles of my feet and cautiously lay down.

I remembered what Essie said her revival preacher had told her, that we should all chat with God before going to sleep, and end the prayer by pledging one very important thing: "God, I am reporting for duty. I'm ready, willing, and able to do what you would have me do when I wake."

There was no doubt I was a draftee, not a volunteer. I wished God would go ahead and give me my marching orders instead of letting me wander in a dark wilderness.

Then again, I knew to beware of what I asked for.

CHAPTER TWENTY-FOUR

"Men zol nit gepruft verren tsu vos me ken gevoint verren."

"Pray that you may never have to endure all that you can learn to bear."

Even though I was deep inside a well-constructed nightmare—something about my medical degree and my heart being stir-fried in a very hot skillet—I was not thrilled to hear a sharp knock on my door from the real world. I sprang up, threw off my towel sarcophagus, and looked at my watch. I'd slept for twelve hours, and it was starting to get dark outside.

My first hazy thought was that Estelle Levitz was at my door, ticked at me for not being at the funeral home when she'd been returned there after her autopsy. The voice, however, was that of a male.

"Dr. G.? Let me in. I've got to talk to you."

Mostly, my patients called me Dr. G. That was not a good

omen. There was no spy hole in the door, and the front windows of the motel were narrow and high. I tried bouncing off the beanbag chair, jumping high to see outside. All I caught was a glimpse of a fairly new black Mercedes with a woman sitting behind the wheel.

There was another knock on my door. Trying to hide in a small Southern town was about as easy as slipping out of a Waffle House without one of the waitresses calling you "sweetie."

I cracked the door to see the neck of a familiar hostage-taker. It was very red.

"Bobby, how did you get out of jail?" I said.

"I'm out on bail. Let me in."

"How the crap did you find me?" I said, opening the door.

My head was pounding from the leaping. Most shrinks wouldn't have been so direct with one of their patients, but I didn't feel like a doctor right then, and I didn't want Bobby to ever be my patient again anyway. I knew I had to regain my composure. My bad-seed visitor was still half Emma's, after all. Bobby smelled like he'd been in jail for too long, and I was sure I didn't smell like roses myself.

"How did you know I was here?"

"Mayor Bloom told Mom."

"How would he know?" I was less than thrilled that Emma and Shel had spoken.

"The rumor in jail was that a doctor from Highland was about to join us. We heard the police had been tailing you. I know you couldn't have killed that old lady. You wouldn't hurt a—"

"Can it, Bobby! What do you want?"

"Mother says you have something Mayor Bloom wants. A little Jew bag or something."

"It's called a *tefillin* bag, Bobby, but I don't have it." Why I thought it was necessary to broaden this walking hate machine's vocabulary was beyond me.

"Dr. G., Mom says she's known the mayor like she has you, from high school. She got him to talk to the judge in my case, and she thinks they'll drop the charges if I cooperate. The mayor has even talked with Dr. Montague about Trinity taking me back, too. You know, I need to be at Highland to stay out of jail on the other charges. All I have to do is get him that Teflon or whatever-you-call-it bag."

If this had been a movie scene, I would have casually lit a cigarette and blown smoke into Bobby's face, waiting for him to collapse in fear. But alas, Gritz, the savior of all flies, had never learned to smoke, and this was no movie.

"Is that your mom waiting in the car?"

"Uh-huh."

"I can't believe she's doing this for Shel Bloom!"

"Why do you say that?" Bobby asked.

I wanted to say, *Because he's your father and doesn't give a crap about you.*

"Look, Dr. G. Just give me that damn bag and I'm out of here. We're supposed to deposit it with some blond chick at Happy Valley."

Emma and the mayor? Candy and the mayor? What was next? Arlene and T disappearing with the *tefillin* bag into the witness-protection program?

"Did he tell you why he wants the bag so badly, Bobby?"

"No, he just said you stole it, and that it was his. He made me promise I wouldn't use any violence."

That was reassuring.

"If it's anything to do with money, you'll find a Jew. That's what Grandfather Raby always told us. I figure the bag must be loaded with gold or diamonds or something. Why else would he want it? I mean, let's face it, if it wasn't valuable or illegal, why wouldn't he just let the police come get you and the bag?"

That was the first thing Bobby had said that made sense. Why didn't Shel tell Talmadge to pick me up for stealing Estelle's bag? And how did he know I had the inner bag anyway, unless he'd located Mutt and his rainbow trout somewhere in the woods?

I heard another car pull up outside the motel. I was all out of leaps. This time, I just swung the door wide and looked out.

A skinny man with a thick red beard and matching satin skullcap popped out of a brand-new BMW Z4, the one that looks like a shark's mouth—not the rabbi, the car. He glanced at Emma in the Mercedes and smiled but said nothing to her as he passed. Emma wouldn't look my way. I glanced over the cars and across the road. The billboard there still read, "Got Milk?" I was surprised it hadn't been changed to, "Looking for Gritz? Turn now!"

Shlomo brushed passed me like he was on a mission, had to use the bathroom, or both. His *yarmulke* fell off. Bobby automatically picked it up and handed it back, holding the cap out in front of him as if he'd just pulled it from a dirty toilet. Shlomo smiled a toothy thank-you grin.

"Mutt at the funeral home said he gave you part of Eddie Levitz's *tefillin* bag, the inside bag," Shlomo said, putting his *yarmulke* back in place. "Estelle is to be buried in an hour. I need it back. Those gravediggers are on overtime. They're waiting at the cemetery. You don't want to make a gravedigger wait, let me assure you. You do have the bag, right?"

"No, I don't have the bag, but Mutt said you wouldn't bury it with Estelle anyway."

I knew it had to be somebody besides a gravedigger who

Shlomo didn't want to keep waiting. Had Shel told both Bobby and Shlomo to get the bag, or did somebody else want it, too?

Bobby looked as confused as I was.

Shlomo looked like he was trying to think of a quick new reason for wanting the bag.

"So you're going to allow the bag to be buried with the body?" I said.

"Well, yes, I think that . . . Well, yes, in this case, it's okay."

"And why is that?"

"Just tell me where the bag is, Gritz." Shlomo's voice was an octave higher than usual, and the fake grin had finally vanished.

I looked at Shlomo and then at Bobby. I wanted to run, but I was already at my hideout. Some hideout.

There was another knock on the door. I jerked it open so fast I almost crushed my hand against the wall. I might as well have put out an open-house sign.

It was Arson. He had a plate of fried okra and barbecue in his hands.

"Jennie Mae said you slept so long you missed lunch. It's paid for with the room."

"I'll be over in a minute. Take it back to the kitchen."

I couldn't believe I'd just ordered Arson to do something. He looked like he couldn't believe it either. After glancing at Shlomo and Bobby, and without saying a word, he lifted my plate high in front of him and flipped it over, splattering the contents on the carpet. Then he handed me the dripping, empty plate.

"By the way," Arson said, reaching around to his back pocket and retrieving a rolled-up bunch of papers, "some old broad came by riding one damn expensive orange cycle. She said not to wake you. Said your son printed this up for you." He turned to walk out.

I flipped through the pages, barely hearing Bobby's jabbering about going back to jail and Shlomo's babbling about how he'd rushed home from Charlotte and how Estelle's burial was delayed because of a lack of cooperation from me.

"Dad, I hope this helps," was printed on the top of the first page. Nate loved to do research on the internet. At least I was pretty sure he was actually looking things up, and not watching *Naked News* from Canada. He'd scribbled this on the same sheet of paper: "My film class at school has been picked to help broadcast Mayor Bloom's speech at the justice center. We're going to set up the equipment and everything. Cool, huh?"

If God was testing me, I was about to fail. I looked at the butter and oil oozing from the okra into the carpet and just started shouting, "Everybody out! Now! Out, now!"

They did leave, but none too happily. I hated to send Emma off like that, but what was she doing running errands for Shel anyway? I watched Bobby and Shlomo go to their respective cars and pull out of the parking lot in a huff, like two riled pups after the same bone, the wheels tossing gravel against the motel like parting rounds of artillery.

I plopped down in the beanbag with Nate's papers and began reading a very strange story.

The seven-page printout stated that, in the 1940s, General Electric, in cooperation with a German corporate ally, had been charged with and later convicted of conspiracy to monopolize the market of a commodity critical to the war effort, raising the price of carboloy and driving out the competition. Carboloy, also known as tungsten carbide, was critically needed by both the United States and our enemies. A hard metal made from scrap-metal by-products, it was used in cutting dies and machining metal. Carboloy was particularly valuable in the production of munitions and tanks.

General Electric and Friedrich Kripp A.G. of Essen, Germany, co-owned the patents and thus constituted a carboloy cartel. According to secret documents, General Electric agreed to produce carboloy for the Western hemisphere, send royalties to Kripp, and block out all competitors. This quasi-monopoly at just the time we were gearing up to enter the war caused the Allies' price to skyrocket from $48 a pound to $453 a pound. Gustav Kripp, the owner of Friederich Kripp A.G., reaped heavy profits that he reportedly funneled to Adolf Hitler's war chest.

I recalled the letter to Paully from Kripp that had fallen out of Moses' album. If Pete Reid was right about a business partnership of some kind between Moses and Paully, it was becoming clear why a senatorial candidate wouldn't want such a letter suddenly showing up.

Nate had hit the jackpot with this stuff. Another report stated that next to gasoline, steel was the element most needed in the war effort. Carboloy was a vital part of the machining of hardened-steel products. Without it, making parts for weapons and tanks was almost impossible.

Nate included excerpts from several Hearst newspapers, one of which commented on the diplomatic initiatives by Roosevelt: "Many Americans believe that the president stands virtually unopposed in his international policies, but the truth is that though he enjoys tremendous popularity among the American electorate, he has a host of powerful and influential enemies within his own government, as well as outside it." The list of those who disliked FDR included a hodgepodge of kooks including Dr. Frank Buchman, founder of Alcoholics Anonymous; a notorious fascist, Father Coughlin; and none other than the chairman of the United States Senate Committee on Military Affairs, Robert Rice Raby.

I used to like playing connect the dots when I was a kid. One thing I never forgot was that if you drew enough lines among those dots, a picture sooner or later always emerged. The picture that was starting to appear before me at that moment was pretty ugly. If carboloy was composed of scrap-metal by-products, then having a handy resource to supply scrap metal would be step one in the whole production line. What if a Jewish-owned salvage yard in a little Southern town—a town that just happened to be the home of a senator—was that supplier? It would have been one of the least likely places to look for a traitor for Hitler. As Dad always said, a whole lot can go on when nobody's looking.

T used to say he knew when his daddy was going to give him "a full-fledged whoopin'." He could see it in his daddy's tight jaws, red eyes, and wrinkled forehead. All the kids, he said, would "scatter like pollen on a breezy spring day." In his family, the process of growing fighting mad was called "gettin' whoopsified." The more I conjured up thoughts of dirty money and rotten business dealings, the more I understood what he meant. Like I told my patients, you have to get mad enough to solve a problem, and I was getting plenty mad.

Supper was cooking in Possum's kitchen. I smelled Jennie Mae's peach cobbler. Every September, when the leaves started to fall, Jennie Mae baked the best cobbler I'd ever tasted. I decided to grab a bite before trying to solve any more problems.

I walked in the back door to the kitchen.

"You must have slept like a baby, Gritz," Possum said, flipping a hamburger on the griddle. "Something about you looks different. Are you okay?"

"He's okay," Arson mumbled from the dishwashing area. "He's just fine now." He pulled his good hand out of the water and dried it on a dishtowel, then took a swipe under his armpit before placing the towel over the clean dishes.

"Cobbler cooled off enough yet?" I asked.

"Not cool enough to stop a dollop of sweet whipped cream from melting all over it," Jennie Mae said.

"Had just two customers so far tonight. I'm thinking of closing up early anyway. It's bowl one game and get one free tonight at the lanes." Possum spoke to me but looked at Jennie Mae for approval. "You going out tonight?" he asked.

"Thinking about it," I said.

"You be careful, Gritz. I got a feeling things are about to burst like a boil on a bear's butt. You got to be extra cautious when things collide and open up like they seem to be doing. It's like God gets grumpy and hauls out a sidewalk sale on misery."

"Lord, that does seem to be the way things come down sometimes," Jennie Mae added. "But you know, it also seems like those are the times that the most good finally gets done."

"The truth speaks out even when the victim can't," Arson said.

I figured he knew what he was talking about, since he'd seen enough victims in his day.

"I'll be okay," I said.

A week ago, it seemed like nothing in my life ever changed. But right then, it seemed like nothing was ever going to be the same. I wasn't sure which was worse.

"Let Arson drive you," Possum said. "That police chief has his eyes on Pearlie Gates, wouldn't you think?"

"You've got a point. Can I use your phone for just a minute?" I asked.

Possum reached under the bar and handed it to me. It had a brown stain on the receiver and smelled like chitlins.

"You got to get used to it. Not everybody likes them," Jennie

Mae said, noticing my nose twitch as I dialed the phone.

"Goldberg residence," Arlene said.

"Goldberg's hideout," I replied.

"Gritz, are you okay?"

"Not too bad. Kids okay?"

"Yes, they're fine. Did you get the papers Nate sent you?"

"They were a great help, but I need to see that *tefillin* bag again."

"That could be a problem."

"Why?"

"I dropped T at Wilson's Funeral Home about a half-hour ago. I was just leaving to pick him up now. He said he was thinking that since there was nothing in the bag except what there was supposed to be, Estelle's wishes ought to be fulfilled. When you get older, you get more sensitive about having things done the way you want them, especially when dealing with death."

"But the secret can't die with her."

"What?" Arlene asked.

"I'll explain later. Don't bother picking up T. I'll get him. Sorry, Arlene, but I've got to go," I said, hanging up abruptly. "Save some cobbler for me, Jennie Mae. I'll be back in a little while."

I looked around for Arson.

"I've done talked to him about driving you," Possum said. "He's waiting outside."

I found Arson sitting in the driver's seat of his Subaru Brat with the engine running. I got in the passenger side and crouched on the floorboard inches from his unlaced, dirty, red canvas Converse athletic shoes.

"I'd better stay out of sight," I said.

"I hear you," Arson answered. "I've lived most of my life out of sight."

"Do you know where Wilson's is?"

"Yeah, they hauled my wife's lover there. Corner of Merrimon and Broadway."

"That's it. Take me there as quick as you can, but don't get pulled over."

You can go just about anywhere in Asheville in fifteen minutes.

Arson's feet were downright foul. I tried to make small talk to keep my mind off the smell.

"Arson, what did you serve time for?"

"Manslaughter, but I killed a woman."

"Oh," I said.

"Found my wife sleeping in our bed with a white man. He pulled a gun on me, right off my own night table."

"Your bullet missed him and hit her?"

"No, my first shot missed. He died of natural causes. Had a heart attack. I shot her second."

"I see," I said, trying to curl up tighter. It was time to change the subject. "I've been trying to clear the name of an innocent man."

"I wasn't innocent."

"I know," I said.

"What?" he shot back.

"I mean, the circumstances are somewhat different. I lost a wife, too."

"Killed her?"

"No, somebody stole her away."

"I don't plan on killing anybody else. One's enough."

"There are plenty of women out there. You'll find another one."

"I don't think so."

"Keep the faith, Arson."

"It ain't that. In prison, I discovered men ain't half bad. Plus, they don't keep after you like a woman. You like men?"

"Not sexually," I said firmly.

"I'm not queer, though. I just don't see no reason not to take advantage of the situation you're in. You see what I mean?"

I saw it only too well.

"Ever see a psychiatrist in prison?" I asked. "Sometimes, we really do help people with their struggles."

He grunted.

As we approached Wilson's, I raised my head over the dashboard and saw an old man sitting on the edge of the landscaped terrace beside the doors.

"I know that guy," Arson said. "That's T Royal."

"Pull up beside him," I said.

I popped out the passenger side. "*Oy vey*," I said, stretching.

"I was balled up for two days straight one time," Arson said. "Got stuck in a drop ceiling over a drugstore safe."

"T, did you already leave the bag?" I asked.

"Almost an hour ago. Where's Arlene? I gave it to that kid that went to school with you. I didn't think you needed it anymore. Did I screw things up again?"

"Don't worry. I'll get it. Come in with me." I turned to Arson. "Back us up. We're going in. Watch out for the cops."

"Dum te dum dum," Arson called back. "They made us watch *Dragnet* at Central Prison. Don't you worry, I'm covering your sweet butt."

That's what I was afraid of.

CHAPTER TWENTY-FIVE

"Der shversteh ol iz a laidikeh kesheneh."
"The heaviest burden is an empty pocket."

The funeral-home business was much improved since I'd left Wilson's. The front two viewing rooms were overflowing with people—two dead and the rest living. Jewish people have their share of uncommon death rituals, like covering all mirrors in the house and sitting on low stools for days, but the gentile tradition of survivors standing in a receiving line beside an open casket while the stiff lies all dressed up with no place to go has always seemed bizarre to me. At least the dead have an eternity of privacy to look forward to.

Crowds were no problem in the last room down the hall.

T and I walked in to find two young, lanky men with greased crew-cut hair standing on opposite sides of the casket. Number one was waving his hands wildly. Number two looked like he was about to take off his jacket and fight.

"You damn idiot, how did you let that happen?" number one said.

"I thought you were going to take care of it, asshole," number two replied.

When they noticed T and me, they immediately ceased their argument and reverted to the accepted Wilson manner. Their voices morphed into that of the *All Things Considered* commentators. Number one said in a soft, compassionate voice, "We were just about to take Mrs. Levitz to the hearse for burial."

"I returned a small velvet bag to Mr. Wilson that was supposed to be placed in that casket. And, uh, I need to get it back," T said.

"That makes for a tiny problem," number one said. "We were just discussing the possibility that the bag has been placed in the wrong casket."

"You mean one of the caskets in the front rooms?" I said.

"No, it seems it was put in yet another casket. An indigent man we've already sent out to the cemetery. We rarely have burials this late, but Mr. Wilson wanted to go ahead and bury the poor man. No family, you know. We've had a crazy interment schedule today."

"Which cemetery?" I asked.

"Riverside. That's where they bury the indigents, at least in part of it. Thomas Wolfe's buried in the paid-for section, you know. We're very sorry for the error."

I looked at T and he at me. Then we turned without saying good-bye and scurried out of the funeral parlor as fast as we could.

"This whole thing is making me all kinds of nervous," T said, struggling to stay up with me.

"I think I've figured part of this whole mess out."

"Tell me which part when I get a little breath."

I got outside first and waved for Arson to pull around and pick us up.

"Ride with us, T."

"*Ride*. Sweet word to my ears," T said, finally catching up.

"You boys are such pussies," Arson sighed as we piled into the Brat and explained that we needed to get to Riverside. "That man's dirt hasn't had time to settle in, even if he is buried. I've dug up many a body in my day."

"You have?" I said. "Why?"

"You wouldn't understand."

He was right. There are some questions that just shouldn't be asked.

"With one arm?"

He glowered at me.

That was another question that shouldn't be asked.

So off we went, two pussies and one giant cock in search of a tiny velvet bag. If we were lucky, we'd collect a stay-out-of-jail pass for me and maybe even a key to a murder.

When we got to the cemetery, a worker was maneuvering a small backhoe into a storage shed while another man leaned on a shovel and watched. Arson searched one of his nostrils with his index finger, then pulled it out and waved at the two.

"Rude bastards," he said. "I hate people that don't wave back. Didn't their mama never teach them manners?"

We drove by a newly dug grave that I figured was prepared for Estelle. It was in an area enclosed by a black wrought-iron fence and had no floral arrangements around it.

"That must be the Jewish section. We don't allow flowers at funerals," I said.

"Cheapskates," Arson mumbled.

We drove down a steep hill and pulled up to a grave covered with fresh dirt. The grass was taller than in the other sections, and weeds had infiltrated the cement paths among the graves.

"Arson, why don't you let T and me off here and go back and catch those two guys?" I pulled two hundred-dollar bills from my pocket. It was all the money I'd brought with me to Possum's. "Give them each a hundred. Ask them to come back and dig this poor guy up."

"Hell, when I was down at Central, I could have contracted the killing of Talmadge Livingston for that kind of dough." He jerked the Brat to a stop and let T and me out, then screeched the car's wheels and headed after the gravediggers.

"I think before we dig up this casket, we ought to say a little prayer, don't you?" T said, looking at the fresh grave below us.

"I don't think the Lord listens to me most of the time," I said.

"Have you listened to him? That's the real issue."

"Like how?"

"You know, when you were a teenager, you didn't talk much, and when you did, it wasn't always what somebody wanted to hear."

"I was a real jerk, wasn't I?"

"What's important is that I always knew when you were around, even when you didn't spit a word out. And when you weren't around, well, the hole you left behind was the size of Lake Julian."

That was the nicest thing anyone had ever said to me.

"What I mean is, it's not the amount of conversation, it's the shadow you throw off that really counts. God don't have to talk for us to know he's around. And it's the devil that does most of the talking anyway. I suspect the majority of these people in here did a heap too much talking in their lives and not near enough listening."

T took off his ever-present cap, revealing a large bald spot that surprised me.

"Dear Lord, we're sorry to have to disturb the eternal peace of this man here below us, but like you told Abraham when he was supposed to offer his son Isaac, 'Just do what I say and get on with it.' Well, that bag in the casket ain't supposed to be there— well, you know that anyway—and Gritz here really needs it. Of course, you know that, too, but what I'm trying to get across and doing a mighty poor job of is that once we get the bag back, we'll let this poor soul rest in peace." T swallowed and then went on. "And if it ain't a whole lot of trouble, could you help Mordecai Moore back at the hotel go ahead and take leave of this planet? I mean, he's got to be getting awfully tired of the Battery Park and all, and besides, he's scaring a bunch of people who don't have such good hearts to begin with. May it be your will, amen."

Just as T finished, I saw Arson's lights heading back toward us. Actually, light—just one headlight was working. A pickup truck followed him closely.

The two men took shovels out of the bed of the pickup and without asking a single question went to work. They dug until the top of the burial vault was accessible, then pried it open.

"Hell, for as much as they charge for these things, they ought to seal them up tighter than that," Arson said.

"Hold your breath. He's not been embalmed," one of the diggers said.

"Jews are weird," Arson said. "Why would y'all do a stupid thing like that?"

"Don't think he's a Jew," the other worker said. "If nobody pays, they don't embalm. There are ways of getting around the law."

"The law, the law—that's all anybody wants to talk about," Arson said.

The men quickly got the casket open. Arson jumped down into the pit, reached right in, and pulled out the missing blue velvet bag. Even in the dark, he looked like he'd just opened a box of Cracker Jacks and found a neat blue plastic whistle. Eddie Levitz's embroidered lettering glittered in the moonlight.

"I got it, but I tell you right now, I ain't doing this again! I mean, if you're going to steal something, it ought to have some gold or silver in it, at least."

"Let's get on out of here. Cemeteries make an old man shaky," T said.

Arson tried to knock the dirt off the bottom of his shoes by kicking someone's gravestone.

"There's always a spigot at the entrance to the Jewish part of a cemetery," I said. "We're supposed to wash our hands on the way out."

"Another law?" Arson said.

I pushed a little dirt back onto the top of the reclosed casket before we left.

"That's kind of rude, don't you think?" Arson said.

"Tradition."

"Yeah, I saw that play one time on television. 'Tradition!' " Arson bellowed. " 'Tradition!' "

I feared he was going to start snapping his fingers and doing a Tevye jig. I was beginning to like the silent Arson better.

"Don't all this just make you feel like a big plate of eggs and bacon?" he said, getting back into the car. "Let's go back to Possum's. If he's still bowling, I'll fix us all something. I cooked quite a bit at Central."

Our mission hadn't whetted my appetite like it had Arson's. But I did need to inspect the bag, so Possum's wasn't a bad idea. I let T sit in the middle, just to make sure Arson didn't mistake my cramped-leg rubbing as an overture of intimacy.

As we exited the cemetery, a hearse turned in.

"I bet Estelle's finally getting buried," I said.

"Duck," Arson said. "You two don't want to be seen, do you?"

We scrunched down as best we could, but Arson's heavily tinted windows kept us pretty safe anyway. Shel and Candy were sitting close to each other. He'd said he was leaving her for his lifelong love, but the way Candy had her head on his shoulder, it appeared she was winning him back. Also in the car were two old men, one wearing a plaid flannel shirt.

"Was that who I think it was?" T said.

"I'm thinking it was," I said.

"Did Pete Reid even know Estelle?"

"He knows something."

"If y'all don't mind me saying so, it don't take a college education to figure this mystery out," Arson said. "If that lady going into the ground tonight had anything to do with some kind of shady pie somebody cooked up, well, whoever is left has a bigger piece of that pie. It's that easy."

"A bunch of people are going to need a damn good lawyer, I think," T said.

"I never had one, but they told me at Central that a Jewish lawyer could just about raise the dead."

I resented that inference but hoped this Jewish doctor might be getting closer to helping one particular dead man rise.

Lying on a table in the mostly darkened kitchen at Possum's Café among two very full platters of fried eggs, bacon, hash browns, and biscuits, the much sought-after prayer bag appeared almost defiant. Like it had a mind of its own, the tiny pouch seemed to dare us to touch it, to unzip it, to poke around inside. *You've already ripped my guts, what else do you want?* it seemed to say.

Arson wasn't going to take on the challenge anytime soon. He was eating so voraciously I thought he might choke. T, on the other hand, was totally the opposite. He was playing with his runny yokes with his fork, watching a yellow river meander around the potatoes and biscuits.

"I don't see how there could be anything else in there, Gritz. I mean, the beanie and the prayer shawl were in the outer bag, so all that's in this one are those little black boxes," T said. "What could fit in them?"

T knew what he was talking about. He'd watched me learn how to use the *phylacteries* as part of my bar mitzvah training. Before I got the hang of it on my own, it was he who was always around to straighten out the straps.

"I checked on what normally goes in a casket, since Shlomo seemed so dead set against letting the *tefillin* bag be buried with Estelle at first," I said. "According to law, he was correct. All that's allowed to be buried with the dead is a prayer shawl, and even that's for men. It must be cut in four corners, to show it's no longer fit for normal use."

"I could never be a Jew," Arson said, his mouth full of biscuit and at least four eggs. "Too many rules. I mean, what's everybody worried about? Only a graverobber would ever get hold of one of those shawls, right?" He didn't wait for an answer. "How much could a sliced-up shawl be worth at a flea market?"

I unzipped the bag slowly. It did contain the two small, black leather-covered boxes with the leather straps attached, just as T remembered.

"Kinky," Arson said.

I emptied the bag and pressed it flat on the table to see if I'd missed anything when I checked the lining the first time. I hadn't.

"You mean, after all this, the only thing in the bag is what's supposed to be in it?" Arson asked. "And to think I gave up trying out for a band tonight. Possum wants music on Saturday nights after the cockfights. I taught myself how to sing in Raleigh, and this other guy I know—he just got out, too—he can play a mean electric guitar. We were going over to this woman's basement. She plays stand-up base. We even have a name. The Stolen Blues Trio."

"Should we look inside the boxes?" T said. "I mean, something real tiny could fit in there. A note or something, I suppose."

"You're right, T. If somebody can write small enough to get a good part of the Old Testament inside, there could be something else. The problem is, I don't feel comfortable tampering with those boxes. Would you cut them, Arson?" I asked.

"Is that superstition, or another law? Give me those things. I'll do it." First, Arson took a soupspoon and carefully rounded the edge of his plate, scooping leftover yoke and biscuit. "What belongs in these boxes, anyhow?"

"Four passages of the Bible," I said. "Exodus 13:1-10 and 11-17 and Deuteronomy 6:4-9 and 11:13-21. They're written by a scribe on parchment, calligraphy-style, on small scrolls. One of these little boxes even has four compartments within it."

"You shittin' me?" Arson said.

"By placing them on the forehead and forearm, they show devotion to God," I said.

"Jews are downright kooky."

Arson jabbed the leather tops of both boxes with the end of his spoon. I looked away.

"You think you're going to turn into a pillar of salt?" Arson chuckled. "You two pantywaists wouldn't last a day in Central. You can't be afraid of your shadow all your life."

"It's what's in the shadows you got to be worried about," T said, sounding like he was getting tired of Arson the sage.

"Feels good," Arson said, rubbing the soft leather of one of the boxes between his thumb and forefinger.

Two tightly rolled, minute scrolls fell out, and from one of the boxes a black plastic object about the size of a tiny thumb. It resembled a cigarette lighter.

"I suppose that's the New Testament for smokers," Arson said.

"Let me see that," I said, grabbing it. It bore no writing but did have the symbol for a USB interface on the side. "This is one of those new minicomputer storage devices. This little chip could hold ten Bibles on it."

"I don't know anything about computers, but I'd bet my next Social Security check there's something on that thing Moses and the mayor are scared of," T said with a slight smile. "And now we've got it."

"This is very new technology," I said. "It couldn't have been made more than a year or two ago."

"How do we read what's on it?" T asked.

"You and Arson run this over to Nate. He'll be up late. Ask him to download it and print it out so we can have a hard copy."

T didn't seem to fully understand what I was saying, but he didn't ask for clarification.

"I don't give a rat's ass what's on it," Arson said, hash browns sticking out the side of his mouth.

"What did you just say, Arson?"

"I said I don't give a rat's ass."

In fact, a rat's-ass solution was exactly what we needed. I remembered when Aunt Fay tried to instruct Mom on how to get rid of a persistent vermin she couldn't catch in our kitchen. "Lily, a rat's not a smart animal," she said. "All you have to do is leave out what it wants—a piece of any cheese—and then have a smart-enough trap so the dumb animal catches itself." I remembered Mom looking at me like it might not be the rat she really wanted to get rid of.

Arson collected the remains of his last biscuit and a few strands of hash browns, pushed the concoction into his cavernous mouth, and stood up.

"Let's go, T. I don't want to be around when Gritz meets up with this devil of his. It's getting close. I can feel it in my left big toe. My feet never lead me wrong."

I wasn't sure if Arson was clairvoyant or arthritic, but I was afraid it was the former.

CHAPTER TWENTY-SIX

"Di roitsteh epel hot a vorm."
  "The reddest apple has a worm in it."

While Arson took T to my house to deliver the itsy-bitsy teeny-weeny storage device, I went back to my room and plopped down with a thud onto the orange beanbag chair. It had been an incredibly long day of chasing the past while being bombarded by the present. I decided that, in my exhausted state, it was pointless to juggle theories as to what might be on the storage device. Nate would know exactly what it was as soon as he downloaded the information. Whatever it turned out to be, it must have been Estelle's power over Moses. On the other hand, she must have felt her own share of guilt, or why wouldn't she have exposed him years earlier? Estelle's plot to take her secret to the grave had been no small task.

The more pressing issue was what to do with the information

from Nate. I could go to the police if it was criminal—which it surely was—but I needed to tend to that little matter of saving my own butt first if I was still under suspicion for Estelle's murder. I'd need to take the information right to its source—to the Blooms—and get them to confess. That wouldn't be easy. My body begged for sleep, but my mind would have no part of it. The more I thought about the scum ring that unfinished history sometimes leaves, the more I felt the need for a quick, thorough rinse.

It's amazing how many creative thoughts come to you when you're naked and sudsy and have a stream of cleansing hot water running over your neck. Well, the water wasn't that hot, and I couldn't find any soap, but still . . . The rattling in the dumpster outside my bathroom wall—a band of rats, I felt sure—kept me focused on making a plan. Moses and Shel were surely more rat than human. I had the cheese. I just needed a good trap. In my sleeplessness, I started a mental list of people I thought I might call upon for help. I envisioned them adding up to my own militia, just like Paully had. I'm ashamed to say I even called out the title of Commander Gritz Goldberg to see how it fit. It didn't. I thought about those who might have been part of the original pack of rats. Almost all of them were dead. Or were they?

I stepped out of the tiny shower and felt like I was drying off in a steam room. I tiptoed across the dirty carpet and the remnants of fried okra Arson had dumped and flung my door open. The cool evening air felt good.

Seeing the lights still on upstairs at Possum's, I yelled toward the apartment windows, "Possum, are you there? Possum?" I held the towel tightly about my waist.

After a couple of minutes, Jennie Mae leaned out the window, her bosom a little too visible in the moonlight. "What is it, Gritz?" she said in an annoyed voice.

"I need to use the phone. Can I bother you one more time?"

"You already have," she said. "Possum, go downstairs and get that boy a phone. What? Just forget about it. Getting out of bed is about all you're going to get tonight."

By the time Possum came downstairs and opened the door, I was starting to shiver.

"Here you go, Gritz," he said, handing me the mobile phone.

"Sorry, if I interrupted something."

Possum looked at his bare feet. "It's just . . . Have you ever felt like life was just a marathon of dodging disasters? The more you dodge, the longer you live, but then you're still faced with the question of what you've got when you get it."

"Sounds like something's got you down in the dumps, Possum."

"Ah, I just get this way when Jennie wants to be feisty in bed and the best I can do is bark."

"I've got just the thing for you. There's an amazing blue pill out now."

"I don't want to become no addict, not at my age."

"No, this is legal."

"Is it what done Rush in?"

"No, that's something different."

"Okay, then. I guess it's worth a try. How about I swap you some third-class accommodations for a few pills?"

As Possum went back up the stairs, I noticed more of a spring in his step. If Highland didn't take me back, it looked like I had a promising career in gerontology as a legal drug pusher.

I had a militia of sorts to muster, so I took the phone into my room. Just as I did, I heard a noisy cycle turn into Possum's parking lot.

"Come on in," I said, uncomfortable about not being dressed.

"What exactly are you doing here, Dad?" Stef said, getting off the bike and looking around.

I didn't answer but grabbed some clothes out of my suitcase and fled into the bathroom. As I closed the door behind me, I heard Nate say, "Cool." Stephanie replied, "Gross!"

"Dad, I didn't nearly finish printing out everything, but I thought I'd bring what I had. The dates on these go back to the thirties and forties. What is this stuff?" Nate spoke loudly enough that I could hear him easily.

"Give me a minute, and I'll tell you."

As I came out of the bathroom, Stef was zipping her sweater high under her neck.

Once again, Nate had a stack of papers for me. These appeared to be scanned ledger sheets, business records of sales and payments to and from Levitz Salvage in the late 1930s and early 1940s. Big sales, too—literally tons of scrap metal worth hundreds of thousands of dollars, all apparently transferred through a web of other salvage yards across the country, evidently so the money couldn't be traced to one company. There were also pages and pages of photocopied canceled checks, more than a few endorsed by Gustav Kripp himself. Those were the early ones. Many other checks, some pretty current, were made out to Moses Bloom. Lots of other current checks were made out to people I'd never heard of: Elbert Lantz, Evan Long, Eben Little. The checks made out to Evan Long were the most recent; one of them even had a telephone number scribbled on it. There were also old records of what appeared to be exchanges of valuables. One noted a shipment of German silver coins, another a shipment of several oil paintings from Warsaw. Most went directly to Levitz Salvage, though some art went to the personal homes of Senator Bob Raby, Sheriff Hurt Bailey, and Professor Hieronymous Sardano. The paintings had surely been stolen by the Nazi government and traded for other things, perhaps scrap metal for carboloy. Talk about having the goods on somebody! Still, I knew Moses and Shel would say I'd somehow concocted the evidence, that I'd made it all up. With the Blooms, I'd need nothing less than a flat-out confession.

As disgusting as the facts in front of me were, they somehow energized me. No wonder Shel and Moses didn't want information like that floating around. There was no way Mayor Shelburne Bloom was going to be Senator Shelburne Bloom if news of his family's Fuhrer footsie ever got out. Estelle must have held onto the proof as part of a lifelong extortion plot. Maybe Estelle's e-mail to Candy was her conscience wanting to spill the beans. Or maybe Estelle threatened to tell and Shel had no choice but to kill her, since he likely didn't know where the evidence was.

I filled in the kids on what had happened to me over the last few days. They were amazed so much had "gone down," as Stef put it.

"Seems like it takes a year to get from Monday to Friday at Asheville High," Nate said.

"Just wait till you're fifty," I said. "Can you borrow some of your school's audiovisual equipment for a couple of hours?"

"I guess so. Why?" Nate said.

"I need to get a confession, and I need it on film."

"Awesome," Nate said. "My dad is another Jackie Chan."

"You're acting really weird, Dad," Stef said. "You're not going to do anything criminal, are you?"

"Dad wouldn't harm a fly, Stef," Nate said. "The drama queen must be afraid of a broken fake nail."

"Knock it off, Nate," I said.

He seemed surprised. I meant it more for the fly thing than in defense of Stef's honor. I was going to have to work on my image when everything calmed down, maybe even go skeet shooting with Talmadge or something. Killing clay pigeons would show them.

"Are you sure all this is worth the trouble, Dad?" Stef asked.

"Does nomnom crunch?" I said.

She shook her head and put her helmet back on. "Be careful, Dad," she said. "Let's go, doofus."

The night desk clerk at the Tunnel Road Holiday Inn seemed suspicious. He was young—probably a college kid—with a white shirt bunched into his jeans. His sloppy knot indicated he didn't wear a tie anywhere but at work. I don't know if he saw Arson waiting for me outside the office or not, but he was cagey about giving out Emma Whitaker's room number. Finally, he called her.

"There's a man here who'd like to talk to you. Says he's a physician, a Dr. Goldberg."

There was a short pause, and then he handed me the phone.

"Uh, Emma, I need to see you. Yes, I know it's late, but it's important. Thanks, I'll be right up."

I rode the elevator with a young couple, obviously not married, who were French-kissing while caressing each other's butts. They didn't appear to notice me. There I was on my way up to Emma Whitaker's motel room late at night. Forty years earlier, we could have been that passionate twosome. But it wasn't forty years earlier, and at that moment, I needed her cooperation more than her love.

Still, as I approached her door, her proximity triggered the usual response. My heart raced like I'd just run a 5K race.

When the door opened, it was Bobby who greeted me. My heart still raced, but with murderous intent.

"Hello, Dr. G.," he said. "This feels funny. I'm letting you in a room, instead of vice versa."

It was entirely too much trouble to even acknowledge Bobby as I walked by him. Emma was sitting Indian-style on one of the beds wearing an oversized gray sweatshirt that came under her bottom and down her naked thighs. She wore a pair of furry pink bedroom slippers that looked like they were made from dyed alley cat. Without makeup, she looked a lot like I remembered her mother. I dismissed the thought that I saw a faint purple vein perilously close to the butterfly inked above her ankle. First loves tend to remain fifteen-year-old virgins in the eyes of those whose hearts they've stolen.

"Emma, we need to talk. Privately," I said firmly.

"Bobby, could you?" Emma said.

"Mama!" The thirty-three-year-old sounded like he was twelve.

"It's not about you," I lied.

I wasn't in any rush to break the news to Bobby that his grandfather might have been a traitor to his country, and that his grandfather wasn't really his grandfather anyway, because his father was really this Jewish mayor who'd deserted him before he was born. All that seemed a little heavy to dump on a patient, even one I hated as much as Bobby.

He left the room, but none too happily.

Emma smiled and invited me to sit on the bed beside her by patting a spot where the sheets were turned down. In my younger days, that would have inspired at least five years' worth of wet dreams, but life being the jokester it is, it just seemed like a place to sit.

"Emma, I really need your help."

"You know I will if I can," she said softly. Her words floated out of her mouth and seemed to land on the sensitive, ticklish part of my ear.

I told her my suspicions, including the possibility that the father of her child had murdered Estelle, and that Bloom history might involve trading with an awful enemy, and maybe plotting to kill the president of the United States, and maybe even committing an actual murder.

"Horrible," Emma said, shaking her head. "Just horrible."

"Shel never told you anything about this?" I asked, unsure whether I really wanted to know.

"Gritz, how could you think that of me?"

I was ashamed of myself, but I did think it.

"Would Shel open up to you?" I asked.

"Well, he never has, but I could try."

"I need it on tape. If he does talk, he may never say it again."

"You want to wire me?" she said in a Southern drawl that made it sound like I'd asked her to slap her grandmother.

"No, I think it would be safer to have the room bugged. This could be dangerous, but I feel sure you'd be the last person he'd ever hurt."

"I don't know if I can do this, Gritz."

"If anybody can, you can. Get him to meet you at the Battery Park tomorrow. In the late afternoon. I need a little time to set things up. I'd like to do it upstairs in the Raby ballroom. Tell him you have a plaque you need to hang honoring your late husband's family, or something like that. Tell him you can help him practice his announcement speech while you're there. More importantly, tell him I called and said I found out some terrible information about the Raby and Bloom family histories, and that I wanted to tell you about it. Tell him you need him to explain before you meet me."

"What about Bobby? Shel promised he'd help me with his legal problems. Gritz, he's my son."

"As soon as this is over, the police chief will owe me a big favor. I think I can get him to recommend more treatment at Highland instead of jail. Trinity won't press charges because of the publicity."

"I need to tell Bobby the truth about Shel and me," Emma said.

"Are you sure? You'll be asking Bobby to rewrite the whole screenplay of his existence that's been running in his head all his life."

"Gritz, we thought life was complicated back in high school, didn't we? Do you ever wonder how things would have turned out if it was just you and me?"

Only about ten million times, I thought to myself.

I leaned over and held her in my arms against my chest. I didn't attempt to kiss her delicate neck. I didn't say a single word. I focused on the two ugly slippers and the spectacular purple butterfly that seemed to be hovering just above the fur. I held on for dear life, and she did the same.

For the first time in my life, I think I did the right thing at the right time.

CHAPTER TWENTY-SEVEN

"Az me muz, ken men."
    "When one must, one can."

The sun rose over Possum's Motel the next morning just as it always had. The dew covered the grass sprouts that poked through the gravel in the parking lot just as the day before— maybe a little more or a little less, but who was going to measure? All over Asheville, parents were yelling that time was running out before the bus would be down the road, and that if their kids missed it again they would surely flunk school. Mothers and fathers were saying that it was absolutely the last time they would issue such a warning, though it was understood by all that there would be at least five thousand more warnings before graduation. Four babies were born at Mission St. Joseph Hospital overnight. One would probably go on to be mayor of Asheville in about thirty-five years, one would likely take to a life of crime and imprisonment, and the other two to lives of spiritual dedication coupled with frequent bouts of absolute boredom. It was mostly just a regular day.

Still, when I awoke, I knew that one tiny bit of Asheville history was ready—almost asking—to be tinkered with. This feeling did not arise from my left big toe, as it might have with Arson, but I still knew it to be real. It was the day to take down Shel and also, if things went well, to give Mordecai a send-off. I couldn't explain the feeling of confidence, but I felt it.

I'd barely opened my eyes before I heard Jennie Mae at my door.

"Gritz, it's the phone again. I ain't complaining, you hear, but we just haven't had boarders that needed the phone as much as you do."

"Sorry, Jennie Mae. I've been trying to stay off my cell phone."

I cracked the door. Jennie Mae jammed the phone into my gut, turned, and sauntered over to the dumpster, where she slipped off one of her wide-width shoes and pounded it against the container. "Damn rats! I'm . . . going . . . to . . . get . . . you!" she yelled, as if slow enunciation would be more understandable to them.

It was Emma on the phone. I'd wanted to spend the night with her, but bringing her back to Possum's hadn't seemed right, and I couldn't stay at her motel with Bobby coming back.

"Gritz, I called Shel first thing this morning. He's going to pick me up, and we'll be at the Battery Park around four o'clock. He was thrilled that I offered to help him practice his speech. He said he has to take his dad to a doctor's appointment before he comes by for me, so he'll have to bring Moses along. Is that okay?"

"Perfect! The more Blooms, the better."

"He said he could explain everything, and not to believe a word from you. He said he's getting tired of you being in his way every time he turns around."

"Likewise," I said. "And Bobby? How did he take your news?"

"He refused to accept any of it. He says you must have made up the story and talked me into telling him. He said it has to be some kind of stupid therapy you thought up. He's really upset."

"Is he there with you now?"

"He's out somewhere. He's setting up some kind of meeting for this afternoon. You know, that awful FAWNS group he's gotten into. I heard him on the phone."

Perfect, I thought. I didn't want him to screw up my plans.

"Gritz, are you sure about all this? I mean, I've always trusted you, but this is like some ugly monster rising out of a polluted lake."

"Just remember who the monster is. And it's not you or me."

"Okay, so exactly what do I do?"

"Get Shel to start practicing his speech. Tell him you and he can talk about me, but that he needs to get his speech down pat first. Make a minor change or two in it, and just keep him talking. Tell him you can't wait to see him as senator, that nothing's going to stop him now. Tell him you fantasize about being in Washington with him someday. He'll eat it up, trust me. And then just wait."

"Wait for what?"

"You'll see."

"That's not very reassuring," she said.

Actually, it was. This time, my left toe was really throbbing.

I called Nate after Emma hung up. He and Stef were heading out to school.

"I need you two to borrow that equipment we talked about and meet me at the Raby ballroom on the top floor of the Battery Park at two o'clock sharp. Tell your teachers I'm the mayor's new campaign manager. Tell them anything you think they need to hear to allow you to bring the cameras. You can get everything ready in a couple of hours, can't you?"

"If I can't, it's my bad," Nate said.

"Cool," I said, trying to match the modern vernacular.

"Gotta go, Dad. Stef's driving. You know how anal she is."

The boy scared me. He could talk a better Freud than me.

I called Pearlie to pick me up at one-thirty. I filled him in on what I'd learned about Levitz Salvage.

"I'd better wear my uniform then," he said. "I was an MP, you know. Just had it pressed the other day in case of invasion."

"Great," I said. When you grow up in the clothing business, you never forget that clothes *do* make the man.

I told Pearlie he'd report to Arson, and then I called Arson and told him about Pearlie. Arson said he didn't have a uniform other than his orange prison jumpsuit, but he assured me he could steal just about anything I needed for the job.

"Jeans are fine," I said. "There are six exits from the Battery Park. I'm going to send you somebody for each one, and I want you to make sure they block them."

"No problem. Who are they blocking, anyway?"

"Mayor Bloom and anyone else in his party."

"I just love a party," Arson said, hanging up the phone.

I called T and Arlene. They agreed to pick up Perrier and Arnie Bigmeat, as well as Essie, Frank from The Hard Lox, and Jesus McFarland. Essie was so slight she probably couldn't stop a flea, but then again, she had the Lord on her side.

"It's coming to a head, ain't it?" T said nervously.

"Feels that way."

"Nate told me you're going to trap the mayor. Is that your plan?"

"Well, it isn't really a plan. It's more like a hunch that I hope turns into a plan."

"What about Mordecai? Is he ever going home?"

"I guess that will be up to him."

"You know, an old man can get bored real easy, but the same ol', same ol' is looking pretty good right now."

"I know what you mean, T."

"Gritz, remember what I used to tell you when you had to do something you didn't want to do?"

"You said, 'Take a deep breath, say nomnom backwards four times, breathe out, and go for it.' "

"It might not hurt to try it now."

I followed his advice and made my last call.

Though he was in full uniform, Pearlie seemed to slump in the driver's seat of the cab.

"I got to watch out. I ain't supposed to be wearing this. Not on active duty and all."

"I'm authorized to activate you right now, Pearlie," I said.

"You *are* an undercover agent! Even in high school, you worked for them, didn't you?"

We made the trip to the Battery Park in record time. Pearlie was anxious to get back into the business of rooting out insurgents.

"I haven't been in there in years," Pearlie said. "Buildings are like people. Some change, most don't. The only difference is the number of layers of plaster hiding their age."

Out of the mouths of babes and lunatics . . .

Arson was waiting for us at the elevator along with Nate and Stef, who both were carrying electronic equipment. Pearlie saluted Arson. Arson hesitated a moment, then saluted back. I filled him in on who was coming and then sent Pearlie on his mission.

"Be at the airport at three. He'll be looking for you."

"How will I know?"

"He'll know you. I told him to look for your uniform."

"Yes, sir!" Pearlie said, saluting one more time, then marching out.

Stef, Nate, and I got on the elevator and headed upstairs. Stef appeared uncomfortable.

"This place has a sadness about it. You can feel it the moment you walk in. I bet it's had more than its share of spilled tears," she said in a low voice.

"You don't know how right you are," I said. I told her briefly about the murder.

"So you and T are sort of exorcising the place," Stef said.

"Not of demons, but maybe tears."

"Yeah, well, that makes me kind of proud of you, Dad."

"I'm proud of you, too, but I'd be even more proud if you laid a twenty on me for this surveillance work," Nate said.

The slow elevator finally reached the top floor, and my kids went to work making sure the Raby ballroom had more bugs than just cockroaches.

"The tape will last about four hours. You won't be any longer than that, will you?" Nate said.

"No," I answered. "You two better get back to school."

"Can't we stay and watch?" Stef asked.

I shook my head. The Battery Park poker club was about to convene for one last hand, and the stakes were too high for bystanders.

Nat and Stef regretfully left just as my ragtag militia was arriving. Frank even brought everybody a bottle of mineral water. He said things had worked out with Hesh and that he wouldn't need therapy from me. That was music to my ears. Now, if I could solve a sixty-five-year-old murder and get myself off the hook for another, I expected to hear a stanza of "Happy Days Are Here Again."

I parked myself beside one of the large, arched windows in the far corner of the Raby ballroom. I stayed mostly behind one of the formerly rich green velvet drapes, which were now more of a dead, faded green. From there, I could see when Emma and Shel arrived and also watch for Pearlie. The sun beamed through the enormous panes, making me hot, nauseous, and uncomfortable. Being alone in a room that held so much history and probably an equal number of secrets was a little eerie. A hotel offers shelter to such a multitude of people. Merchants and miscreants, convicted innocents and scandalous scalawags, professors and politicians, writers whose words danced and dancers whose elaborate steps spoke volumes had all walked the halls of the Battery Park and slept in its rooms. And then one day in one room, something happened that shouldn't have. I knew I wasn't going to change history that day. But if I could cause the past to stutter a fraction of a second, just long enough to straighten out the tiniest crook in the flow of what should have happened instead of what did happen, then I had to try.

I saw Shel's car pull up to the hotel. He jumped out of his side and started around the back. I thought he might be rushing to get Emma's door, but I was foolish to consider him capable of such a gentlemanly task. He pressed his remote key lock, and the trunk flew open. He reached in, pulled out a collapsed wheelchair, and set it up. Then he opened the right back door and helped Moses get into the chair. Moses, wearing the same plaid flannel robe and brown corduroy bedroom shoes he had at the funeral home, put the white cowboy hat he held in his lap on his head in a slightly crooked fashion. Shel didn't wait for

Emma to get out, pushing Moses up the handicapped ramp until I lost him as he entered the front doors. I was getting worried that Emma hadn't come when the front passenger door popped open and two long white legs in black fishnet stockings stretched out of the car. Emma had no shoes on, and even from the fourteenth floor I could see the smallest glimmer of toenails painted bright red. She reached back inside the car and pulled out a pair of black high-heel pumps. I hoped the style of her shoes allowed at least a little toe cleavage.

In just a few minutes, Shel and Moses appeared at the ballroom entrance. Shel was dressed in cuffed, wrinkled khakis and a dull blue outdoorsy plaid shirt with the sleeves rolled up to his elbows. His usual attire was a suit and tie, so I figured some political guru must have recommended he start dressing like an environmentally sensitive but hardworking Senate candidate.

I pulled the drapes a little tighter around me. Even across the large dance floor, I could see Shel's eyes grow wide at the sight of the old, elevated stage, a platform that had hosted its share of big-time jazz greats. He abandoned Moses in the middle of the room and made bounding, awkward strides toward the stage, hopping on just like any seasoned politician might think would look good to a crowd of cheering supporters.

"I love stages," Shel said to his dad. "I see one and my heart starts pounding."

My heart was pounding, too, but for a different reason.

Moses pulled a sub sandwich out of his robe and unwrapped it.

"Dad, let me know if you think I should change something," Shel said.

"Leave me alone," Moses replied.

I watched out the window nervously. Pearlie was still nowhere in sight.

"Let's start from the beginning," Emma said. I thought I heard a slight crack in her voice.

"Don't slump," Moses said, clearing his throat. He looked at Emma like he was curious, but not curious enough to stop eating his sub. Bright yellow mustard clung to both sides of his mouth.

I didn't really care about the content of Shel's speech. What was important was that he should never have the chance to give it publicly. He really hadn't made a bad mayor. He'd done some good things and some bad, as they all do. Schoolyard bullies tend to grow up to be effective politicians.

I did care that my rattrap worked. Unfortunately for historic preservation but fortunately for high-tech snooping, the ballroom's old tin ceiling had grown loose at the seams in a few locations— just the right ones to allow cameras to roll.

"My fellow Ashevillians," Shel began, "today marks a time in history that has never before been seen."

"What the hell does that mean?" Moses said around a mouthful of food. "Every moment in time has never before been seen."

"Dad, just wait till the end, will you?"

Moses shook his head and took a big bite of his sandwich.

"I think that I speak for most of you when I say that Washington has grown out of touch with us. Asheville needs a senator—North Carolina needs a senator, the United States needs a senator—with the same vision, the same goals as a former senator from North Carolina, a former senator from Asheville we are all here to honor today. When Robert Rice Raby was our senator, he spoke just like you and I, he acted like you and I, he *was* you and I."

He wasn't I, I thought.

Emma pounced just as I spotted Pearlie pulling up outside.

"Shel, we need to work on your grammar," she said. She asked for his written speech, pulled out a pencil, and began making marks on the paper like some mad English teacher. I knew Emma was on my side.

Down on the street, Pearlie double-parked and opened the trunk just like Shel had. This time, what emerged was not a wheelchair but a bright red collapsible motorized scooter like they sell on infomercials, the ones that guarantee purchasers their lives will once again be mobile. Pearlie set the Medicare marvel beside the back passenger door and helped an old man emerge. Nothing about the elderly man seemed unusual—nothing except his black ten-gallon hat.

It had been a stab in the dark when I'd called the number off the latest of Estelle's check records. I asked the man who answered if he knew Estelle Levitz. Of course he did, since she was the one who sent him the checks. But I had a feeling there was more to it.

At first, he acted ignorant, but when I told him she'd passed away, he voiced genuine concern: "Oh, no. Who's going to send me my checks now?"

I heard the scooter before I saw him. He looked a lot like Moses Bloom except that he was dressed.

Shel stopped his speech when the man rode into the room. He looked on with disgust, as if the man were interrupting something important on his unimportant way to bingo. "What do you want?" he said.

"I need to talk to him," he said, pointing at the back of Moses' head.

Moses swung his wheelchair around as if he knew the voice.

"Eddie Levitz! You're dead!" he said, spitting food.

"Legally, I suppose I am. But then neither of us needs to be buying any green bananas."

They looked at each without saying anything else for a minute or so. Moses strained to see Eddie. Eddie seemed to have less trouble with his vision, but only thanks to heavy lenses attached to broken frames held together by very worn Band-Aids. At first, it seemed almost funny, two aged cowboys who'd swapped their horses for handicapped vehicles and their liquor for Metamucil in a final face-off well past high noon. But the reality of it wasn't funny at all. The truth of their lives, their unclean hearts and dirty hands, quickly took any humor out of the situation.

Even after Eddie had admitted his real identity, he still had no desire to come help me. But after I explained what would happen to the remaining money once Shel took control of it for his campaign, he softened and agreed to hop on the next plane to Asheville. Though I'd told him I was sure I could get him immunity from prosecution, I wasn't sure at all. I didn't promise him any of the remaining pot of filthy money, yet I didn't discourage him from thinking it might be his either.

"What the hell are you doing, showing up after all these years?" Moses finally said.

"Who's going to send me my money now?"

"What are you talking about?"

"My money. With Estelle gone." He paused. "I had to leave. I knew my life wasn't worth a dime after I saw Paully shoot that girl. I don't know why I went with him to her room. I knew if anyone found my whereabouts, I was a goner, so I've kept moving and changing names. I'm a tired old man now, but I'm still around."

"I should have known!" Moses said. "Estelle showed me the books once a year. I never could make head nor tail of it when she did."

"Estelle never missed a month," Eddie said in an almost taunting voice.

"I told Paully when it happened that you never let a witness disappear. You *make* a witness disappear," Moses said.

"Thanks, brother-in-law."

"If Paully hadn't been such a hothead, it would have never happened. I told him to pay her off. She wouldn't have turned in her uncle."

"It might surprise you, Moses, but not everybody can be bought off."

"If you'd just stopped him . . ."

"If, if, if. If the girl hadn't had trouble sleeping and come to see the professor while the card game was on. If she hadn't overheard us talking about having FDR knocked off. If she hadn't gone to the manager to tell him. If the manager hadn't told Paully that the girl knew. A few less *ifs* and Senator Bob would have been President Bob."

There was one more *if* Eddie hadn't covered.

"And if you hadn't killed Estelle, Shel," I said, stepping from behind the drapes.

Shel looked at me, then at Emma, then at his dad.

"I didn't kill her." He paused, then said in a high voice, "Dad did it."

"Me? You little shit! I can't even pee straight. How could I have killed her? Not that I didn't think about it," Moses said.

Shel looked at Emma for support but got none.

"How could you?" she screamed.

"Dad told me to talk to Estelle. Well, not talk. We sat next to each other in her room in front of the computer and typed out what we had to say. She always controlled the Levitz Salvage funds. There was a lot of money left, too, even after all those years. But Aunt Estelle liked to act poor. That's why she made Dad pay for Happy Valley. I knew I was going to need all the money I could get my hands on for the Senate race. I always thought Aunt Estelle liked me, but when I asked for money, she typed out, 'Hell no!' I begged her over and over. 'Over my dead body!' she typed out on the computer. I've never been so mad. I had that bottle of Xanax in my pocket that I took out of your kitchen, Gritz. I'd been siphoning off Xanax from Marsha's meds for months. I'm hooked on them. Take eight a day. That's why I stole them from you in the first place. But when Estelle shut me out like that, it came to me that I could force those pills down her damn throat and she'd be out of the way for good. It surprised me how easy it was. And when I saw your name on the bottle, well, that was like killing two birds with one stone. I decided not to cover it up but to let the blame fall on you. And then all the money would be mine." Shel glanced at Moses. "Well, mine and Dad's."

"And mine," Eddie said.

"Dad reminded me we needed to find those records Aunt Estelle always threatened him with. Even if she wasn't alive to do anything with them. You know how politics is. If there's something your opponents can dig up, they will. We needed to destroy them but couldn't figure out where she kept them. When Candy mentioned that last e-mail, and then when Shlomo told us about the *tefillin* bag, we figured that must be where she hid the records."

I wanted to yell, "Cut!" Hollywood couldn't have directed a better confession.

"Renegades," Pearlie said from across the ballroom. "I just hate renegades."

I do, too. But they looked great on the six o'clock news that night.

EPILOGUE

"A gelechter hert men veiter vi a gevain."
  "Laughter is heard farther than weeping."

My life changed quite a bit, after all was said and done.

When the Southern Nazi Jewish black version of "Who's on First" finally came out in the media, Trinity actually called me to come back and offered me the job of chief of staff. Dink had been nabbed in his running shorts at the mall with a Britney Spears CD in his crotch and was fired. I thought about the offer overnight and accepted, after coming to the conclusion that I really did care about my patients—excluding Bobby Raby, of course, who was back at Highland after Emma made a large contribution to the Trinity Foundation.

Essie's church designated a Sunday as Gritz Goldberg Day, but I decided it was safer for me to send Pearlie as a stand-in, just in case the congregation's generosity morphed into forced baptism.

Shel went to prison for life for doing away with Estelle, but Moses was not prosecuted, due to the complexity of the 1939 murder and the illegal trading scheme. Same for Eddie. The district attorney said that disgracing the Bloom and Raby family names would have to be sufficient, since the only two witnesses left were the perpetrators, and it wouldn't be worth the taxpayers' money to try the cases at their age. Eddie stayed in Asheville but changed his name one more time, to Edgar Linney. I still see him sitting in the park sometimes. The skateboarders and the little kids in the sandboxes have no idea how close they're playing to a man who indirectly played such an important role in World War II. The district attorney came up with a deal whereby the remaining illegal money was dispersed to the Sardano and Moore descendants. Mordecai Moore was granted a postmortem pardon.

Marsha divorced Shel before he even went to prison. People tell me she's dating Shlomo. I did notice that Shlomo was no longer wearing that toothy smile the last time I saw him.

T and Arlene are engaged but haven't set a wedding date. They want to give their new business venture a chance to succeed first. T's Kosher Nomnom is selling well everywhere but New York and Jerusalem. They were able to finance the business after Perrier and Arnie had a successful séance and reached Arlene's late husband, who reluctantly shared where he'd hidden the untaxed money all those years.

Aunt Fay won second place with her Paully presentation. Big Fay won first. Little Fay told her cousin to wait until next year, when she'd get her nephew to come and tell a story nobody could top. Big Fay said she'd probably be dead by next year anyway. That way, she could go out a winner.

Dad moved in with the *shiksa* from Iowa, and they seem happy. How bad could it be, not living with Aunt Fay?

Possum and Jennie Mae decided not to retire for a few more years. That's working out well, because Arson and I turned out to be one hot duo. No, not that way. The band he was going to form didn't work out, so he and I organized a little house band for Saturday nights at Possum's. I mainly play the maracas. Cage and Candy join us sometimes. We call ourselves Dr. G. and The InkBlots.

Emma went back to Tarboro. We agreed to keep in touch and go out to dinner when she comes to visit Bobby. Maybe something will develop, but I've had this horrible premonition that Stef, who just broke up with a guy with a nose ring, might go for Bobby if they ever meet, and that will be more than I can bear. I transferred Bobby to another doctor, so when Emma comes to town we won't have to discuss Nazis over filet mignon.

Mordecai has never been seen again at the Battery Park. I got Talmadge to persuade the city council to halt the naming of the Raby Justice Center. I'm getting petitions for a new name. The Moore Justice Center has a nice ring. Talmadge was not successful in removing the oil portrait of Hurt Bailey from the police-office entry, however. Old political bosses die hard.

Pete Reid stopped by my office the other day. He wanted to thank me for finally solving the Battery Park murder. Pete was never charged with anything, though I still harbor suspicions as to how much he really knows. He said there are at least ten unsolved murders he'd written about over the years, and that I have potential as a private eye. I got defiant at the suggestion and told him I have no interest whatsoever in that kind of work. I told him I never want to solve another mystery as long as I live. But just as I said it, the sweetest-smelling perfume wafted through my office. It didn't leave until I glanced at the day's *Citizen-Times*. Local police have discovered a body floating in a pond near the Vanderbilt Forest Golf Club. They've refused further comment, except to say an arrest is imminent.